Other Titles By
T. T. Henderson

AMBROSIA

PASSION

PATH OF FIRE

SOMETHING SO RIGHT (AFTER THE VOWS ANTHOLOGY)

TATTOOED TEARS

Too Much Hennessy

T. T. Henderson

Parker Publishing, LLC

Noire Allure is an imprint of Parker Publishing, LLC.

Copyright © 2007 by T. T. Henderson

Published by Parker Publishing, LLC
12523 Limonite Avenue, Suite #440-438
Mira Loma, California 91752
www.parker-publishing.com

ISBN 978-1-60043-008-4

First Edition

Manufactured in the United States of America
Cover Design by www.mariondesigns.com

Dedication

To my father, Boozie, whose Jazz club Piccolos is still a happy memory. To my Grammy, Ella Louise, I added just a dash of mystery. And, finally, to my muse…thanks for being just as excited about this book as I am. And thanks for dreaming up the Blues 'N Booze.

Chapter One

Karlem "Boozie" Walker was bound to die at the hand of some no good woman. But no one expected her name to be Katrina or for her wrath to be so widespread and devastating. Not a soul suspected the horrors Katrina would bring save the oracles and psychics who dared only speak of her in hushed voices in darkly veiled rooms. And only then when they were guarded by charms and spells.

For one horrible night in late August, a page of the Bible was brought to life as the hurricane blew merciless winds through the heart and soul of each of New Orleans' parishes. After exhausting her anger, she sat over the city for a while, crying buckets of sorrowful tears; flooding the streets, topping the levees, and drowning all that was precious and rare in the Crescent City.

On that August night, Boozie Walker had decided to ignore the Mayor's repeated evacuation orders and take his chances with Katrina. He'd insisted on staying because he knew what would happen if he didn't—his club would become fair game for looters. Besides, he'd lived through hurricanes before. Betsy had been a whopper a while back, but he'd taunted her all night—"Take yer best shot!" he'd shouted to the wicked dark winds. The following day, he and his bar were still standing. He felt sure Katrina couldn't be any worse. He'd told his son just that the day before the storm.

Maybe Boozie Walker, like the city he lived in and the bar for which he was nicknamed, was too full of life. Maybe he'd enjoyed too many sins without apology or atonement. Lord knew he was definitely no saint. He was a man who'd loved more women than his God allowed, gambled away a small fortune once a year, and made Blues artists famous just by appearing on his club's stage. At least that's what the folks on the streets would tell anybody who asked. The all night jam sessions were legendary at the Blues 'N Booze and for years he'd brought good music and good times to the heart of New Orleans.

He'd also brought a son into the world who had worshipped the ground he walked on. Hennessy James Walker stared at the narrow brick building off Elysian Fields Avenue, holding tight to the ballooning grief and pain inside his chest. Suffocating because he felt so much all at once. He was afraid to let even one teardrop fall because he thought he might never stop crying.

Never in his life had he seen such horrible devastation. To the city, to the parish, to the building that had housed every dream his father had dreamed. The Blues 'N Booze no longer hosted a hall full of patrons swaying and singing to the sounds of the Blues drifting on the good natured New Orleans night air. Now, its main room was filled with debris; torn walls, blown-out windows and stained wood floors. A week that had stolen his fathers life.

Yet, the Blues 'N Booze still stood.

"Mamma always said the B&B was Daddy's one true love," Hennessy said absently. "She thinks he died happy because he died here."

"Yeah, I'm sure she's right," Marcus "Teardrop" Marshall, one of his father's oldest friends, acknowledged his agreement. "Helluva man, your daddy. Helluva man."

Hennessy stepped inside the dark building, immediately overwhelmed with the smell of rot and the sight of devastation. Silt covered the floor; in places, mold had begun to climb the walls. Broken chairs and glasses were everywhere and even the huge bar had cracked and been moved by the floodwater to an awkward angle on the warped wood floors. His father had never been a religious man, but a Bible, a rosary and a crucifix lay near an overturned table by the stage.

"Where…um, where'd they find him?" Hennessy asked his companion.

"The storeroom," Drop said knowingly, "They found him layin' face down on the floor between the racks of liquor. I always said this place'd be the death of him."

"Everybody always said that." Hennessy frowned. "I thought this was the first place they looked after the flood. Why did they just now find him?" It had taken a full three months to be notified of his father's death.

Teardrop shrugged. "I 'spose they were more thorough the second time around. You know the government ain't done nothin' right from the get go."

The Federal Emergency Management Agency had come under fire by the press in the early weeks of the disaster, as had the New Orleans police force and Mayor Ray Nagin. No one had been fully prepared for the havoc named Katrina. And no one had any idea how difficult it would be to sort things out as the whole of New Orleans had been awash in floodwaters for days and days.

Hennessy had been waiting for months for news about his father's whereabouts, but found it difficult to get answers from any agency he'd contacted. Instead, taking matters into his own hands, he'd spent months combing the lost Hurricane Katrina victims website and watching CNN, hoping for a hint of where his father might have gone after the storm. He'd hoped to get news that his father was in a shelter in Baton Rouge, Texas, Tennessee, anywhere. Unfortunately, after three long months, news had finally come, but not the news Hennessy wanted to hear.

Hennessy placed his hand on the inside wall of the old building. It felt cool…just as he'd remembered it. How many times had he sneaked in with his friends, Rayne and Earl, on sweltering summer nights to sit on the floor with his back against the wall to listen to the bands? More times than his mamma gave him whippins for, that was certain.

The club had always been cool, no matter how hot the place got with all the dancing, drinking, fighting and singing. Hennessy and his friends would buy five-cent soda waters at the K&B drug store and sit just in the back corner and listen to the music. He remembered most the bass and the drums…how they'd felt like rhythmic heartbeats through these walls, bringing life to the club and music to the street. Even now, he tried to imagine the sounds of the music that had meant life to him as he'd grown up. All he could make out now were ghostly echoes of forgotten voices, chords and riffs.

Most of all, he missed the way it felt to have his daddy walking the room, talking to everybody, telling jokes and patting backs like each and every one of them were his very best friends. His daddy had always been one of the biggest draws at the B&B no matter who was playing on stage.

"What the hell was he thinking, Drop?" he asked, his heavy heart laden with the loss of all he'd cherished. "Why did he stay here when he could've evacuated?"

Teardrop patted him gently on the shoulder. "Love is a funny thing. Sometimes ya think ya can protect sumthin' just by bein' there." He planted his feet. "That's hardly ever the case."

"I asked him to come to California to stay with me. I should've come and got him. I knew how stubborn he could be."

"Looka here, son," Teardrop's tone dictated that Hennessy turn to face him, "Your daddy couldn't save the B&B, though Lord knows he was bound and determined to try."

Hennessy found himself swallowing back a hard lump in his throat.

"And wasn't nuthin' you coulda done to save your daddy, either," he added softly.

"I know," he admitted. "But I damn sure could've tried harder, couldn't I?" Self-disgust and pain for the loss of his father hit Hennessy hard. He ducked his head to stab at a tear. "We can go now," he managed, as grief thickened his voice.

"Yeah you right." Drop led the younger man to his truck. The bed was filled with an odd assortment of wood. Since his old company had decided not to return to New Orleans after the hurricane, Drop had been forced to take on odd carpentry jobs to pay the bills. "Better take ya by your mamma's house. She'll be worried I didn't bring you straight on from the airport."

They took off down the narrow street and Hennessy took in the horror and ruin of what was once a great city. He was stunned to see either rubble or vacant land where house after house, business after business had once stood. It was mind-boggling to know an entire city could be virtually wiped off the map in a matter of days. Suddenly, Hennessy wanted nothing more than to get the funeral over with and get out. It was far too depressing to stay.

"So, I 'spose you know Boozie intended f'you to have the B&B if anything ever happened to him?"

His daddy had put Hennessy on the deed years ago. "Yeah. He told me."

"So, ya need some help renovatin' her, I'll be glad ta help."

Teardrop's offer was no doubt mainly out of loyalty to an old friend, but Hennessy sensed the man could use whatever money work on the club would bring. Still, he had no intention of staying. "I'm due to start touring in California in a few weeks," he said honestly. "I won't be staying."

"Awright, awright." The older man nodded as if assessing the situation. "Your band doin' well, then?"

"Very well." Pride forged a smile on his face. Glad to be on a different topic, he continued. "We're booked in clubs all up and down the coast and in Los Angeles."

"You still playin' the horn?"

"Yeah. And the slide guitar now." Hennessy had carried his instruments onto the plane. He never took the chance of having them stolen out of his luggage. He didn't care how much security the airports claimed to have…he loved them too much.

"I always said you had a voice for Blues but a heart for Jazz."

The thought made him smile. "Yeah, you did, old man. You sure did."

They talked companionably during the short drive to the heart of St. Bernard Parish. Homes still stood in this neighborhood, though he could see piles of rubble and destroyed yards every block or so. Lila Walker Ellis was out on the covered stoop of her large house. She nearly jumped all the way down the stairs at the sight of the truck. No easy feat for a woman of her size. "Hey, bayyyyyby!" she shouted.

Hennessy rushed out of the truck to hug his mother. "Hey good looking!" he said as he sank into the softness of her plush bosom. She smelled sweet and warm. She smelled like home.

The second he released her she began slapping his arm. "Why you wanna go and worry your mamma? I expected you over a half hour ago."

"I took him over to see the Blues 'N Booze, Lila," Teardrop pulled out the trumpet and guitar cases from the side of his truck bed. "Man has a right to see where his father met his demise."

Lila shook her head. "I fought to get attention from Boozie for fifteen years because of that club. I didn't expect to fight that place for my son's affection too."

Anyone who met her, didn't take no time at all to realize Lila was a woman who demanded attention. She was probably about two hundred and thirty pounds, but she made sure her long hair was always curled and her creamy brown face was made up even if she was just going down to the grocery store. Lila would never be caught in a housecoat and curlers. She was an attractive, curvaceous size 22 who could still turn heads. It had taken her no time to find her second husband, the very devoted—some said, whipped—Antoine Ellis.

Hennessy gave her a loud, wet kiss on the cheek. "You know my heart has always belonged to you, good looking. Hey, Drop, let me get that." He took hold of the bag holding his clothes.

Lila frowned. "That's not a very big valise. You're not planning to stay long?"

"Nuh uh. I told you, Mamma, I've got a gig lined up next week. I'll be touring California when I get back." The smell of gumbo hung heavy in the air as they entered the house. Hennessy was a child for a moment, reminded by how much that smell meant comfort and home to him.

"Smells mighty good round here," Teardrop pushed his dark nose into the air. "I think I might have to see what's cookin' 'fore I head out."

"Come on the both of ya." Lila hustled back to the house. "I got some gumbo on and some French bread. Get something in your stomach before we head out to the funeral home."

Panic wrenched Hennessy's gut. "I thought the wake wasn't until tomorrow," he said, struggling to keep up with his mother.

"That's right." She nodded. "But that woman he was livin' with—what's her name?"

"You know good and well what her name is," Drop said holding the door open for them to enter. "Deja Devine."

"Why does that name sound familiar?" Hennessy struggled to remember.

"Anyways, she up and disappeared," Lila dismissed his question. "So it's been up to me to make arrangements since your daddy hasn't got any livin' relatives other than us." Lila passed through the living room and passed the bathroom. "You're the only one with a key to your daddy's house and we need to see where his life insurance policy is. The funeral director says he needs payment in full today or proof of a life insurance policy before he can proceed."

Stopping at the doorway, Lila ushered Hennessy into the spare bedroom. The toy box bursting with colorful playthings in the corner and the Bob the Builder bedspread left no doubt he was putting his nephew Teray out of his bedroom.

"Ray Ray can sleep with his mother for a few nights," Lila answered his unspoken question. "Heaven knows where that girl is, I sent her to the store hours ago."

Teardrop handed Hennessy His trumpet case and headed toward the back of the house where wonderful smells wafted from the kitchen. He hadn't eaten all day, but Hennessy wasn't hungry. Ordinarily he would've raced Drop to his mamma's gumbo, but all he wanted to do was lie down and rest for a while. He'd never felt so tired in his life.

"Teardrop, rinse off your hands 'fore you get in that pot," Lila yelled after him. She stood quietly in the doorway with crossed arms for a moment. "This is hard on you, isn't it, dahlin?"

Nodding, Hennessy buried his face in his hands.

Lila was immediately by his side sitting on the bed with her arm around his waist. "Well, death is just another fact a life, baby. All I can tell you is that it gets easier to bear with time."

He looked into her soft brown eyes. She'd divorced his father some fifteen years before and had since remarried, but Hennessy felt horrible and empty. He wanted—no needed—someone else to feel his pain at that moment. "Are you sad, Mamma?"

Too Much Hennessy

"'Course I'm sad, dahlin. There's a part a your daddy that never left me alone no matter how hard I tried to forget him. He was a charmer, your daddy was," she sighed softly.

"We had good times with him, didn't we, Mamma?" Hennessy thought back to the days when he was young. Seemed like his daddy always had his friends over for jam sessions in the back of the house. His mamma would always have some good food cooking and there would be laughter and music well into the night. "I remember that time Dad came home and insisted you put your finest dress and stockings on."

Lila chuckled. "And I did. Put on that black dress with tiny straps and tight skirt. Ohh, how your daddy went on about how fine I was."

"You so fine, I could sop ya up wid a biscuit," Hennessy mimicked. "He asked 'Is that a new dress?'"

"An I told him 'No. I been havin' that.'"

"Which was a lie, 'cause I saw you throw the tag in the back of your closet."

She laughed. "Yeah, you right."

"Then he took you out on the stoop and there was the Hardesty Trio right there in our front yard."

"Ha, Hah! That was the best party our block has ever seen to this day."

"That's for sure, Mamma."

"I've missed that man since I left him. I could always count on having a good time when Boozie was around. 'Course don't be telling that to Antoine." Her current husband had proven to be far more stable if significantly less fun than her ex-husband. "Boozie was built to be a man for everyone. He could never be happy with just me."

Hennessy kissed Lila's cheek. "That was one big mistake he made," he said honestly.

Lila shrugged. "I don't hold any grudges against him. Fish gotta swim, birds gotta fly, they say. I found me someone who gives me all the attention I need and in case you hadn't noticed, I need a powerful lot of attention." Lila laughed heartily.

Hennessy smiled sadly. "I'm sorry I haven't been around all that much, Mamma."

"Hush now. Don't apologize for being young. Just do your mamma a favor."

"What's that?"

"When you do decide to settle down, don't be having my grandbabies off in California or Chicago where I can't see them as much as I like. You hear?"

"All right."

They hugged again for a long while before Lila pulled away.

"I better go check on Teardrop. Man might clean the pot the way he eats. You comin'?"

"Not just yet. I think I'll rest a while."

She left the room and it seemed the light went with her. Bowing to fatigue, Hennessy lay down on his nephew's Bob the Builder bedspread and stared up at the ceiling. This was really happening. He was going to bury his father in a couple of days. It didn't feel right. His thoughts were unsettled, like unmade beds in a messy house. He didn't know what to think about, except everything at once. His father was found in the back storeroom of his club…seemed to Hennessy like he would've been up front to protect the place from looters like he told him he was planning to do. Maybe he'd heard something and had gone back there to check it out.

And his father had been dating a new woman. Deja? He'd heard the name before, but not from his father. Of course, Daddy wasn't one to be without female company. He had no idea how to be alone. Surely this Deja was one of the curvaceous, long haired, café au lait eye candy, his father usually trophy-ed around on his arm.

Hennessy closed his eyes and tried to quiet his brain. He'd been gone far too long. Everything had changed. A song was inside somewhere. One day, when he could make sense of things, he'd write it down. He drifted off to sleep with the *duh, dah, dah, dah duh* of a blues tune playing in the recesses of his brain.

Too Much Hennessy

It had to be here. Rayne Walker put the lid back on the coffee can and hopped down from the kitchen counter. Dusting coffee grounds from her jeans, she began pulling out drawers to see if the papers had been shoved into one of them. Silverware, spatulas and knives, the inevitable junk drawer holding exploded batteries, a rusty flashlight, destroyed matches and other odds and ends, but no papers.

Think, Rayne. Where would he put them?

Any normal person would keep important papers in a desk or something, but that was apparently too obvious for Boozie Walker. She'd already checked his roll top desk and had only found water-warped insurance papers and bills. Maybe, his bedroom…

She trudged across the molding floor rug, around furniture ruined in the flood and into what was left of her daddy's bedroom. The bed was pushed against the far wall and the black lacquer furniture was toppled and severely water stained. Still, she had to try. Pulling out drawer after drawer, she sifted through sour smelling clothing. Though she'd already had to go through this exercise in her own mother's house, she couldn't help but recoil at the touch of the ruined materials. Finally, she found his underwear drawer…not surprisingly she also found women's bras and panties mixed with his boxers.

"What the hell are you doing?" A man's voice from the doorway demanded.

Startled, Rayne turned. One hand went instinctively to the pistol holstered at her ankle. She held the other hand up in the air for distraction. "Sorry…" she began and then she recognized him. "Hennessy?" she asked. She hadn't seen him in years. He looked the same; tall, creamy brown complexion…Except, he now wore long, neat dreads that framed the strong angles of his cheeks and jaw and hung past his broad shoulders. He'd filled out and looked more like a man than the young, skinny boy she'd grown up with. "I was just looking for something of mine I left here."

He cocked an eyebrow and stared at what used to be a pink lace thong dangling from her finger. "Is that it?"

Rayne frowned. "Hardly," she said, shaking the offending material from her hand and releasing her grip on her ankle. "I was looking for some papers."

"Right," Hennessy said skeptically. "In the bedroom?"

Embarrassed to be found going through their father's underwear drawer, Rayne felt herself warm under his scrutiny. "Yeah…well…it's not here." She moved toward him, hoping to slip past him and out of this awkward situation. The last time he'd been in town, they'd had words and she wasn't in the mood to have more.

He grabbed her arm and held it firmly so she couldn't pass. "Mamma thought you were at the store. Where've you been? Where's your son?"

"I was at the store." She looked into his eyes and felt uncontrollable anger building as it always had where Hennessy was concerned. Rayne was the oldest. How dare he treat her like she was a child? Hennessy's eyes were the same dark brown as she remembered, with gold just around the edges. But there was something new in the way he looked at her, some-thing raw and angry. Rayne pulled her arm loose of his grasp. "I have some things Daddy was holdin' for me. Why you sweatin' me so bad?"

"Because I know you, Rayne. If this was for real you wouldn't have to sneak around behind Mamma's back, would you?"

"Get the hell out of my face," she shot back, growing more disturbed by his close proximity. "And don't be getting all up in my business, hear? I ain't got nothin' to say to you, Hennessy."

"Well, I've got plenty to say to you, but first tell me where Ray Ray is."

"Who the hell are you, getting all demanding?" Rayne placed her hands on her hips. "My son is being takin' care of, all right. That's more than you have a right to know about him."

"Now you two knock it off." Lila Ellis came into the room wearing her not-puttin-up-with-this-nonsense look. "For the next couple of days, ya'll need to get along, if not for my sake, for the sake of your dead daddy's memory. Now hush up and let's find what we're looking for." She looked back and forth between her children. "And, Rayne," she turned a frown on her daughter, "You go get my grandson from whoever's house you left him at and bring him home."

Too Much Hennessy

Rayne crossed her arms and pinched her lips tight. She knew better than to sass her mamma. Lila wasn't a violent woman, but she delivered a good backhanded slap when her good temper wore out. The last time she'd been on the business end of her mamma's right hand, Rayne had seen stars for over an hour. Her best course was just to leave, she decided. Besides, this house didn't have what she needed…and all of the sudden it had more than what she wanted. "You two enjoy yourselves. I'm outta here." She rushed toward the door.

Hennessy wanted to remind her about his nephew, but knew it would be wasted breath. She was already halfway up the walk. He knew because she'd left the door gaping open on her way out. Not that it mattered. There was no need for privacy or security at this point. Hennessy was surprised by how much his sister had changed. As a teenager, she'd worn glasses, had bucked teeth and had been skinny as a rail. But now…now she looked like some supermodel with high cheekbones, a classy short haircut and honey-colored skin. And she was still thin, but not in a good way. She was now bone-protruding skinny—the way Whitney Houston got when she started on drugs.

Not only had her appearance changed but also her personality. Rayne used to be quiet, painfully so, but she'd always been an obedient daughter, until she fell in with her no good Baby Daddy, DeTron, drug pushin' son of a dog. She'd finally divorced the man after their father had spent a night convincing him it was in his best interest. How he'd convinced the thug was still a mystery to Hennessy, but, since then, it seemed like his sister tried her best to find the next DeTron, son-of-a-dog clone to mistreat her and push her back to drugs.

Hennessy's heart broke just thinking about what a mess she was making of her life. It would've been bad enough if she was alone, but she also had a three-year-old son to think about. "She never went to rehab did she, Mamma?"

Getting to happy /
CALL NO: MacMil
34028075950163
DUE: 09/13/12

A love noire /
CALL NO: Tur
34028052489318
DUE: 09/13/12

Too much Hennessy /
CALL NO: Hender
34028065786411
DUE: 09/13/12

TOTAL: 3

"Oh, yeah, she went," Lila nodded and sighed. "She just didn't remember a thing they said two seconds after she left the place."

Rayne thought how horrible it was to see Hennessy again. She managed not to think about her younger brother most of the time since he was gone more than he was home. He was the one who could never do any wrong. He'd gotten all the attention from Mamma and all she got was chores and responsibilities. He would break something and she'd get in trouble for not watchin' him good enough.

Still, one thing she could count on with Hennessy was that he wouldn't be in New Orleans very long. After the funeral, he'd be gone and out of her hair for a nice long while. That suited her just fine since the last thing she needed was for him to get in her way.

She hadn't found the Quit Claim Deed for the B&B, but she would. Then it'd be a simple thing of taking over the place by signing the property into her name. She was Boozie's oldest child and was entitled to it. She knew just how much the place brought in every month because she'd been talking with Earl Grant and making eyes at him when he was cooking the books. *That was it!*

She hadn't found the deed because she'd been looking in the wrong place. If anyone knew where her daddy had kept important papers it would be Earl Grant. The man had managed the books at the Blues 'N Booze for years. The thing was, she didn't know how to find him—or if he was even in town.

So many who had evacuated New Orleans before Katrina had still not returned. But there had never been a doubt in Rayne's mind that she would return. New Orleans was her home. It frightened her to think about starting a new life in a place as big as Houston or Dallas. Besides, when she just needed to be off by herself she needed someone she trusted to take care of little Teray. Her friends were good for a few hours, but when she needed to take a few days—sometimes a week, she much preferred he be with her mamma.

Rayne turned and headed for St. Augustine, the oldest church parish in New Orleans and a Katrina survivor. Inside, students of Tulane University had set up a sort of grocery store where anyone in town could make groceries without charge. Everyone in the parish knew about St. Augustine's. And if anyone had seen Earl Grant, it would be Sister Alveta Flowers, who had worked at the church since it had begun its first relief efforts for the community. Rayne figured it was the woman's way of not feeling like a victim—a way of making a difference in the face of adversity.

"Hey, Rayne baybeee!" Sister Alveta had spotted her from clear across what used to be the nursery room of the church. "How you doin', sugah?"

"Awright, Sister Alveta," Rayne replied to the typical Ninth Ward greeting before submitting herself to the grand hug of the older woman. She always smelled like rosewater. "How bout you?"

"I'm doin awright, dahlin. How your Mamma'n'em?"

"Fine, ma'am. Mamma's good, so's Mr. Ellis." He didn't say too much and Rayne found that a nice characteristic in a stepfather. "Ray Ray's good."

"Good. Good." Sister Alveta's salt-and-pepper wig was slightly askew atop her head. Sometime around the age of sixty-three she'd decided it wasn't worth fussing with her own hair and she'd been wearing wigs ever since. The one she donned now looked a bit matted and messy—definitely past its prime. The old woman frowned, bringing wrinkles to her chocolate complexion. She leaned in conspiratorially, "You been stayin' away from them drugs, dahlin?"

As always, embarrassment over having her business all over town, shot through Rayne's body, but she managed to find a little 'polite' to add to her tone. "Since Rehab, I've been doin' just fine," Rayne said. Though she hadn't been completely off drugs since getting out, she was doing way fewer hits than before. She was sure she could stay off of them forever if she could just get through the stress of her daddy's funeral. Through no choice of her own, she'd been sober for the past two days. She hadn't gotten paid yet and was without a sugar daddy at the moment to get her over the hump. Maybe her dealer would give her a hit on credit. It wouldn't hurt to ask.

Rayne needed to change the subject because the need was growing stronger the more she thought about it. "I was wondering if you've seen Earl Grant around, Sister," she said quickly, before the woman could ask any further questions.

"Earl Grant?" She scratched her head, pushing her wig further back to expose the white of her real hair. "What he look like?"

"A little taller than me, five ten, he's slender, always wears sunglasses…"

"He light-skinned?" she asked.

"Very," Rayne acknowledged. "He worked at the B&B every night before the flood."

"Oh, I know that boy," she said as recognition dawned. "He always runnin' about in that sports car of his with his nose in the air."

"That's him." Rayne grew excited. Earl had always been flashy. Seemed he enjoyed whatever money the club was making a whole lot more than its owner ever had. Daddy had spent a small fortune on jewelry for his many girlfriends, Rayne knew this firsthand, but he hadn't been showy. Earl however, had moved to the Jefferson Parish in a new town-house. He drove a flashy little Lexus convertible and wore a huge diamond stud in his left ear. Rayne had always wondered if it bothered her daddy. "Has Earl been makin' groceries here?"

"Oh no, dahlin. I ain't seen him. And I seen just about everybody who's still around."

"Okay," Rayne said, disappointed. "If you should see him would you let him know I'm looking for him? It's important." She wrote her number down on a piece of paper and handed it to the woman.

"F'sure, dahlin. I'll let him know if I see him," Sister Alveta assured her. She proceeded to stuff the paper into the safety of her brassiere. "I heard about the wake they havin' for your daddy tomorrow."

Rayne nodded.

Sister Alveta shook her head slowly. "I told Boozie 'You need to turn away from all that sinnin' you doin' and turn to God' that's what I told him."

Rayne was certain Sister Alveta hadn't been the only one out to save her daddy's soul during his lifetime. The one thing she'd always appreciated about her daddy was that he'd done exactly what he pleased, when he pleased. "Yes, Ma'am."

"That's what happens to a man who grew up in the streets around all them hoodlums. He didn't know anything but the dark side of life."

Nodding politely, Rayne let the woman talk, though she didn't share the same sentiment about him. In her eyes her daddy was a man among men. He'd done her many kindnesses over the years. The kind she'd had no hopes of ever repaying except— He'd asked her a favor two days before the hurricane. She'd promised him she would get clean and stay that way. She had every intention of honoring the promise she'd made—right after his funeral. She would go cold turkey right after the services.

When the woman finally ended her rant, Rayne took the opportunity to be on her way. "Well, thanks, Sister. I have to be going now."

"You need anything 'fore you go?"

Rayne looked around at the impressive stacks of canned and dry goods lined up around the room. All had been donated from families across the nation. Not for the first time she was embarrassed that her whole community had been reduced to the same social status as beggars. Except Antoine Ellis. Her stepfather had sold his businesses right before the hurricane. It seemed he had enough money to do just about anything he wanted. "No. Not today, Sister. But thanks again."

Climbing back into her truck, Rayne made her way back to Jefferson Parish to get her son from a friend. She'd get him a pizza from one of the restaurants that re-opened. Afterward she could easily get around to Elysian Fields where the club still miraculously stood. One last look there and she'd have no choice but to call it a day.

Chapter Two

After a three-month stay with relatives in San Antonio, Earl Grant clearly saw his welcome had worn thin. Earl could tell from the moment he'd stepped into the house that he and his brother had very different ideas about things, but he hadn't expected the man to be downright resistant to his attempts to liven up their dull lives.

His baby brother, Trey, had a boring job at a bank and drove to work every day in a boring minivan. Though he made enough money to afford his nice four-bedroom home, the man monitored every dollar like it was going to grow legs and walk away. Since he'd started making a paycheck, Earl had decided money existed only to be spent. If he didn't spend it, what was the point?

It made him very happy to buy his sporty Lexus convertible last year and its safety was one reason he'd decided to vacate New Orleans when the announcement about Hurricane Katrina hit the news. The car made Trey's kids happy too. He'd never seen three happier kids as they screamed their heads off with their hands waving in the air while cruising Highway 281 in search of a McDonald's Playland. Trey and his wife Loretta acted like he'd committed the crime of the century for not putting them in car seats.

But yesterday, they'd had a fight and when Trey wouldn't even listen to his side of things, Earl knew the time to go had come.

Earl eased back in his car seat and grew a little uneasy at the thought of coming back to New Orleans. Not that he'd given this much thought, but he didn't care for San Antonio. And like he'd told Trey, he couldn't take just *any* job. Having grown accustomed to the finer things in life, Earl wasn't in a hurry to go the other direction.

Though he didn't know what to expect now he'd returned to New Orleans, he knew old Boozie Walker would be good for some chump change while he decided upon a course of action. With any luck, the old man had the Blues 'N Booze up and running again. In the last three months he'd heard that more and more business owners were choosing to reopen. If Boozie could find a way to open, he'd be sending the Blues out into the street the first opportunity he got. Earl hadn't received a call from the old man, but he'd chocked that up to the fact that he'd probably been fixin' up his beloved bar. Earl would be happy to help…as long as most of the heavy work was out of the way.

Driving slowly down Elysian Fields, Earl grew disheartened. Many of the buildings on one the side of the road had either been torn down or bore red tags. Most just sat looking haunted with dark vacant windows. Things weren't looking promising.

Debris-clearing crews were scraping shredded insulation, wall frames and tangles of electrical wires from the foundation of homes everywhere he looked. He knew for certain his old apartments were unlivable. He'd contacted the property manager and found out they weren't planning on having apartments for rent until mid 2006.

Fortunately, he'd planned for this. Earl had been approved for a Federal Emergency Management Agency trailer before he'd left Texas. Heaven knew where he would put it. He guessed Boozie would allow him to park it in his driveway if he asked.

"Thirty years old and I'll be living in a damn trailer. Just what I was trying to avoid all my life."

Hopefully the Blues 'N Booze had made it through the flood all right. Managing that joint had been the easiest gig ever. Boozie had trusted him like his own son. And why wouldn't he, Earl scoffed. He'd been working his behind off at the place since he was a boy, wiping down tables, sweeping and mopping the floors and emptying the trash. All while Hennessy sat talking to the band members and begging his daddy to let him jam with them. Of course, more often than not, Boozie gave in to Hennessy.

Hennessy, he thought bitterly, was a man who'd never had to work for anything his entire life. Went off to college for four years then wasted the education to go on the road with his two-bit Jazz band. And what does his old man do about that? Does he give him a few punches to the gut or head? Naw, not Boozie. He tells Earl to "Make shore you send Hennessy his money." He'd tell him the same thing every month—as if Earl was likely to forget after ten years.

Yeah, good old Hennessy got money just for being born so it seemed that a working man like himself was due the extra twenty here and there he'd taken from the till. He'd worked hard every night, managing the waitstaff and bartenders. He did the books so Boozie didn't need to worry over a single thing. Earl made it so the old man hadn't needed to lift a finger except to book Blues bands for the club—a job he insisted on handling himself.

That suited Earl just fine. After a while, the twenties he'd been pocketing doubled, then tripled. The more money the club made, the more "allowance" he took and Karlem had been none the wiser—or worse off, he reminded himself smiling. The Blues 'N Booze had made them all pretty wealthy over the years. Still—if he'd thought to listen to anything his sorry janitor father had told him before he'd died years ago, it would've been to save some of that money. Before August 29, it'd never occurred to Earl the good life he was living would all come to an end so quickly.

Of course, with all his money, Boozie Walker had kept on livin' in his old home in the Lower Ninth Ward all these years. He'd said it had "history" or something. To Earl that just meant it was old. As far as he was concerned half the houses down there needed to be knocked down and new ones built instead. As he drove down Claiborne Avenue and crossed the Industrial Canal into the Ward, he was surprised by seeing bits and pieces where whole houses used to be.

"Damn," he said under his breath, it was like having his thoughts brought to life, but not in a good way. With almost no traffic on the streets, Earl started to think he wouldn't find Karlem Walker at his home, after all. "That would be just my luck," he sighed as he turned onto Boozie Walker's street, "To come all this way for nothing."

His mood brightened considerably when he saw a vehicle parked on the street in front of the house and not overturned in the yard. "Hey, hey,

Earl Grant. You are one lucky dog," he sang happily and parked his Lexus on the opposite side of the street. The place was nothing to look at. The floodwaters had pushed the house slightly off its foundation and it seemed to tilt the closer he got to the old shotgun style house.

The door had been left ajar so Earl didn't bother knocking before entering. "Anyone home? Boozie?"

"Is that you, Earl?" A man came from the direction of the bedroom. It took a moment for his face to come out of shadow. "How are you, man?"

. "Hey, Hennessy. I'm doin' awright, partnah. Doin awright." They clasped hands, butted chests and patted each other's backs in greeting. "Where your ole man at?" Earl asked.

The smile fell swiftly from Hennessy's face. "You haven't heard?" The question was rhetorical. "He passed away during the flood, man."

"Oh, man," Earl felt bad for Hen, but worse for himself. That meant he had no place to put a trailer and no way to get a few easy bucks. "I had no idea," he said truthfully. "I'm sorry, Hen. What happened?"

"They found him in that club of his," Lila Walker suddenly appeared to stand next to her son. After twenty years, she was still the finest mamma he'd ever laid eyes on. "Surprised you didn't stay too, as much as ya seem to love that place," she said disapprovingly.

"No, Ma'am. I hit the road when they first started talking bout that hurricane comin' our way. I told Boozie he should hit the road too, but he said he couldn't leave the place unprotected. Last I saw him, he had a couple of guns sittin' across his lap and he was watchin' the front door."

"Look like Boozie was the only one needin' protection," she said wryly. "I found the insurance papers," she said holding up a handful of water stained pages. "Let's get out of here, Hennessy."

"Found 'em in the roll top?" Earl asked.

Lila nodded. "That's right."

"I'm surprised," Earl said. "He usually kept his important papers in the bank safe deposit box."

Hennessy frowned and gave him an odd look. "How do you know?"

Earl laughed. "Work with a man for ten years, you get to know a thing or two about him, right?"

"That's true," Lila agreed.

"Awright, Mamma." Hennessy pulled some car keys from his pocket. "Let's get those to the funeral home."

"Now, Earl if you get a chance, the wake is tomorrow afternoon at four and the funeral is the day after at two," Lila informed him as they all walked out the door. "After the services we're getting together at my house since this place isn't livable."

"Yes, Ma'am. The services gonna be at St. Augustine's?"

"Yes, Lawd. I hope the place won't catch fire as sinful as that man's soul is."

"Stop it, Mamma," Hennessy chided. "Daddy's dead. Wasn't it you that said if you can't say anything good about a person, don't say anything at all?"

"Yeah you right. I'm sorry, dahlin," Lila apologized. "I should show more respect." She turned to Earl. "Where you stayin', baby?"

"Executive Suites for tonight," he answered. "I got a trailer from the emergency agency, but they need somewhere to park it that has electricity and water hookups."

"Park it in the alley behind the bar," Lila said matter-of-factly. "They got hookups from when bands used to park there back in the day."

Earl smiled and gave the woman a loud smack on her smooth, creamy brown cheek. "Beauty and brains all in one fine package. I tell you what, if Antoine Ellis hadn't snatched you up, I woulda had to take a shot myself."

Obviously pleased by the compliment, Lila pushed her hair back from her face. "There was a time when I woulda fell for a smooth talker like you, Earl, but no more. I'm much wiser in my old age."

Hennessy sighed and shifted from one foot to the other, "Come on, Mamma. We've gotta go." He opened the car door to let his mother in. As he moved to the driver's side, Earl stopped him.

"Hey look, man. You planning on rebuilding the B&B?" he asked.

Shaking his head, Hennessy eased into the seat and closed the door. He spoke through the open car window. "Naw, man. I'm not stayin'."

"Well, if that's the case, why don't you let me buy the club?"

A disgusted look stole across Hennessy's face before he managed a more civil demeanor. "I don't think so, Earl," he said simply.

"What? We can't talk about it?" Earl pressed.

"Not right now," Hennessy said. With that, he started the car and sped off down the street.

"Well, I'll be John Brown." Earl pushed his sunglasses on his face and watched the white Ford disappear down the road. "If I didn't know better, I'd say that man has something against me." The thought made him smile. He had no idea what was bugging Hennessy, but it was always a good day when someone thought more of him than they did themselves. And it was a great day when that someone was Hennessy James Walker.

Taking a deep breath of clear air, Earl decided the day would end just right if he could find some female company to take to the Suites. Though the cost would be a good chunk of his monthly government money, he decided the money would be worth it if he could get a woman to warm his bed. It had been nearly impossible to get any play at his brother's house. He'd wondered how Trey'd managed to have three kids since he and his wife didn't seem to have any time together. Heck, the kids slept in the bed with them.

Anyways, first things first...He needed to stop by the Blues 'N Booze to see if the hookups were working and if there was enough room for the trailer. Given Hennessy's reaction to his question about buying the place, Earl was surprised he didn't voice any objection to him taking up parking space in the back. 'Course, it was hard for any man to go against his mamma. And damn, he had a fine mamma.

By the time he reached the B&B, Earl had worked up a nice lusty mood. His next stop would be the Quarter. Some bars had to be open there...and there had to be someone good looking enough to take home. Hell, at this point, good looks were optional.

An old white Taurus was parked in front of the bar. Earl smiled as he recognized it. Rayne was here. The sight of that fine black woman was certain to do nothing but raise the level of his lust...and he didn't mind that a bit.

He rushed out of his car and up the sidewalk. "Rayne?" he yelled pushing his way inside. "You here?"

No answer, but he did hear noises coming from the office behind the bar. Wrinkling his nose at the smell, he made his way across the bar carefully. He didn't want to mess up his Italian leather shoes. The two thousand dollars a month he got on a Visa card from the government wasn't enough to replace them worth anything. "Rayne?" he peeked inside the office.

She turned away from the desk with a handful of water-stained papers in her hand. "Earl!" Her face brightened. "I'm so glad to see you!"

To Earl's delight she flew into his arms. He was immediately aroused. "It's good to see you too, dahlin."

"I was hoping you were in town." She stepped back and adjusted her blouse. Just enough creamy brown cleavage peeked out from the v-neck to send Earl's lust into high gear. "Did Sister Alveta tell you I needed your help?"

"No." *But I sure need yours*, he wanted to say. He knew better than to move too fast. After all these years, Rayne would think he'd lost his mind if he suddenly started mackin' on her now. But Boozie wasn't around...and she was sure looking good in those jeans. "What can I do for you, Rayne?"

"I'm looking for the deed to the B&B." She went back the desk, careful not to trip over the overturned file drawers. The floor was covered with a pulpy mess that had once been paper and manila folders. "I hope it wasn't in there."

"I doubt, it," Earl offered. "It's probably in your daddy's bank safe deposit box."

"Really?"

She looked so pretty and hopeful, it made Earl ache. "Yeah. I suppose Hennessy could get in now the old man is dead."

"You don't have access?" she asked. "That's surprising. I thought you took care of all his business matters."

Maybe he imagined the extra bat of her eyelashes or the shift of her hips, but Earl didn't think so. He knew when a woman was comin' on to him. "Naw. Not everything. Just the B&B, here," Earl looked around. "What a mess, huh?"

"Yeah. It's a real shame." Rayne dusted her hands off and moved past Earl into the bar. She brushed him gently with her breasts as she passed. "But I plan to renovate it."

"Really?" Earl followed her with renewed interest. "Hennessy told me he wasn't planning on rebuilding this place."

"Oh?" Rayne lifted a lovely dark eyebrow. "Well, not everything's up to Hennessy."

"Do tell," Earl sidled up next to her. She was saying some sweet things and he didn't want to miss a word. "Who's it up to then? You?"

"Once the deed is in my name it will be." She gave him a knowing look.

"What about Hennessy?"

She gave a lovely dismissing noise. "You know that boy…he ain't stayin'. He'll be headin' back to California on the first plane day after tomorrow."

It fit with what Hennessy had told Earl. "So, what's your plan?" he asked, enjoying of her breasts as she adjusted her blouse for no good reason 'cept to tease him.

"I was thinking that once I put this place back in order you could go back to running it like you did before." She looked up at him with her wide, pretty brown eyes.

Hell, he was about to say he'd work for free if she kept that up, but reason found it's way through all the haze clouding his head. "Temptin' offer," Earl said, raring back on his heels, "but I believe I have a better one."

She turned and crossed her arms. A hint of a smile played at the corners of her lips. "What's that?"

"A partnership. You and me. Fifty-fifty."

Rayne tucked her chin and looked skeptical. "You got fifty percent money to put up?"

"Naw," Earl laughed. "But, you're gonna be busy with other things—watchin' that boy of yours, you know? I think it's worth fifty percent if I have to do all the work of running the place. Whaddya say?"

"Let me think about it," Rayne offered. "But, first, we have to find the deed."

"That shouldn't be too hard." Earl moved closer to the front door. The smell of the place was getting to him. "Have your brother take you to the bank and get in that box."

"All right."

"But I think it best if you not mention our little side deal," Earl said quickly.

"Why?"

"Seems like Hennessy's got something against me having anything to do with the place. I already offered to buy it from him today."

"Really?" Rayne raised her brows. "I thought you said you didn't have any money."

"Don't," Earl smiled, "but that shouldn't stop a man from asking, should it?"

"Anyway…" Rayne gestured for him to continue.

"Anywayyyy," Earl teased, "he told me he didn't think so. All nasty like."

"Why would he care if you owned it?"

"Who knows? Maybe it's because your daddy died. You know I've seen more of his old man in the past ten years than he has." Earl stepped out in the fresh air. Rayne followed and closed the door behind them. "I'm lucky he's allowing me to park my government trailer behind the building." He walked around the front and started down the alley. "Which is why I came here. I've got to check the hookups."

Behind the building the wide concrete pad was relatively unharmed. Other debris, including tree branches and broken furniture had been left in the wake of the flood in the yard, however.

"Nice view," Rayne teased.

Earl turned the faucet and was thrilled to see the water was still running. "This is a good sign. I wonder how I can test the electricity."

"Wait." Rayne ran back up the alley and came back a few moments later with tools and some kind of gauge. "Since we don't have anything with the right kind of plug, I'll test the wires to see if there's a current." She quickly had the cover off the plug and had stripped the wires enough to put the probe from the gadget on them. "They're hot," she announced. "Looks like you're in business, Earl."

"Thanks, Rayne." He was growing as attracted to her handy work as he was to the way her behind looked when she bent over to put the outlet cover back on. "Where'd you learn to do that?"

"DeTron had a friend who was an electrician. And we lived in a house with a lot of electrical problems. I got to know a lot about fixin' things…and about that friend before my divorce." She shrugged as if her confessing to having an affair was no big deal.

"What're you doing for dinner tonight?" he asked impulsively.

"Nothing special," she shot over her shoulder. "Why? You wanna hang out?"

"Why not?" Earl tried to sound nonchalant. "I was thinking about going over to the Quarter to see if anything was open."

"Sounds good." Rayne grunted as she put the final twists on the screws. "I've been dying for some crawfish since I've been back."

"Then it's a date." Earl's lustful mood was back and pressing hard against his BVDs. It had been one great day and Rayne in his bed would make the night just as great. Suddenly, he was thinking anything could happen. He was back in New Orleans, baby. *Let the good times roll.*

Buddy Guy's "Cheaper to Keep Her" played, announcing an incoming call on Hennessy's cell. The clock on the nightstand told him it was nine o'clock. "Hello?"

"Hey, Hennessy, it's Jack. How's it goin'?"

Jack played the keyboard in their jazz trio. It was good to hear his voice. "It's going all right. You know…considering."

"Right, right. My heart goes out to you and your family, man." Jack spoke quickly, always had. But he was speaking even faster than usual tonight, which meant he was nervous about something.

Hennessy sat up in the small bed. "What's going on, Jack? Everything good with you and Johnnie?"

"Yeah, we're doin' all right. But, listen, Hen. I got the gig in San Francisco pushed until next weekend, but here at Yoshi's, they're not happy with us. They're threatening to sue us for breach of contract."

"Well, screw 'em, man." Hennessy hadn't had a good day and this was the last thing he wanted to hear. "My father died, what do they expect me do?"

"Calm down, brah. It'll be fine. Look here, me and Johnnie found us a singer and the thing is, he can play the piano, too. He said he'd be happy to step in till you get back."

"You replaced me?" Hennessy couldn't believe what he was hearing. "Just like that, after all—"

"No, no, man. It ain't like that at all," Jack insisted. "We made it clear with Terry that when you come back he's out and he's cool, Hen. Really, man, it's all good."

"Terry? You replaced me with Terry Pryce?" Hennessy was on his feet, pacing furiously around the small room. "You know he got kicked out of his own band because he's a damn junkie. Have you guys lost your minds?"

"Damn, man, what's wrong with you?" Jack was angry now. "The man's gonna keep us outta trouble 'till you get back. He swears he's fresh out of rehab and won't be doing any drugs. We haven't replaced you permanently so would you please chill out?"

Hennessy stopped pacing and took a deep breath. Jack was right. What was he having such a fit about? He'd be back in California in three days, so everything would be back to normal then. Being back in New Orleans was suffocating him. "I'm sorry, man. I…it's just that I'm so stressed since I've been back…sorry."

"All right, all right. That's better. That's the man I know and love. Look it's cool, man and I understand how you must be feeling, but look here, you need to get out take your mind off things. Go find you a woman, have a date and work some stuff out. You hear what I'm saying, right?"

He heard him loud and clear. "You know, sleeping with a woman doesn't solve all of life's problems, Jack."

"Maybe not, man, but I don't remember ever feeling bad when I was getting my groove on. You know what I'm sayin'?" His laughter crackled across the line, making Hennessy feel better.

"You're right, man. I think I'll take your advice and get out of the house for while."

"That's good, man. I'm glad to hear it. We'll be checking with you later." Before he hung up, Hennessy heard Johnnie's voice asking, "How'd he take it?"

"Negro nearly lost his damn mind," Jack replied, then the line went dead.

Hennessy laughed, folded his phone and placed it in the holder on his belt. He hadn't bothered to get undressed because he hadn't been sleepy. Opening the door, he stepped out into the darkened house. The light snores he heard from the living room couch let him know he wouldn't be able to ask his stepfather's permission to take his car. His mother had left for a friend's house a half hour before. Better to ask for forgiveness later, he decided.

He eased into the living room, taking care not to make more noise than the television. The *Antique Road Show* was on, but Antoine wasn't hearing a word about the 1870 glassware one woman was having appraised. Kicking the coffee table, and running into the edge of the couch was all the damage Hennessy managed to inflict upon himself as he made his way through the room and into the kitchen. With growing fondness for the sight impaired, Hennessy felt around until he found the light on the stove hood and pushed it on. Antoine's keys were on the hook by the back door.

In less than a minute he'd pulled out of the carport and was heading down the street toward the French Quarter. If anything was happening in the city this time of night, it would be there. The Quarter had been the first area to open after the hurricane and for some unexplained reason, people and some tourists had come back to bring life to the city.

And lively it was.

On Bourbon Street, Jazz drifted from bars, laughter filled the streets, as did dozens of people who danced to the tunes of roving street performers. If he didn't know better, he'd think the hurricane never happened. But, the Quarter hadn't been the area hardest hit by the flooding. The Orleans and St. Bernard Parishes, where his father had lived had been damaged the worst.

Here, it looked as if most of the business owners had chosen to come back and rebuild. The thought still amazed Hennessy given there didn't seem to be much progress or interest in making the city's levee system hurricane proof anytime soon. In a matter of a few short months, it would be hurricane season again with no guarantee that a repeat performance wouldn't wipe New Orleans off the map permanently.

But, for the moment, he was here in the New Orleans of old and the neon sign for Arnaud's Remoulade blazed like a beacon in the clear November night. A beautiful antique mahogany bar dominated one wall of the bar where a respectable number of patrons enjoyed drinks and talk. A perky waitress was there in a minute to whisk him to a vacant granite-topped table. Hennessy ordered a beer then scooped up the menu.

His stomach rumbled reminding him of his neglect. That afternoon, when he'd gotten back to his mother's house from the funeral home, Antoine and Teardrop had managed to clean the gumbo pot—not that he'd felt much like eating after seeing the coffin his father would be buried in.

Shaking off depressing thoughts, Hennessy tried to hold on to his newfound good mood. Just as he was narrowing his choice to pizza or a shrimp po-boy, he heard the unmistakable cackle of his sister's laugh.

Looking up, he was shocked to see Earl and Rayne across the room. He didn't care at all for the way Rayne was resting her breasts on top of her arms like an offering to the gods of lust. Nor did he think too much of the way Earl's eyes seemed to stay locked on them, like she was that evening's special.

The waitress came over with his beer and asked to take his order. "Shrimp po-boy," he said taking the drink from her.

"You want that dressed, dahlin?" she asked, smiling sweetly and just a tad seductively.

"Yeah, put everything on it," he instructed. "Oh, and could you deliver it to that table there?" He pointed at Earl and Rayne.

"If you say so, sugah," she said with a smirk. "But it seems to me like you may be bustin' up a pretty good party."

That was the point, but she didn't need to know. "Yeah, well, trust me, I'm always the life of the party."

The waitress gave him a quick once over. "I'll just bet on that. I'll have your order right out."

Collecting his napkin and silverware, Hennessy marched over to his sister's table. "You don't mind if I join you, do you?" He pulled out a chair and sat down, ignoring their surprised looks.

"Not at all, brah," Earl recovered quickly. "Have a seat. You want me to call over a waitress?"

"I've ordered." Hennessy smiled, but felt no humor. "So what brings the two of you out tonight?" He tried to make the question casual, but knew it hadn't come out that way.

"I ran in to Earl at the B&B and we decided to hang out since it's been a while since we've seen one another," Rayne answered simply. "Why? Is that a sin?"

The B&B? Why had she gone there? "I thought you were going to pick up Ray Ray."

"He's at a friend's house who has a little boy his age. He begged to spend the night. I let him."

The lie slipped out of her mouth like melted butter. If she hadn't avoided looking at him, Hennessy might have believed her. "I'd like to see him before I leave."

"Fine. He'll be back tomorrow," she said.

"Great." Hennessy said.

"Hey, Hen," Earl leapt into the narrow wedge of silence. "You remember when we were kids, you used to stop by the bar before school and pretend to play a trumpet up on the stage?"

"You were there?" Hennessy seemed more surprised than upset. "I never saw you."

"I was usually finished with the sweeping your daddy paid me for by the time you came by. I didn't want to disturb you since you'd taken such pains to keep it secret."

"Why didn't you want Daddy to know about it?" Rayne asked.

The humor left his face. "Because he didn't approve."

"What?" She was shocked. "He lived for music. Seemed like to me he was awfully proud when you got your own band."

"He loved the music, but he saw what a lot of the musicians were into. A lot of them were addicted to drugs and liquor." He didn't mean to pester, but he couldn't help but give her a preaching look. "He didn't want me—either of us—to have any part of that, remember?"

Rayne looked past him toward the bar. Her mouth moved from side to side as if working to swallow all the things she didn't want to say. When her eyes filled, Hennessy felt bad, but hopeful. Maybe he would get through to her after all.

"Anyway," he continued. "Daddy was real disappointed to find out I'd been playing in a band at night while I was at LSU. We had a big fight about it back then. For years, every time we talked he asked me to come back and help him manage the bar. Not that you weren't doin' a good job, Earl," he was quick to add. "He just wanted to watch over me, I think."

Earl nodded and pretended to take interest in the drink on the table. He remembered overhearing Boozie talking on the phone with Hennessy about coming back and running the bar a few days before the hurricane. Earl had asked him about it when he hung up. "What about me?" he'd asked. "Your son comes back and I'm out of a job like that?"

Boozie had just looked at him for a minute. Then he'd said, "I have eyes and I have ears and all of them work jus fine, son. I hope you don't think I haven't noticed how much less we're makin' ever' night than we were a year ago. I hope you don't think you're puttin' anything past me."

Of course, Earl didn't take too well to being called a thief. What he'd taken, he was owed—least that's the way he looked at things and he had no problem saying just that to Boozie. The old man had let him raise hell, and then shook his head. "Straighten up. Fly right," he'd said, "and I won't press charges."

Because Boozie had a soft spot and Earl knew how to push it, he'd immediately dropped the attitude and pleaded with the man to let him keep his job. He'd promised not to take another dime out of the till. Boozie had said he'd think on it and get back to him.

Earl never had the chance to talk with him again. The next day the mayor was evacuating the city, then Katrina blew through. What surprised Earl was finding out the old man hadn't told Hennessy about their conversation. He thought maybe that was why Hennessy had acted so funny when he'd asked to buy the place. But sitting here talking with him, Earl realized Hennessy had no idea about that last conversation.

"So, I didn't get a chance to ask you what you were up to while you were gone, Earl," Hennessy said. "Were you with family?"

"Yeah, I was." Earl confirmed, knowing Hennessy really wanted to know why he was here with his sister. "But it was definitely time to go. They wanted me to take any job I could find out in San Antone, but I just couldn't do it. A man's gotta keep up appearances." He pulled at the collar of what had to have been an expensive shirt. "Ya can't do that working at McDonald's, you know?"

"I dunno," Hennessy leaned back to let the waitress serve their meals. She winked at him when she strode away from the table. Hennessy smiled at the woman, but didn't take any real interest. "I heard McDonald's managers make pretty good money," he kept up the small talk. "And, let's face it, there isn't much opportunity around here."

"You're right," Earl agreed. "But I found out you can get government money to rebuild your house and start up a business if you came back. I plan to be my own boss."

"Seems a little foolish, Earl. They haven't made firm plans to fortify the city's levees to take a level four hurricane. You could be right out of business come the next hurricane."

"No more foolish than thinkin' you can make a livin' playin' a guitar in a band," Earl half-laughed to hide his irritation. "Both things take a lotta faith."

"He's got a point there, Hen," Rayne chimed in. Earl thought she looked pleased he'd been able to come back at Hennessy. "How is that band of yours anyway? What's the name?"

"Whiskey Sins Trio," Hennessy answered. He'd noticed the quick exchange between Earl and Rayne. The two of them were cooking up something and he was sure it was no good. "It's sort of a play off our names. Hennessy, Jack Daniels and Johnnie Walker." It was a huge coincidence he and Johnnie had the same last name. A bit of butter dripped down the side of his mouth before he caught it with the corner of his napkin. "We're touring some joints in California for the next couple of months. We should get some real good exposure."

"Seems like you're making a fair living at it," Earl observed, feeling as if he'd proven his point. "Nice watch, nice threads."

Rayne shook her head. "Leave it to you to notice anything that even smells expensive, Earl. What I want to know, Hen, is how you like all that traveling? Seems like you'd get tired of it after a while."

Hennessy shrugged. "I do sometimes. I can't stand flying and tour buses are too slow, but what're you gonna do? I love playing. It's like I get up on that stage and all my worries and anxieties disappear. I'm transported to another world—to another reality."

He closed his eyes and a satisfied smile lifted one corner of his mouth. "It's like the music is deep inside me and it wants so bad to come out that I have to play and play…" He moved his hands as if playing his guitar was in his hands. Then he opened his eyes just enough to look at Rayne. "*Dweeee-dee-da-da-da. Da-da-da. Da-da-da. Da-da-da,*" he sang the tune in his head. "It's mystical. It's magical. You know what I mean?" he asked, his voice a husky whisper.

"Whatever," Rayne clucked her tongue. Something so compelling threatened to suck her in when he spoke about his music. When they were kids, she used to sneak into his room when she couldn't sleep and he would tell stories and make up songs until she fell asleep. But she was a grown woman now and wasn't in the mood for fairy tale stories that would never come true. "Must be nice to bounce around like that—all carefree and stuff. Just when I think life is going good, some damn hurricane blows in and makes a mess of things."

Hennessy hated the look of hopelessness creeping into her eyes. "We may not be able to control the weather, Rayne, but we can choose to evacuate when we know its coming. Your hurricanes have names, too. Male names like DeTron and Tyrone and you walked right into them."

"You're so full of it, Hennessy."

"I'm full of it?" he asked, nearly shouting.

She lifted the palm of her hand to his face. "I'm in no mood for your preaching tonight."

Hennessy grabbed her hand and pulled it down to the table. "Don't disrespect me like that."

"Hold up, hold up, hold up." Earl put up both hands and waved the arguing to a stop. "I hate to break up this here love fest, but I think you're scarin' the other customers," he joked.

Hennessy looked around. He saw people turning their heads abruptly back to their meals. "Yeah. Right." Now wasn't the time for this conversation anyway. "We'll talk about this later." He released her.

Rayne scowled at him and massaged her hand. "Let's get outta here, Earl." She pushed away from the table and grabbed her purse from an adjacent chair.

"No problem, baby. No problem." Earl reached for his wallet. "The night's still young and I got plans for later. Don't want you all riled up—unless it's in a good way."

Hennessy didn't like the way Earl's gazed roamed his sister's backside when he spoke.

"See you later, Hen," Earl said, tossing a twenty on the table.

Hennessy reached for his own wallet, realizing as he picked up the ticket that Earl had given just enough to cover his own meal, but not Rayne's. He cursed beneath his breath and put down enough to cover the remainder plus tip. He was getting a real bad feeling about Earl and Rayne. Real bad.

Chapter Three

Dejanette Devine found herself in a smoky bar navigating between gyrating hips and dancing feet being led by seductive lyrics and deep, throaty moans. A Jazz trio played a sexy, soulful tune. The bass, drums and piano were the perfect backdrop to his down home voice, rich with the ancient soul of New Orleans.

She weaved in out of the tangle of happy spirits, nearly a lifetime seemed to pass before she reached the edge of the crowd. They parted as if on command, allowing her a glimpse of the man with the magical voice.

Magnificent, she felt her thoughts whisper. Though inadequate, it was the only word that came close to describing the man. Trumpet gripped firmly, but carefully in his right hand, and the left caressing the microphone like a lover, he sang to her. The words were difficult to make out, though the deep, throaty voice resonated clearly throughout her being.

She took a step closer to the stage, wanting suddenly to put a hand to his slightly whiskered jaw and trail her fingers along the neat dreads hanging just past his wide shoulders. As she felt the urge grow stronger, he opened his eyes and caught her in his chocolate-brown gaze.

His eyes were magic eyes, brown irises ringed with gold. He became aware of her then as his eyes pierced into her soul. *Of course,* she thought. Her soul was all he *could* see at that moment. In this plane—in this reality—things felt less solid, less certain, so she didn't blame him for believing her to be a dream.

As he lifted his trumpet to his mouth, Deja found herself wishing to be in the instrument's place…then she became the instrument, pressed against those strong, firm lips, feeling his breath against her skin.

Her pulse raced in time to the tune his fingers played against her now naked spine. His music blew through her being whipping life into places she'd forgotten existed. She felt herself sparkle. She shimmered green, then red, then gold. The feeling went beyond sensual, beyond sexual—it was—erotic. And, good God, it was wonderful. His tune grew more intense, his fingers traveled faster. He hit a high C note and millions of bright white lights filled her. She stretched taut as he held that note…and held it…Overwhelmed, Deja cried out releasing her ecstasy into both the worlds in which she resided.

Panting, Deja opened her eyes and stared at the top of her narrow trailer. "Jeezus," she pushed her hair back from her face as she lay in her bed. That had never happened before. In all her travels, she'd never had an experience quite so satisfying. For the first time in a long time, she felt as if all of her chakras, her power centers, were pure. Which surprised her. As recently as yesterday, she'd done a crystal cleansing. Yet, last night in the plane less tangible, she'd found the mere thought of the man's hands to be more real than anything she'd felt in a very long time. "That means he's close," she said to the black cat who'd just jumped onto the bed next to her pillow.

"Rrrrowww," Jazmeen replied lazily. She curled herself into a contented black ball of fur and started to clean herself.

"How many times have I told you not to do that on my bed?" Deja got out of the bed and picked up the cat. "You can leave all the hair you want on your own bed," she scolded gently before dropping the cat onto the pillowed perch at the front window.

Crossing the narrow FEMA trailer to the kitchenette, it could hardly be considered more, Deja turned on her laptop then started a pot of coffee. The Internet took forever to come up because she had to plug it into a regular telephone line. "I miss high-speed cable," she said, petting her cat companion now occupying space on one of her two dining room chairs. She took the other, opened her journal to the list she'd made on January 1, 2005 and waited patiently.

She didn't have much use for her gifts these days. With precious few tourists visiting her shop on Bourbon Street and no radio stations calling her to do readings lately, they too were struggling with rebuilding their stations to get back on the air, Deja found herself with lots of time on her hands.

Too Much Hennessy

Her AOL came up at about the same time her coffee maker finished brewing. Pouring a cup of black coffee she typed in NOLA.com and selected the obituaries. "Damn," she said dismayed. She ran her finger down the page of her journal and found the name—just as she'd predicted.

Services for Etta Jane Williams were being held Wednesday at 5:00 P.M. at the Lake Lawn Metairie Funeral Home. Deja made a note that in lieu of flowers the family was requesting donations to the hospice that had cared for her in her last days.

She was about to click off of the depressing page, but a name caught her attention—it stilled her heart. Walker. Karlem James. The name was next to last on the page. "Oh no." She hadn't anticipated this death, hadn't even had a hint of it happening. "Not him."

Jazmeen seemed to sense her alarm and moved into her lap, letting her soft, furry tail wrap around Deja's arm. She sat down heavily and began purring as if to ease the distress.

Deja pet the cat mindlessly for a while, not wanting the information to be true. Eventually, she took a hesitant hand to her touch pad and clicked to open the notice. Karlem Walker's service was to be held on Tuesday with visitation happening the day before. That was today, she realized.

Quickly she jotted his name on the back page of her journal along with the name of the funeral home. She paused, closed her eyes and willed herself to be still. With her hand over the page, she waited patiently. She felt no vibrations, no images, nothing at all that confirmed Karlem's death. Something wasn't right.

Her cell phone rang and she jumped from her chair. The movement startled Jazmeen who dug her back claws into Deja's legs as she leapt to safety on the floor.

Deja cursed as she ran to the bedroom, but managed to retrieve the cell from the bottom of her shoulder bag just before it went to voicemail. "Hello?" she tried not to sound out of breath. Hopefully the program manager at one of the radio stations would be asking her to come back to their morning show.

"Hello? Zhooreena?" Ivalou Devine was on the other end of the phone and her slurred speech evidence that she was having another "episode".

"Hi, Mamma." Hopeful thoughts of a job disappeared. Deja repositioned herself on the floor and slumped against the bed. She rested her elbows on her knees as she talked. "Did you take your medicine this morning?"

"Yup. I shore did," she confirmed. "Lishen, babee. Where'ya at? I ain't seen you…you…in a long time."

"I'm back home, Mamma. Remember? I'm in New Orleans."

"Yeah…Yeah." There was a long silence on the other end of the phone.

"Mamma?"

Her soft sobs filled the empty space.

Deja's heart grew heavy with sadness. "Don't cry, Mamma. Please."

"I'm so sorry, babee," she wept mournfully. "Sorry for…for evrathing I done."

"There's no need to be sorry, Mamma. We're going to be all right. Both of us. I'm going to find a job and get some insurance—"

There was a thud on the other side of the line. Then the sound of her Aunt Billie calling her sister's name in the distance. "Ivalou?"

"Mamma?" Deja rose to her feet, feeling panicked. "Mamma what happened?"

"She fell down, Dee." Her Aunt's voice came across the line in a crisp, irritated tone. "It's been happenin' more and more. We need to talk about makin' other arrangements."

At first, her Aunt Billie had been more than happy to take them both in when they'd arrived after the hurricane. But, she'd had no idea the amount of care and attention her mamma required. Not all the time, just when she had her little episodes.

Ivalou was on medication to allow for fairly constant bowel movements. Her liver wasn't functioning right and wasn't flushing out the ammonia that built up like it was supposed to. When the ammonia levels became elevated, her mamma's speech slurred, she became moody and her muscles weakened. Most people thought she was drunk because she exuded a strong alcohol-like odor when this happened.

Deja discovered quickly during their brief stay that her Auntie Billie was not a nurturing woman. She'd had every intention on bringing her mamma back to New Orleans with her, but Billie's husband, George, had advised against it. "Your mamma needs good medical care," he'd said. "You don't know what you'll find back in New Orleans." He'd insisted that she get settled before coming back for Ivalou, which turned out to be very sound advice.

But her Tee Billie was clearly running out of what little patience she had.

"You're right, Tee," Deja called her Auntie by the nickname she'd used growing up. "But I haven't been able to get a good job yet and I need to get insurance so we can put Mamma on the transplant list."

"Do whatever you gotta do, Dee." It sounded like a command.

"I will. Would you have Mamma call me back when she's feeling better?"

She received a grudging agreement and they ended the call.

Deja closed the small phone and let it drop into the pile of what remained of her life inside her purse. Then she fell, arms spread, back onto her bed. "What am I going to do?" she asked, hoping an answer would fall into her arms. Or, at the very least, make its way into her conscious thoughts.

She lay there for a long time, staring up at the ceiling. By the time she rose to get another cup of coffee, she knew the one thing she had to do. She had to attend the visitation for Boozie Walker. Doing so had no possibility of helping her with her own problems, but for whatever reason, everything in her was insisting she go.

"So be it." She said aloud. Now the only problem was to find something black to wear.

You never knew about a man until he died, Hennessy thought. For the past hour and a half he'd learned more about his father than he had in his entire lifetime. For a man rumored to be "godless" and "no-account," it seemed Boozie Walker had made a lifelong habit of doing good for those around him.

"Yeah, I used to be at the Blues 'N Booze ever' night." The man speaking was tall and thin and missing a few important teeth. His name was Crazy Willie and Hennessy knew the man had been chased from nearly every legitimate business in the city. "I'd beg me a few dollahs offa da tourists down at da Quartah and come in to get a drink, you know?"

Hennessy nodded and waited patiently for the man to finish coughing long enough to continue his story. The man looked sober now, if a bit worse for wear, after decades of drinking.

"But, yo daddy never would let me have a drink at his 'stablishment." Willie shook his head and stared at Hennessy with rheumy eyes. "He'd tell me to sit a while, listen to the Blues and think how my problems weren't no worse 'n the ones they was singin' about."

"He'd give me some soda water and a bit of food 'cause he knew I didn't care much 'bout eatin' back then. Probably saved my life, you know? He'd say, 'Gotta eat something, Willie. Give that liquor something to eat on 'sides your liver.' Purdy soon, I figured yo daddy was right, but I din't have no idea how to stop wantin' likker, you know?"

"Sure, sure," Hennessy acknowledged, impressed that his father hadn't thrown the man out like everyone else had.

"Seem like whiskey tasted just like butterscotch it was so good." His old eyes brightened at the thought. "But it was jus the voodoo my wife done on me what made it so hard, you know? But Boozie took me to a priestess ovah da river in Algiers. She took dat spell right offa me," he said with wonder. "I ain't had a drink since, but that spell hung onta me for a whole week. Had me shakin' and stuff. Boozie'd stop by ever' day ta make sure I took da medicine the priestess give me and to make sure I had food. He'd sit a while and tell me 'bout what band was playin' at the club." The old man took out his handkerchief to cover his next bout of coughing. "He was a good man, yo daddy. Good man."

Too Much Hennessy

Hennessy offered his hand to old man. "Thank you, Mr. Willie. I appreciate your kind words." As the old man moved on there were more people with more stories of how his father had helped them in some way or another. Many a musician stopped by to say how his daddy had discovered them and helped them get gigs at other clubs in the city. His neighbors talked about how he kept their kids out of trouble during the day after school—just like he'd done when Hennessy had been a kid.

Because of the hours he kept, Daddy had slept during the day. By the time school let out, he would be dressed and ready to help Hennessy with his homework. He always let him bring home friends as often as he liked, which drove his mamma crazy. Usually, Rayne would insist on hanging out with him and his friends. Once they'd finished with homework they'd go outside to play stickball, or go skateboarding and he'd allow his sister to go as long as she didn't act like a girl and start whining and crying over the smallest little thing.

He looked over at his sister who was talking with some his father's old band friends. She looked lovely in her simple black dress, though it worried him to see the bones of her spine so plainly above the scooped collar. She seemed sober enough, but her hands shook ever so slightly as she gestured.

She'd sat Ray Ray down in one of the chairs along the wall. He seemed content to play with the small cars he'd brought along, racing them up and down his extended three-year-old legs and making car sounds with pursed lips and puffed out cheeks. He was a good boy and most of the time Rayne took really good care of him. Still, Hennessy was afraid for them both. Afraid Rayne would continue using drugs and afraid of the effect it would have on her son.

A shrill woman's voice brought Hennessy's attention back to his greeting duty.

"I remember your dad used to fix all the flat tires we'd get on our bikes, back then." Sheree, now a welfare mother of three, reminisced. "You boys stop all that runnin' around!" she yelled. One of her boys, a child of about Ray Ray's age was running around the casket screaming while the other, at least a year older, chased him. Her third child she held firmly in the folds of her plump arms. She was about the cutest baby Hennessy had ever laid eyes on.

"Your dad never did change. Before this," Sheree continued, glancing quickly at the coffin, "he would still talk with my kids and give 'em money for snow cones every Friday."

"Is that right?" Hennessy nodded politely noting her other two children were still running amuck.

"Jason! Lysander!" she screamed with more volume this time. "Could you hold her?"

Before he could answer, the sweet-faced baby was in his arms and Sheree was chasing down boys and grabbing them by their collars.

The baby looked up at him with wide brown eyes.

"Hey, pretty girl," he said, a little nervous about how she'd react to being thrown into a stranger's arms.

She cooed and gave him a gorgeous smile.

Relieved, Hennessy settled her onto his hip. "Don't ever grow up to be like your brothers, okay?"

She giggled with delight and bounced a bit in his arms.

If he was guaranteed to have a child with this disposition, Hennessy thought it wouldn't be so bad to have kids. But Sheree's boys—well they were like taking a year's worth of birth control all at once. Sheree finally got tired of managing conversations between yells and left with all three of her children in tow.

In another thirty minutes, the visitation would be over, but Hennessy knew the memory of this day would live with him forever. Today, the better part of the community had come out of their hurricane-battered homes and troubled lives to pay respects to a man who, on the face of it, had done nothing more than run a bar. In fact, his father had touched many lives in a positive way. The whole thing was overwhelming.

Hennessy felt shamed. Ashamed he'd been in such a hurry to leave home and start his own life. Ashamed he'd been so caught up with his band and the road that he hadn't stuck around to get to know this Boozie Walker. Hennessy refused to look toward the coffin, certain he'd let his father down.

Too Much Hennessy

Feeling closed in, he looked around the room. Thank goodness the crowd was thinning. His mother stood talking with a couple and there were only a few other people around, including Teardrop. Soon he'd be able to get out of there and get a few drinks. A little liquor would help him sleep better than he had the night before, though for a while he'd had the best dream…

A strange feeling prickled the back of his neck, like a door had just been opened. He turned his attention to the front entrance. He blinked twice when he saw her, thinking he was imagining things. It was the woman from his dream. But how was that possible? Hennessy was sure he'd never seen this woman before, yet she looked so familiar.

Though she wore a wide-brimmed black hat, tilted just so across her face, and a large pair of sunglasses, he knew for a fact it was her. He'd dreamed of her pressed against his lips and his fingers playing along her beautiful creamy brown spine. He'd played her softly until she'd moaned then played her fast until she'd screamed. He'd awakened with the most amazing hard-on that morning.

As if she'd heard his thoughts or sensed his stare, she turned to look at him.

She looked the way Jazz sounded on a warm, summer night in her breezy black dress and her strappy sandals with sparkling black beads. She walked toward him in what seemed like slow motion. Her long, elegant neck was wrapped in white pearls, her shapely caramel legs glistened beneath the soft folds of her outfit.

A song sprang to his mind as he fell captive to her sexy sway. It had a strong, stealthy beat, he decided. Yeah, that's it—something bold and sexy. He heard a piano playing, accompanied by a soulful saxophone. And then the lyrics—*Sexy lady, I-I-I don't know your name. (No I don't) Bu oh-ohhh honey! I gotta have you just the same. I remember your sweet lips and the way you felt beneath my fingertips, awww-oh-oh babe, you've like to drive this man insane.*

She stared deep into his eyes as she walked past him to stand in front of the casket. She seemed to be deep in thought, almost trancelike as she stood there. After a while, she placed her hand on the casket, closed her eyes, and froze.

Shaking loose of his hypnotic trance, Hennessy wondered about the woman. What was she doing with her hand laid gently on top of his father's casket? It seemed like she was trying to feel for movement beneath the smooth, polished steel.

Curious, Hennessy walked up beside her. "I'm Hennessy Walker." He offered his hand.

The woman opened her eyes slowly behind the dark lenses as she turned to face him. It seemed she took a moment to catch her breath. Hennessy found that surprisingly erotic.

"Dejanette Devine." She took the hand he offered and tilted her head slightly as if waiting for something.

You certainly are, he wanted to say, but checked his lustful impulse. He recalled briefly that her name had come up when his mamma and Teardrop had talked about his daddy's latest mistress, but he didn't linger on that detail. Their palms met and it seemed to Hennessy like his dream had come to life. His body remembered being with this woman, his fingers recalled tingling as they'd played along the soft, silky skin of her back.

A tiny moan escaped Deja's lips. Her voice was just as he'd dreamed it—1-900 soft and sexy.

"Nice to meet you, Miss Devine." Every male part of him seemed eager to do in real life what he'd dreamed the night before. Hennessy released her, hoping to calm himself in the process. Ever so casually, he brought his hands down in front of his "boys" to make sure she didn't see how enthusiastic they were becoming.

"The pleasure's all mine." She said calmly, coolly. "I have good news for you."

At first her comment didn't register with Hennessy. Good news? Was she kidding? His question must have shown on his face.

"Your father is very much alive."

Hennessy looked at the casket. Had she actually felt something in there? Of course not, he dismissed the thought quickly. The woman was clearly some sort of religious zealot. Inwardly he sighed and his hormones became significantly less energetic. Why did the gorgeous ones have to be crazy?

"I know," Hennessy decided to play along and tell her what she obviously wanted to hear. "His spirit lives on, I'm sure."

She bit at her very tempting bottom lip and managed a slanted smile. "I'm being quite literal, Mr. Walker."

Really crazy.

"Okayyy," he drew the word out like he was talking to his three-year-old nephew. "Who's in the casket then?"

Looking back at the box, Deja breathed deeply and frowned in concentration. "A man whose ill intentions were turned upon him," she finally replied. Then with a smile she added, "Your father killed him."

Hennessy was no longer amused. "Who are you and why are you here?" he demanded

"I'm a friend of your father's. I saw his obituary and I knew it couldn't be right," she said in a rush. "I'm not crazy, Mr. Walker," Deja insisted as if reading his thoughts. "I…your father meant a lot to me. That's all."

"I'll just bet he did." Lila was at Hennessy's side looking the woman up and down.

"You're his ex-wife, right?" Deja turned an assessing look in Lila's direction. "I remember you from…that day."

"And I remember you." Lila lifted her eyebrows in a disapproving way. "But, I'd thought you'd left town."

"I did. For a while." Deja seemed not to notice what Hennessy thought was obvious dislike for her. "Boozie always said such nice things about you," she said brightly.

"How embarrasin' for you." Lila smiled a little.

Hennessy knew the words soothed the hurt deep inside his mamma that had never healed from his daddy's rejection.

"A man has a hard time forgettin' his first love," she added smugly.

Deja nodded, though clearly she was holding back her thoughts on the subject.

Hennessy was truly disappointed. This crazy but gorgeous creature had been his father's mistress. His heart sank to the soles of his feet as all the sensual images of her popped out of his mind like the air from a balloon.

Rayne walked up then. "Did I hear you right?" she asked the woman. Her eyes were wide with wonder. "You're THE Deja Devine? The psychic?"

"I am," Deja sang out happily. Obviously she had been anxious to be recognized.

It all clicked into place for Hennessy. He'd also recognized her name because he'd heard her on the radio. Deja Devine was a local celebrity prior to the hurricane as listeners to any of New Orleans major radio stations could testify. Hennessy, a true skeptic, had always considered her "readings" to be nothing more than really good leading questions. "So, you knew my father?" he asked her, not sure if he expected her to come right out and say she'd been his mistress.

"I wouldn't be Deja the Devine Psychic if not for Boozie Walker," she said. "I'm relieved to know he's all right." She reached inside the large black bag draped from her shoulder for her wallet. Pulling out a business card, she handed it to him. "Come and see me tomorrow so we can talk."

"But I—"

"California can wait," she said, stopping his protest. "Eleven o'clock will fit into my schedule just fine."

The entire Walker family watched in speechless wonder as she headed out the door.

"Now I've seen everything," Hennessy said, pushing the dreads away from his face. "She's crazy as hell."

"I dunno, Hen," Rayne looked at him warily. "They say she's the real deal, not like some other psychics."

"Oh, please." Hennessy held up both palms. "She's a New Orleans marketing gimmick. They make a big deal of her because all this psychic stuff seems cool to the tourists."

"But what if she's right and Daddy's not laying in that box?" She stared at the casket as if she could see inside.

"Well, the police said—"

"The police jus say they found the body in the bar," it was Lila who spoke. "We assumed it was Boozie."

"Yeah, we did." Teardrop had appeared from across the room to join their little group. "'Course they said they found his wallet on the body."

"A body too bloated and decayed to really identify," Rayne added. "What if we're about to bury somebody else's daddy?"

Doubts rose in Hennessy. "How long do you think it would take to get dental records?" he asked, a small glimmer of hope began in his chest.

"I dunno." Teardrop scratched at his shiny bald head. "Lots of dentists ain't open yet."

"There's gotta be a way to find Dr. Weenig," Hennessy said, starting to believe in the cause. "I'm supposed to head back to California tomorrow night. But I could try to change my flight if this takes a little longer." He frowned, wondering about Deja Devine's last comment. "California can wait." How did she know? Probably she'd heard about him from his daddy and knew where he and his band were touring. Yeah, then she would be able to guess he was going back after the funeral.

She was very good.

"But what about this funeral?" Lila put hands to her shapely hips and looked around the flowered room. "If yo daddy ain't dead, how we gonna pay for it?"

"Why you wanna pay for buryin' somebody else?" Teardrop shot out. "Seem to me like that's the problem of dis here funeral home."

Hennessy had to agree. It wouldn't be their fault if Boozie Walker wasn't in that casket. The New Orleans police department would have to take the blame.

"I guess the best place to start is the dentist's office, right?" He looked to his sister for confirmation.

She nodded. "Let me come with you. Mamma, would you take Ray Ray home with you?"

"All right, dahlin, but I hope ya'll ain't getting your hopes up for nuthin'."

Tucking Deja Devine's card into his pocket, Hennessy thought something good might yet come out of her visit. "You have your car?" Hennessy asked Rayne as they left the church.

"Uh, no. I'm using a friend's."

The sight of Earl Grant's flashy black Lexus brought Hennessy up short. "Dang it, Rayne. Please tell me you didn't sleep with that man."

"Last I checked, I was over twenty-one years old," she said. "If riding in Earl's car is beneath you, I'll be happy to go by myself."

Hennessy cursed and climbed into the passenger seat.

"Buckle up, little brothah," Rayne smiled and slipped on her new sunglasses. She'd bought them because they looked good on her when she rode around in this car. "This bad boy rides like buttah."

The top was down on the convertible and the wind made the trendy spikes of her short hair dance as she navigated the car toward the Central Business District, or the CBD.

Hennessy was struck by the fact this was the first time since he'd arrived that his sister didn't look stressed or angry. How odd, but she seemed at peace driving the car, letting the 75-degree wind blow against the smile on her face. At the sight of such a simple pleasure he nearly forgot to be angry at how she'd come to possess the car.

He wondered about Earl. "Why wasn't Earl at the visitation?" he asked.

The smile fell from Rayne's face in one second flat. "He's tryin' to take care of some business. All right? He's planning on comin' to the funeral tomorrow to pay respects to Daddy—if there is one," she added.

"All right." He pulled back, feeling her become defensive. "I'm not tryin' to start a fight."

She looked at him for a moment. "Oh."

"Nice ride," he complimented, hoping to bring the smile back to her face. She was too young to look so serious. She was only two years older than he was, but her hard life was carving grooves under her beautiful dark eyes—grooves that disappeared when she smiled.

"It is a beauty, isn't it?"

Diverting his gaze outside the vehicle, Hennessy found himself more successful in carrying on a conversation rather than an argument. "You know that Deja Devine kind of pissed me off."

"Really? Why? Because she claims to see into the future?" Rayne seemed amused.

"No, because she didn't bother to say she'd been stepping out with Daddy."

"So? What did ya expect her to say? Hello, my name's Deja Devine and I'm your daddy's mistress?" she asked.

"Maybe," Hennessy admitted.

"Oh. I get it." Rayne laughed. "Sister-girl was getting you all hot and bothered and it cooled you off to find out she'd been with Daddy, huh?"

"Don't be stupid," he said, angry she'd hit the nail right on the head. "I'm also mad because she had the nerve to come up to me and tell me Daddy was alive."

"What's wrong with that? We wouldn't be out here tryin' to prove it's him in that casket if she hadn't said that."

"I know," Hennessy leaned his head against his fist. "But, what if she's wrong? How cruel is it to give people false hope like that?"

"What if she's right?" Rayne countered. "What if she's for real and Daddy's still alive?"

"Then where is he?"

"I dunno. But you know what I'm startin' to think is strange?"

Hennessy looked at her and waited for her to continue.

"How is it a body could be so damaged from water, but stuff in a wallet comes out intact?"

"His drivers license was laminated," Hennessy argued.

"You ever wash one of them things?" she challenged.

Hennessy's heart raced. She was right. His license would've stood up to the water for a while, but ultimately it would've broken down after days and days of being soaked. This could all be a mistake. His father might really be alive.

"There's Dr. Weenig's office." He pointed at an empty parking space in front of the building. He was so excited he jumped out of the car as soon as Rayne brought it to a stop, not bothering with the door. "Damn. It doesn't look open."

A notice hung on the boarded up double doors.

"What's it say?" Rayne ran up beside him and pulled off her sunglasses to read the small print.

The sun was setting and the words on the paper had long ago been washed away. The light print remaining couldn't be read in the waning light. "Can't tell," Hennessy sighed, feeling the swell of hope dipping low like the late afternoon sun.

"Maybe I have his number in my cell," Rayne said hopefully. She pulled the phone out and beeped her way down a pretty long list before finding the dentist's name. She selected his name and called.

She had the phone set to Speaker, so when the ringing stopped, both of them heard the message. "Due to Hurricane Katrina, Dr. Weenig is no longer open for business. We apologize for the inconvenience."

"Inconvenience?" Hennessy pounded a fist against the wood. "It's a helluva lot more than that."

"Chill out, Hen." Rayne folded her phone and tucked it carefully into her small purse. "There's gotta be another way to identify him. What about DNA?"

"Okay, but how do we do that?"

"I've got a friend who's a nurse. We could ask her."

"Okay, cool." He agreed, though it was starting feel like they were on a wild goose chase. "Let's go."

"Say, Hen," she said as she pulled the Lexus back onto the street. "What if Daddy wanted everyone to believe he's dead so he planted his wallet on the dead man?"

Hennessy frowned. "You're taking this a little far, aren't you?"

"Maybe that's why he's keeping a low profile," she continued.

"If that were the case, he'd want us to go through with the funeral," Hennessy said with a sigh.

"Exactly." Her eyes were shining under the street lamps that had come on. "Before the storm, I was in the B&B office with Daddy. He got a call from some man, I know cause I answered the phone."

"Yeah?"

"So, Daddy made me leave the room. He said it was a private conversation. But I could hear him yellin' even outside the office door."

"You were eavesdropping," Hennessy taunted.

"I didn't have to," Rayne said with a laugh. "Right before he came out, he'd said something about 'I'd like to see you try it!' and then he'd yanked the door open and came out to the bar for a drink."

"A drink? You sure about that?" Hennessy knew his father never drank when he was at the bar. He'd always said he needed his wits about him because there'd be too many others getting theirs soaked in whiskey.

"Oh, I'm sure," she stated confidently. "I remember thinking how mad he must've been to take that drink."

"God, Rayne." Hennessy pulled his dreads back from his face and blew out a long breath. "Do you know how crazy this all sounds?"

"Pretty crazy," she admitted. "But it's kind of fun too, right?"

"So, you're saying we shouldn't call off the funeral because Daddy may have some grand scheme in mind." He looked at her, checking for agreement.

"Right." Rayne nodded. "Plus, that way no one starts to think we're losing it if we happen to be wrong."

Well, that was something. At least she wasn't so far gone on her theory she didn't realize it was a little bit out there. "But you think we should get your friend the nurse to get a sample and test it for DNA?" he continued.

"Exactly."

The whole situation was ludicrous and Hennessy couldn't help but laugh. "Check this out, we're like CSI New Orleans all of the sudden because of some crazy psychic chick."

Rayne laughed along. "But what if she's right?"

"If she's right, I'll sing a Blues song about her and call it Miss Devine." He closed his eyes at the thought and let the tune he'd heard earlier come back to mind. *Now I know your name, and babeee, you're certifiably insane...but I still can't get you off my mind. Oooh, no not you, sweet, sexy Miss Devine...*

Chapter Four

Rayne reached for her purse and pulled out her cell phone. She flipped it open. "Pamela Flowers," she said to the phone. A moment later, a female's voice answered.

"Where are you?" Rayne asked Sister Alveta's granddaughter.

"Having an intimate moment with my pillow. Why are you disturbing my sleep, Rayne?" Pam seemed about as cranky as usual.

"Because you're always in bed," Rayne said half-teasing, half-serious. She'd never known a person who slept as much as Pam. "Now, get up," Rayne demanded. "I'm on my way over with my brother. We need your help." She looked over at Hennessy who simply shook his head.

A few choice curse words were the sum of her friend's reply before hanging up.

"You sure she's okay with this?" Hennessy asked skeptically.

"Perfect," Rayne assured him, before tossing the phone back in her purse. "We'll just need to toss a very strong cup of coffee into her trailer before we go inside."

Hennessy thought she'd been teasing about the coffee, but twenty minutes later, they were walking up the short steps to one of many trailers in a FEMA reserved lot, a cup of steaming hot java clutched in Rayne's hand.

A short, light-skinned woman wearing sweatpants and an oversized T-shirt answered the door. Her naturally wavy brown hair was pulled into a tousled ponytail. Despite her extremely casual attire, she managed too look adorable. "This better be impor—" She stopped and looked up and down the length of Hennessy before letting a sleepy, yet seductive smile replace the scowl on her face. "Well, hello Hennessy," she said.

"Hi." Hennessy couldn't help but smile back. He remembered Pam from when they were kids. She hadn't changed much. She was still cute with heavy lidded hazel eyes. She hadn't grown much either. She was a very petite woman who he guessed barely topped five feet. She'd been the only girl who would play with Rayne back in the day. Hennessy was glad she'd taken pity on his skinny, buck-toothed sister.

"Enough chit chat." Rayne pushed the cup of coffee in Pam's hand. "Here. Can we come in now?" she asked, then turned sideways to enter the trailer before her friend could answer.

The adorable Miss Flowers didn't seem to mind Rayne's rudeness. Nor did she seem inclined to move from her spot in the door.

"May I?" Hennessy gestured to go inside.

"Yes, you may," she said sweetly. She didn't move.

Seeing no other option, Hennessy turned sideways to enter through the narrow doorway. Despite pressing his back against the door, he brushed gently against the woman as he entered her trailer. "Sorry," he apologized.

"For what?" she asked coyly.

"Pam?" Rayne crossed her arms impatiently.

"What?" Her eyes were wide with feigned innocence.

"Knock it off."

"Fine." Her friend made a sour face then plopped down on the sofa. "Have a seat. I'd offer you something, but I haven't had time to make groceries this week. Things are so busy at the hospital I've had to pull double shifts."

Hennessy and Rayne sat in the two mismatched chairs in her sparsely furnished living area. The trailer was only slightly larger than some of the hotel suites Hennessy had called home for the past few years.

"That's okay," Rayne said. "Like I said on the phone, we need your help."

"With what?" Pam took a tentative sip of the hot coffee. She seemed satisfied and took another.

"We need you to take a sample from a dead man and check his DNA."

Pam wrinkled her adorable forehead. "Check it for what?"

"To see if it's really our Daddy," Hennessy chimed in. "There's a possibility there's been a mistake."

"Well, then I'd have to take your blood too," Pam said. "And probably your mamma's."

"What for?" Hennessy asked.

"To see if it's a close match to the dead man's. See, there's no need in taking a DNA sample unless you're comparing it to something else. And, since it's supposed to be your father, we can expect to see a lot of similarities in the DNA."

"Well, let's get started," Rayne said, rubbing her pitifully thin arm.

"I'm a nurse. I can't do stuff like that. Ya'll need to go to get an expert in this type of thing to perform a DNA paternity test." Pam took another sip of her coffee and made no move to leave her spot on the sofa.

"That'll take forever." Rayne seemed disheartened.

"How long will it take, Pam?" Hennessy wouldn't be daunted now that he knew something could be done. "We've gotta know before we have this funeral."

"Not as long as you think," Pam said. "You can order a collection kit for free online and then it takes about four or five days for the lab to send it back to you."

Rayne raised and eyebrow as she looked at her friend. "And you know this because…?"

Pam rolled her eyes. "Once upon a time I had a friend who needed to know who her baby's daddy was, so I ordered a kit on my credit card. Stupid, huh?" She didn't wait for an answer. "Turned out the little boy looked exactly like his bighead daddy, so there wasn't any need. Anyway, I'll let you have the kit. That'll take a few days off the process for you."

"Well, that's something," Rayne said as Pam rushed into her bedroom. "But, I thought this would be easier."

"I guess we have to start somewhere," he said, looking over at his sister. "I guess we don't have no choice," she agreed. "But the funeral cover will be blown for sure if we find out that dead man ain't Daddy."

Pam walked in at that moment and gave her a strange look. "Funeral cover?"

"I'll explain it all later," Rayne waved her hands and pushed her way out of the chair. "Thanks, Pam. You're the best. Let's go, Hen."

"Looks like my taxi is leaving." Hennessy rose and nodded his head in Pam's direction. "Good seeing you again, Pam."

"The pleasure's been all mine." She gave him an exaggerated wink.

She was the second woman who'd said that to him today. The first one still haunted him.

"I do like your friend," Hennessy joked as he and Rayne headed for the car.

"Yeah. I got that."

The air had cooled as the sun left the sky. Rayne pushed the button and suddenly the car had a roof again. "Could you lock that side?" she said pointing at the mechanism.

He did as she asked. Maybe because they rode in silence a few minutes too long, Hennessy started to think about Earl Grant again and how much he disliked the thought of he and Rayne together. "You know…" he started, trying to find the words she would listen to without getting defensive. "You're a very smart, capable woman, Rayne. And Earl—"

"Hennessy?" she jumped in softly.

"What?"

Her quiet, tortured voice carried softly across the darkened interior. "I was having a good time with you today. Don't blow it. Okay?"

Reluctantly, he settled back in his seat. "All right. But, can I say just one thing?"

"Sure," she sounded tired.

"I love you, Sis. No matter what."

Hennessy had no idea how she'd taken his declaration, because she remained silent on her side of the car. It didn't matter, though. It just needed to be said.

Earl was relieved to hear the sound of closing car doors outside the Ellis house. Not that he hadn't enjoyed Lila's cooking or her husband Antoine's boring banter before he'd drifted off to sleep on the couch—it was the kid. Little Ray Ray had shown him every toy he owned and was now staring up at him waiting for him to send his car along the little yellow racetrack on the living room floor.

"Its your tern, Mistah Url." The little boy handed him the black racecar with white stripes.

"Okay. Just this last time." Earl tried to be insistent, but it hadn't worked in over an hour. Making car noises, because it sent the kid into fits of laughter, he *vroomed* his car along the figure eight track until he reached the finish line. "I win," Earl shouted pumping his fists in the air. Ray Ray rolled on the floor in an explosion of giggles.

That's how Rayne and Hennessy found them when they walked inside.

"Mamma! Unca Hensee!" he shouted and was quickly on his feet. He flew at them, grabbing his mamma's left leg and Hennessy's right.

"How ya doin', little man?" Hennessy pulled the child into his arms. "You been playin' cars?"

"Uh, huh." He gave a big nod and pointed behind him. "Mistah Url played wid me."

"He did?" Rayne said, giving the boy a kiss. "That was nice of him, wasn't it?"

"Uh huh," the child repeated.

"I see you brought my car back, Earl," Rayne moved over the couch her stepfather had vacated not five minutes before to go to his bed. "I guess that means we gotta swap back."

Earl lifted himself off the floor and brushed at imaginary dirt on his slacks. "That's what it means," he said, taking the spot next to her. "Or, you could come home with me."

"Did you get your trailer?" she asked.

"Yeah. I had them haul it in back of the bar."

"Aww," she sighed. "No more Embassy Suites."

"The bed I bought is just as good as the Embassy and I made it up myself...same as I had to do at the hotel 'cause they didn't have enough help." He leaned closer to her and smelled her glorious smell. "You wanna help break it in?" he whispered.

"I bwoke my bed one time." Ray Ray had somehow escaped Hennessy and now hung on one of Earl's knees. "Nana said not to jump, but I did and it bwoke."

"Ray Ray?" he said to the child, "I think your Nana said you had to go to bed before she left, didn't she?"

His eyes grew wide and he shook his head. "I don wanna go ta bed, Mistah Url."

"Oh, here comes the fight," Rayne said between clenched teeth.

"The sooner he goes to bed, the sooner we can be outta here," he urged her to take the child and go.

Rayne scooped her son into her arms and tossed him into the air a few times to take his mind off the fact she was heading toward the bedroom. It only lasted until they got there, then the child started to scream bloody murder. He sank back against the couch cushions. "Kids."

"Real mood killers, huh?" Hennessy was slumped comfortably in a chair adjacent to the couch, where Earl sat staring at him.

"Yeah. But they're mostly awright," he knew better than to dis a single mother's child to anyone.

"You got any?" Hennessy asked. He was clearly fishing for information, anything that would make him look bad to his sister.

"Naw, man. I ain't got no kids. Look." Earl stood and adjusted his slacks and looked at the bedroom door impatiently. "You don't have to worry 'bout me disrespectin' your sister, Hen. I'll treat her good."

By the look on his face, Earl knew Hennessy didn't believe him. "You do drugs?"

That was a tough one. Earl decided it was best to go with the truth. "I've been known to enjoy a little weed now and again," he smiled. "You ain't gonna hold that against a brotha are ya?"

"Not as long as you don't do it in front of my sister or her son. You do anything harder than that?"

"Naw, man. I tried crack once...a little X. That stuff jacked me up bad. I ain't done it since," he confessed. "Look, man, I know bout your sister's habit and how she's tryin' to stay clean so why you sweatin' me so bad?"

Too Much Hennessy

Earl threw his arms out like Jesus on the cross. "You know me. What've I done to earn all this hate?"

The air left Hennessy in a long sigh. "You're right. Sorry, man. I…it's just…you know…she's my sister."

"I feel ya, dog. But, trust me. It's all good. You ain't got nothing to worry about." Earl closed the distance between them and held out a hand to Hennessy.

The other man clasped it signaling a truce.

Earl was relieved to have that over but was beginning to wonder if Rayne Walker was worth all this trouble. She had a bad drug habit, an energetic three-year-old and an overprotective brother.

The bedroom door opened and she tiptoed out closing it quietly behind her. His doubts were gone in an instant.

Rayne carried a small bag, which to Earl's delight, meant she had no intention of coming back home tonight. Hennessy frowned when he saw it.

She had changed into tight jeans and a silky, barely there blouse. Earl decided she looked so good he would have to show her off, take her out for a coffee and beignet. Then he'd take her back to his new trailer home and let her "talk" him into letting her borrow his car again. "Um, um, um. You shore look fine," he said, letting his tongue roll around the inside of his cheek.

"Well then, let's get outta here," she said, batting her eyelashes. "Don't wait up, Hen," she said to her brother. "I gave a sample to our little kit and left it in my room for you. I'll be back early."

"No she won't, " Earl said, placing a hand around her narrow waist. "She'll definitely be home late tomorrow morning."

Hennessy's face deepened into a concerned frown, Earl saw it, but chose to ignore it. The man was just hatin'. He got busy talking dirty to Rayne as they left the house. He wanted to make sure she was good and ready when they took his new sheets for a test drive.

Morning dawned bright and cloudless. Calm winds swept across a pristine blue sky. It was quite the contrast to the image Hennessy saw when he looked across the New Orleans' tattered landscape. Homes were in varying stages of repair in his mother's neighborhood. His mother's home had been spared the worst of the damage since Antoine had replaced all the floors in the house with tile prior to the hurricane. He'd also blown the walls dry immediately upon coming back, though they were bowed out of shape and water-stained.

The back patio was prepared for entertaining visitors after today's funeral—but Hennessy already knew there wouldn't be a funeral. At least not for a few days.

Hennessy had pulled out a few hairs and cut them from his dreads for the paternity test kit. He'd also collected a few of his mamma's long hairs from her brush. All that was left was to visit the funeral home that day to get as many types of samples from the dead body as possible in order to ensure an adequate sample size. The kit was very specific about how to collect and label each sample. He'd thought about Rayne going off with Earl. What a waste, he thought for the millionth time. She would've made a brilliant lawyer—that's what she'd aspired to do before she'd gotten into trouble. Instead she was wrapped up with another no-good man and doing nothing to further herself.

Then it struck him—Rayne had been sober all day yesterday. She'd been a little shaky, but better that than have her high. Maybe she needed to believe Daddy was still alive—to have something important to keep her busy.

If that were the case, running down what might end up being a wild goose chase might be worth the time and effort. Actually, Hennessy had something to look forward to as well. It seemed he'd awakened from some dark nightmare to a bright reality where his father might still live. But if he were alive, where was he? Did he fake his own death?

Hennessy shook his head and tried not to get ahead of himself. First things first—he had to find out if the man in the casket was his father or not. Then he had to find out what Deja Devine had to do with all of this. He didn't know if truly psychic powers had led her to the funeral home or something else—he guessed it was more likely she knew something about her father's disappearance and she wanted to keep up pretenses to keep her image intact. Though having her image seemed a pretty useless thing at this point. Who needed psychics when it was clear to everyone in New Orleans what their future was—years and years of back-breaking rebuilding and reshuffling of their lives.

Hennessy climbed into the shower. The smell of mold still clung to the walls in this room, but the soap he used did a fair job of masking it for the short time he was in there. He towel dried, then pulled on underwear and slacks before opening the door and letting the steam out of the tiny room.

"Hennessy?" his mamma called out from the living room.

"Yeah?"

"Have some breakfast 'fore you head out to the funeral home and start all this madness."

"Be right there, Mamma," he called back.

He'd told her when she'd come home from playing cards with her friends they'd had no luck with the dentist, but had found out about the forensic paternity test they could send and have mailed back. She still thought her children were getting their hopes up and wasn't fully on board with the plan. "Best to let bygones be bygones, chil'ren," she'd said.

He heard the front door open then close.

By the time he'd pulled on a shirt his mother and sister were locked in some whispered argument, clearly trying not to let him, or perhaps, Ray Ray overhear.

"I've raised my chil'ren," his mamma said, her hands on ample hips, her lips drawn into a thin angry line. "You get in there and take care of yours."

Rayne stood looking like she'd just turned twelve again, "I…I was going to," she finally answered, clearly not knowing what else to say. "You ain't got to preach."

Hennessy didn't dare say a word. It was clearly an A and B conversation and he planned to C his way out of it. *Way* out of it. He and his sister followed their mamma back to the kitchen.

"Mamma!" Teray scooted off the hard chair and ran to his mother.

"Oh no, Ray Ray," Rayne lifted his sticky hands. "What've you got all over yourself? Syrup?"

"Can't be no worse than whatever you had in yo hands this morning," Mamma said not quite under her breath as she tended to her scrambled eggs.

"I got the message, Mamma," Rayne rolled her eyes impatiently then, with effort, placed a smile on her face to greet her son. "Let's get that stuff off your fingers, all right, baby?" She carried him to the sink, then lifted him to reach the faucet. Ray Ray stuck his chubby fingers under the water, a look of delight on his face.

Hennessy knew Rayne could get away with just about anything, except ignoring her son. His mamma had no problems caring for her grandson, but she felt his parents needed to be responsible enough to raise the child they brought into the world—Hennessy had to agree. He noticed Rayne didn't even attempt to argue. Probably because she knew it wouldn't do her any good.

Gratefully, Lila decided to take on another subject. "It's a damned crazy idea, ya'll sending in a paternity test," Lila said, flipping over the last of her pancakes. "What's everyone gonna think? I can't just call off the funeral with no notice. Besides what'll I do with all this food I got cooked?"

"Have a party," Hennessy said. He proceeded to pile food onto both his and Rayne's plates. Rayne waved him off after only a forkful of eggs and a couple of sausage links. She sat Ray Ray back into his booster seat to finish his pancakes.

"Ummm mmm, this looks good, Mamma," Hennessy said through a mouthful of sausage. He missed rich food. Oakland, California was full of restaurants, but every place had health choices. Even their pizza was made with whole wheat flour and all vegetable toppings. Having some real food for a change was a relief.

Lila chuckled. "Glad to see your appetite Hennessy. I was startin' to worry you'd waste away."

"Where's Antoine?" Hennessy asked, though he didn't really care. The man seemed to keep his own time, rising early, going to bed early and in between he just wandered around town visiting with people about nothing.

"He said he had things to do this morning," Lila said in a long-suffering voice. "I don't know what a retired man finds to do so early."

Rayne put a dainty forkful of scrambled eggs into her mouth. "So, were you able to get your flight changed?" she asked when she'd swallowed.

He nodded. "For a hundred bucks," he confirmed.

"Better than the price of a new ticket," she offered by way of consolation.

"I suppose. I also called Jack and Johnnie last night. I told them I wouldn't be heading back for another week or so.."

"How'd they take it?"

"They seemed disappointed, but said that Terry Pryce was doing just fine filling in for me." He made a sour face.

"You don't like this Terry Pryce?" Rayne asked.

Hennessy didn't look up from his food. "He's a great vocalist—when he's sober." He cringed, not meaning to bring up the subject of drugs.

But Rayne pretended it meant nothing to her. "Is he sober now?" she asked lightly.

Hennessy just nodded.

"Then it's all good, right?" She gave him a telling look. As if to say, don't judge somebody who's trying.

He smiled so she knew he got her message. "I'm just vain enough to want to think the band isn't as good without me," he admitted, taking a long swallow of orange juice. "So what would be good is if they were begging me to come back."

"Big head." Rayne teased, feeling more at ease with her brother than she had in years. She missed the way they'd talk to one another and share their biggest secrets with one another. Even if their biggest secret at the time was stealing a Camel cigarette from their daddy's pants pocket and running into the dog house to smoke it.

"They'd be crazy not to want you back, Hennessy," Lila soothed. She kissed his cheek before taking a seat at the table. "You sing better'n anybody I ever heard at the B&B."

It might have been an exaggeration, but obviously Lila knew the exact way to her son's heart. She'd just made it clear there would never be anyone more important in her life. Rayne had always known it. Up until now, she'd been all right with it, because she knew she always had her daddy's love. A hot flash of grief seized her just then. If only Deja Devine was right and he was alive and well…it was probably a stupid hope, but at the moment it was all she had.

Hennessy rewarded his mamma with a glowing look of adoration and a gentle kiss to her hand. "Thank you, good looking.

Rayne dropped her head, feeling emptiness and jealously.

"If you're done pushing those eggs around your plate, let's get out of here," he said.

Rayne looked up. He was on his feet and looking at her in anticipation.

"I've been ready," she replied, pushing away her plate.

"Can I go, can I, can I?" Teray bounced in his seat.

"Sure," Hennessy said before his sister could think of a good excuse not to take him. A part of him didn't want to see his sister get another tongue lashing from Mamma. And a family outing would do them all good.

After washing Ray Ray's hands once more and wiping off his round cheeks, they headed out. Hennessy was thrilled to see Rayne's old Toyota sitting in front of the house.

Antoine Ellis pulled up in his white Taurus just as they climbed into Rayne's truck.

"Hey, Mr. Ellis," Hennessy called out.

Rayne gave a half-hearted wave then continued strapping the child in his car seat.

Antoine walked up to the car as Rayne started the engine. "You two off to the funeral home, then?" he asked Hennessy through the open window.

"Yeah."

"Didn't seem like there was nobody at the place. I drove by on my way to the store." He held up a couple of small plastic bags.

"That's okay. We'll just sit and wait," Hennessy said cheerfully.

"All right, but keep in mind, son, just because that man in the casket might not be your daddy, doesn't mean he's alive."

That was a depressing thought and Rayne could tell Hennessy didn't want to hear it any more than she did. "I'll keep that in mind, sir," he said, the light had dimmed in his voice.

She pulled away from the curb and headed toward the funeral home. "I'm sorry, Hennessy."

"For what?"

"For getting your hopes up. It might be for no reason."

Hennessy stared at her for a moment. "You don't believe that." His words were more a statement than a question. "Do you?"

She wanted to lie, to say she wasn't so sure anymore, but she couldn't. Even if she was bringing his hopes up sky high only to be dashed on the concrete, she couldn't help but tell him what was on her mind. "Something just isn't right about all this, Hen. I can't explain it, but no. I don't believe he's dead. And I'd really like to go see Deja Devine with you today."

"Okay," he agreed, though a part of him wanted to have the wacky, but sexy woman all to himself. "Wait a minute," he sat up straight. "I didn't tell you I was gonna see her. How'd you know about that?"

"I was there when she told you to show up. I could tell by the way you tucked her card in your back pocket you were gonna go."

"Oh, so now you're the psychic," he teased and eased back in his seat. A moment later, he was smiling again. "To tell you the truth, I can't wait to see what that crazy chick is gonna tell us. She might accidentally tell us something helpful."

They reached the funeral home a few minutes later. An empty hearse was sitting in the parking lot. "Looks like things are going our way, Rayne." Hennessy hopped out of the truck and sprinted inside the building.

Rayne took her time, and paused as she placed a hand on the hood of the hearse. She crossed herself and sent a prayer into the clear blue sky. "Please let me be right about this," she pleaded. Hennessy's spirits were so high right now it would be a long way coming down.

She went to free Ray Ray from his car seat and started up the sidewalk only to be met by Hennessy and the funeral director on their way out. "Someone's gonna have to pay for this man's funeral," the funeral director said, folding his arms across his wide middle.

"I told, you sir," Hennessy said firmly, but politely, "If this is our father, we'll be happy to pay for all expenses."

"And if it isn't your father?" the man asked testily.

"Then you wouldn't expect us to pay for it would you?" Hennessy smiled and hopped inside his sister's car.

Rayne quickly got behind the wheel. "What happened?" she asked her brother as they left the lot.

"I got a tissue sample of some of the man's hair." He showed her his sample collection bag. "Now all we need to do is label this bad boy and mail it off. Next stop, the post office."

"That was quick." Rayne had expected a delay because of Antoine's statement about the funeral home being closed.

"After the post office, what're we going to do?" Rayne asked.

"Go somewhere."

"Where?"

"Anywhere...to the park. Let's let Ray Ray play before we have to head to the Quarter."

"We have about an hour," Rayne said, checking her watch. "That should give us plenty of time."

They found a park where the playground equipment seemed relatively clean. The ground held grooves from where some heavy machine had scraped and cleaned up after Katrina's wrath. A few people were there to watch their handful of kids.

Ray Ray shot off like a rocket toward the curving slide. Rayne and Hennessy stood on the edge of the playground where the sand used to end. Rayne hadn't done anything quite so normal as bring her child to a playground in a very long time. She smiled to see how happy he was just to be with other kids, sliding down a bright yellow piece of plastic, screaming at her, "Mamma lookit me, lookit me!" And at Hennessy, "Uncle Hensy, lookit me, lookit me!"

A huge swell of pride filled Rayne's chest. She'd made that wonderful child. He was hers forever, which was more than she could say for any man—including his daddy—that she'd ever been with. She looked over at her brother and saw the handsome man he'd become. But she saw deeper. He still had the same hint of humor and mischief in his smile he'd had as a boy. She wondered if that's what made her mamma smile when she saw Hennessy. Did she feel the same sense of motherly pride even now? How strange to think she and Mamma might actually have something in common.

Rayne turned back to watching her son, since he was calling her again. But her mind drifted back to her daddy. "He'd said something strange the day before the hurricane."

"Who did?"

Rayne was startled, not realizing she'd said it out loud. "Daddy," she said. "We'd been sitting in the Blues 'N Booze and he was cleanin' his gun and shotgun and telling me why he couldn't evacuate with me, Mamma, Ray Ray and Antoine. He was looking around the room the whole time."

"Yeah, he'd told me he wasn't about to lose the place to looters," Hennessy said.

Rayne nodded. "He told me the same thing. But then he got this sad look on his face and he said he'd sold his soul, not once, but twice, to keep the B&B and if he ever lost it, his sacrifices would be for nothing."

"Sold his soul?" Hennessy scratched his temple. "You think he was just being dramatic like he gets sometimes?"

"At first, I did, " Rayne acknowledged. "But then I realized there was more to the story. I asked him what he meant, but he wouldn't tell me. Instead, he just frowned hard, getting that little V in his forehead, you know? And he went back to polishing his guns." Hennessy thought back on what he knew about how his father had come to own the B&B.

"Daddy said he'd gotten a small business loan back in the '70s so he could buy the bar. He said there'd been some years where he and Mamma could barely make ends meet and he had to get a day job and she had to work at the grocery store. I don't remember much about it, but those hard times might be what he's talking about."

"Maybe," Rayne said. "But I just got the feelin' it was something bigger than that. I dunno," she shrugged. "I'm probably makin' too much out of nothing."

"Don't do that," Hennessy was irritated.

"What?"

"Second guess yourself. I get tired of you always thinking somebody else has a better answer than you. You've been right about lots of things, Rayne." He really didn't want to pick another fight, but he wanted the old Rayne Walker to break through the surface. The Rayne who'd once been full of self-confidence and big dreams was buried inside this…this frail mess of a woman and he really wanted her to come out.

"Name one," she challenged after a long moment of silence.

"One what?"

"One thing I've been right about." She didn't look at him, just stared soberly toward the playground. Her hands began to shake slightly.

At first, Hennessy thought she was kidding, but he could tell by the tense way she held herself that she was waiting for a serious answer. After a moment, he gave her an answer. "You were right about going to college."

"I dropped out," she spit back, still not bothering to look his way.

Feeling something competitive spark within him, he racked his brain for another example. "You were right when you talked Mamma into going to the hospital and it turned out she needed a hysterectomy."

She turned and scowled at him. "That wasn't a decision I made for myself. When have I ever been right about my own life?" she persisted.

"Well…" he looked toward the ground hoping an answer would pop into his head. Having no luck he looked up again, ready to concede defeat. Then he saw his nephew, talking animatedly with his newfound playmate and he knew the answer. He felt a little smug by saying it. "You had Ray Ray."

"Out of wedlock. And then I decided I'd be better off marryin' his drug dealin', wife beatin' daddy. Oh that was a *great* moment in my history."

"Hey, hey. I thought this was supposed to be me saying what's good about you, not the other way around." Hennessy took offense to the sudden attack.

Her eyes filled with tears and her mouth sank with sorrow into a frown like a tiny boat taking on too much water. "Well don't," she ordered. "Stop tryin' to make me feel better. Stop tryin' to lecture me into the person you think I should be. You know, for a moment, I thought I'd start renovatin' the B&B and run it like Daddy did. I thought maybe having Earl on my side would make it possible, but now I know I was only foolin' myself. I can't run a business."

"I'm thirty-three-years old and I don't have the foggiest idea who I am. All I know is I look good on men's arms and that makes them very happy. And when they're happy they give me things to make me happy. I just want to feel good for a little while, Hennessy. And you and Mamma's little digs and preachin' doesn't do it for me."

"But drugs and meaningless sex does?" He couldn't stop the words from leaving his mouth. "Mamma and I are just tryin' to help."

"Well, Mr. I'm-so-perfect-I-can-tell-everybody-else-how-to-live-their-lives, keep it to yourself until you get the hell out of town. Ray Ray! Get over here," she shouted. "Time to go."

And just like that, the beauty of the day disappeared. Hennessy climbed into the car, slamming the door shut and hoping the psychic chick would be easier to deal with.

Chapter Five

Deja looked around the room of her "office." It wasn't exactly beautiful, but the owner of the property had paid good money to have all the side-by-side Victorians on the block fumigated. At least she, and the other tenants who'd decided to come back, wouldn't get the cough plaguing so many New Orleans citizens who were attempting to live in houses still filled with mold. She'd had her mamma's house fumigated weeks ago and the contractor was now making slow, but steady progress in making the necessary repairs to make the house livable again.

The sooner, the better, she thought. She had to get Mamma out of her sister's house and back home where she belonged. She'd be more comfortable here, though most of her familiar things were now gone and Deja was going to be hard pressed to replace them with the government money she received every month.

Even here at her shop, she'd lost all of her furniture and silk pillows to the flood. Luckily, Deja didn't need much to get back into business, such that it was. She'd had enough in her savings to buy fancy pillows at WalMart, which she tossed on either side of a low, sturdy mahogany coffee table. The silk scarves cradling her Tarot cards were intact, as she'd taken those with her when she'd evacuated with her mother. She and this deck had become so familiar with one another, she couldn't imagine losing them.

Sadly, her once ochre, red and yellow walls were dull, having been repainted a safe tan shade. Deja hated the color but was slightly consoled by the light of the sun streaming through the bright orange and yellow sheers draped loosely across her windows. The sign outside was still in place and welcomed visitors into *Deja's View* for Tarot card and psychic palm readings.

Too Much Hennessy

Deja went around the room, lighting the candle-scapes arranged in alternating round and rectangular holders about the room. She used to light incense, but found that many customers thought the smell was too strong. Now she used scented candles. By the time Hennessy Walker arrived—oh, and his sister, she felt her coming as well—the room would smell nicely of vanilla—a nice cleansing smell, though she had no idea if it helped her readings at all.

An old car slid into a vacant parking spot just to the left of her front door. Deja felt a tingle of anticipation of seeing her Mr. Magnificent again. She had intentionally not visited with him in the other realm last night, though she'd been tempted. No. She thought it better the both of them remained focused on this world for the moment. She knew his father needed him and she had to help. When she did a reading for him, he didn't need images of the other place, of their surprising desire, filling his head.

Hennessy backed inside the door of the *Deja's View*, then turned around. A sleeping child was cradled in his arms. Deja felt her pulse skitter about in her veins. Somehow he seemed even more attractive today, his gaze more riveting than before. Each time she saw him, a thin layer of separation seemed to drop away, moving them closer.

Closer to what? She wondered. No answer rang through her conscious mind, though she knew her subconscious would puzzle the question until it discovered the answer.

Hennessy felt the floor shift beneath his feet—at least he thought it had. He blinked hard, trying to decide if the woman standing in the vanilla scented room in a haze of red and orange color was a dream or if she were real. She looked regal, spiritual, sensual, in a dress made of flowing white layers, the sleeves swaying as the wind moved past Hennessy into her domain. But what caught and held his attention was the sexy bustier she wore. The satiny red material appeared to struggle to hold her ample curves. The outfit was unusual, but he had to admit he liked it—a lot.

"You wanna let me in?" Rayne pushed at Hennessy so she could get through the door.

Feeling clumsy all of the sudden, Hennessy took a few steps inside to let Rayne pass.

"Is there someplace we can lay him down?" Rayne asked Deja, the slap of irritation still evident in her tone. The drive over hadn't done a thing to cool her anger. In fact, she seemed to get angrier by the minute. Maybe because she hadn't had drugs in a couple of days…at least he assumed she hadn't. The shake in her hands had grown more pronounced the closer they'd gotten to The Quarter.

Deja either didn't hear, or chose to ignore, Rayne's rudeness. "Come in the back," she said, motioning for Hennessy to follow.

The "back" consisted of a large room with a desk that obviously served as her office. A counter along the right wall separated this room from a small kitchenette. An oversized, round purple chair sat against the back wall and this is where Hennessy carefully laid his nephew. When he stood again, he noticed a door on his left labeled with the typical restroom male and female symbols. But these were seated in yoga meditation postures.

Deja pushed a sliding door of a hidden closet, to pull out an afghan, which she used to cover Ray Ray. Before leaving, she knelt down and looked at his nephew. A soft serious expression was on her face as she studied him sleeping. Finally, she let her fingers trace the length of his chubby cheek before smiling and standing. "Shall we begin?" she asked Hennessy.

"Begin?" Clearly she had the wrong idea and he wasted no time in setting her straight. "I came to ask you questions about my father. I didn't come for any of your psychic bull…stuff." He caught himself before totally insulting her chosen profession.

"Hmmm." She said, her eyes narrowing slightly. "Your sister first, then." Deja moved to the dark wooden coffee table and sat cross-legged on a stack of large colorful pillows. She gestured to Rayne to take a seat on the pillows on the other side of the table. "Please, sit."

Hennessy was so shocked at being dismissed he just stood in the doorway between the two rooms with his mouth hanging open. When Rayne moved obediently to sit across the table from Deja, he found his voice. "Rayne. You're not seriously going to go through with this, are you?"

Deja's quick, searing gaze stopped his protests. "If you want to stay," she said in slow, even tones, "You'll have to be quiet."

She sure was a bossy chick, he thought, irritably. He took one look at his sister and saw something in her face—a sort of desperation that she was managing to keep below the surface—but just barely. She was crazy to think this psychic could give her any real answers, but since Rayne had told him in no uncertain terms to butt out. "Fine." He held up his hands in surrender, then crossed his arms and legs and leaned against the door-jamb. *This oughtta be good*, he thought.

Deja unfolded a blue silk scarf to reveal what looked like oversized playing cards. She began handling them, then stopped. She turned slowly to look at Hennessy.

"What?" he said defensively. "I'm not saying a word."

She smiled and cocked her head to the side. "Would you mind terribly running to the store and getting me some bottled water?" she asked sweetly.

"You have a refrigerator back there," He poked his thumb over his shoulder. "Don't you have some?"

"I'm all out and my mouth is really dry. Would you mind?" she asked again.

He narrowed his eyes at her suspiciously. "You're tryin' to get rid of me, aren't you?"

"You're shooting negative energy flows at your sister. It'll cloud her reading."

Rolling his eyes, Hennessy stood up straight. "Fine. I'll leave. But when I get back, I want a few answers from you. You'll owe me that." He hoped she could tell he meant business.

"That's fine. Let me get you some money." She started to unfold from her sitting position. For the first time, Hennessy noticed her feet were covered in satiny red slippers designed with sparkling beads. He didn't know why, but he thought them the most interesting shoes he'd ever seen.

"Don't worry." Hennessy waved her back to sitting. "I'll take care of it."

He rushed out and started walking down the sidewalk of Bourbon Street. Frustration quickened his stride. The smell of vanilla stayed with him for a while and mingled with the smells of Cajun cooking drifting in the clear air. The day was warm for November, about seventy degrees, he guessed, so it didn't take long for him to start sweating. He slowed down.

What was he in such a hurry about? He probably had a good half hour before Deja and Rayne would be done. He realized then he was low on cash. He'd boldly told Deja "I'll take care of it," with all of two dollars and change in his pocket.

Smooth move, Hen.

A drug store was a few blocks down and his father's bank about a block past it. Well, first things first. He'd get some cash from the joint account he'd had with his daddy for years. He'd never actually done a transaction there. Daddy had put his name on the account "in case."

"In case what?" he'd asked his daddy some five years ago.

"Well. In case something happens to me and you need to get some cash," Daddy had explained. He'd also put his name on his safe deposit box and his savings accounts. He'd told Hennessy there was important information in the safe deposit box he'd need when he was no longer around.

At the time, Hennessy dismissed the thought. He couldn't imagine a world without his daddy. Actually he'd been convinced the man was invincible, which was a thought that had started when he was a child. How many times had his daddy managed to get between drunken men to stop fights when all others could do was stop and stare? How often had he stared down the site of his shotgun at "hoodlums" who'd busted in to his bar at closing time demanding money from his till? Hennessy hadn't been around to see these things happen, having been tucked into bed by his mamma at that time of night, but the newspapers had been full of the stories about Boozie Walker, owner of the Blues 'N Booze and the people who partied at their house were full of tales about his fearlessness.

Too Much Hennessy

Daddy had said all he was doing was "protectin' what was his." He'd said if the police weren't going to help him, then he'd defend himself. It had been years since he'd had to protect the place. The crime in the area had lessened significantly.

Maybe that's why the news of his father's death had hurt so badly. When he'd gotten the call a few days ago, it had paralyzed him at first. He'd lain, staring at the ceiling, on his hotel bed for a full twenty-four hours before he'd finally come out to hit the stage with his band.

And then, all his grief poured out in his music with pain searing through the notes of his trumpet and agony in each guitar strain. The Whiskey Sins Trio played old, familiar sets, but he'd taken extreme liberty with his solos, making them last much longer than usual. Jack and Johnnie kept up with him the whole time and never once complained. They'd pitied him. But he was grateful for their understanding. Grateful they'd let him play and play and play until he was ready to drop from exhaustion.

Boozie Walker, his own personal superhero was gone. Of course, it *had* taken an act of God to do it. Somehow that thought was soothing, consoling.

In case. Daddy's words echoed in his head as he stood in front of the bank's double doors. Well, today was the day "in case" happened. He tugged at one long silver door handle. Nothing happened. Confused he checked the hours posted on the doors and looked through the glass at the tellers he saw behind the counter. One of the women waved and he heard a soft buzzing sound. He pulled again. This time the door opened with ease.

Extra security. With all the looting and the short police staff, things had really changed in The Quarter—and not for the better. Hennessy walked up to the counter, pulling out his wallet as he went. Hopefully, they wouldn't give him grief about making a withdrawal.

The woman who'd buzzed him through the doors offered to assist him. She was a brunette woman with those wannabe blond streaks in her hair. Hennessy never understood why women wanted to look like tigers or zebras. Personally, he found solid colored hair to be much more attractive.

Hennessy slid his driver's license across the counter, grateful it was a Louisiana license and not out of state. He'd never changed his state of residence. He didn't see the need since he'd only been in New York, Atlanta, Chicago, Kansas City and California for months at a time. Always, he'd returned to New Orleans, but never to stay.

The teller was cheerful, but seemed hurried. Quickly and competently she had him complete a withdrawal slip and then processed his transaction. Hennessy placed the pile of twenties into his wallet then decided he needed to do one more thing before he left. "I need to get into my safe deposit box," he told the woman.

He pulled the oversized flat key from a pocket of his wallet. The shape of the object remained imbedded on the soft grain leather.

She took the key and had him follow her down the teller counter to the open vault.

"You know, I've never been in here before," Hennessy confessed unnecessarily.

She gave him a confused frown. "I don't understand."

"My dad brought me in here every time I was in town. But when he got into this box, I just sat out in the lobby."

"Oh," she said simply. Clearly this little piece of his family trivia didn't interest her. Hennessy didn't have a clue why he thought it would. He just thought a little small talk might loosen the woman up. She was rigid with so much efficiency Hennessy thought she might break in a stiff wind.

She escorted him to a privacy booth and laid the long steel box on the counter. Hennessy sat in the hard chair as she closed the door behind him.

A light along the back wall brightened the small space hardly big enough to be called a room. Hennessy stared at the box for a long moment. He felt he was about to open something sacred, something secret that Daddy had entrusted only to him.

Too Much Hennessy

He wondered for a minute if Rayne was bothered that Daddy put him on his accounts and safe deposit box and that he had been named co-owner of the Blues 'N Booze when he'd turned eighteen. She'd been twenty-one at the time and had dropped out of college a year short of her Bachelor's degree to run off with Tyrone. What a jerk he was, Hennessy thought. And he was just the first in a long line of losers Rayne managed to to find.

Daddy had said something about her not being ready for this kind of responsibility when Hennessy asked about her being on his deeds and accounts. "Jus cuz she's the oldest doesn't make her the wisest," he'd said.

Taking a deep breath, Hennessy placed his hand on the lid, paused, then eased it open. To his relief, the items inside looked harmless enough. A bunch of papers mostly, the deed to his daddy's house, the deed to the B&B. He owned both properties free and clear. Daddy had said he didn't want to be in debt to anybody when he died—didn't want bill collectors taking what he'd worked hard to get. Hennessy looked at the papers, taken aback by the sight of his name and his father's listed one under the other, connected forever in public records. More importantly, connected forever in his heart. He thought briefly about Rayne's confession—that she'd thought about taking over the B&B and running it. A part of Hennessy didn't want anyone to own it—not even himself. The Blues 'N Booze was his daddy's place and it only seemed right that it died along with the man.

Because the hurt was returning, and his faith in his sister's idea that Daddy was still alive was fading, Hennessy re-folded the deeds and laid them to the side on the counter. He saw another deed then, one he didn't know about. He unfolded it and looked at the name lines.

His heart caught in his throat, and he felt a strange sort of nothing— the way you feel when you don't know what to feel. On the paper, bigger than life, Karlem J. Walker and Dejanette Devine were declared owners of a home in Jefferson Parish.

Hennessy was so shocked he almost missed the edge of black velvet hiding in the back shadows of the narrow steel box. He pulled out the tiny black box, knowing what he'd find, because only one thing came in such small velvet cases.

He swore quietly as he looked at the wedding set of yellow gold. The engagement ring was simple, with a single white diamond. It was clear then, his daddy had meant to propose to Deja Devine.

Wow. The sexy woman in a red bustier and flowing white dress was supposed to have been his step-mamma—and she still might if it turned out Daddy was alive.

A part of him grieved. His heart had started wanting her even before he'd seen her in person. How else could he explain his strange dream where she'd become an instrument in his hands? They'd made love and music at the same time.

Not twenty minutes ago, the earth had moved when he'd seen the perfection of her face glowing vibrantly in streams of citrus colors. And now, he realized she would never be his, in dream or reality.

Hennessy placed everything back in the box carefully and left the cramped booth.

"All done?" The teller was there in an instant to help him slide the box into place in the vault.

He nodded.

On their way out, the woman paused, her brown and blonde striped hair gleaming dully beneath the recessed lighting. "You look like him," she said.

"Who?"

"Your father," she said. For the briefest moment, she let a smile crack the intense look of purpose on her face.

"You knew him?" Hennessy asked.

"Not very well," she said with a shrug. "I just remember helping him into that safe deposit box the day we were closing up for the hurricane."

"What day was that?" he asked curiously.

"August twenty-seventh," she said with certainty. "The next day we were closed." Suddenly, she was Chatty Kathy. "We just opened up again two weeks ago. It took a while to clean up the place."

"And you haven't seen him since you opened?" he was fishing for any information that might give him real hope that he was alive.

"Nope. Not me. But that doesn't mean someone else hasn't seen him."

Inspired by that thought, Hennessy made a request. "Can you print out a statement on our joint checking account? The one I just took cash from?"

"Sure." She bustled behind the counter and nearly beat Hennessy to her station even though she had further to walk. Her fingers tapped quick, staccato beats on her keyboard with the occasional click on her mouse. The printer droned for a few seconds and she handed him two sheets of paper. "This is the activity for the past thirty days."

"Thank you," he gave her a big smile. "You've been a great help…" he looked at her nametag. "Christine."

"Have a good day, Mr. Walker." She gave one last smile a quick ride on her lips before reverting back to her all-business face.

Excited to know there had been two pages worth of activity on his Daddy's checking account, Hennessy started looking at the entries on his way out the door. *Dang.* Except for his cash withdrawal that day, all of the transactions were automatic—to pay a car note, car insurance, home-owners insurance, cable—Hennessy made a note to cancel that—his home security service, cell phone.

Cell phone.

Hennessy wondered if he could go online to see activity on his daddy's cell phone. Probably all he'd find was all the normal fees they charged just to have the service, but it was a thought.

The second page had a single transaction listed. On October 16, 2005, a check had cleared for five thousand dollars. Hennessy wondered when the check had been written and to who. His father's balance was well over thirty thousand dollars—and this was only one of several accounts he held here. Who knew he was rolling like that? Five thousand dollars wasn't exactly chump change. "Could I get a copy of this check?" He pointed the item out to Christine the teller.

"Oh, sure, Mr. Walker." She went about tapping her keyboard with quick, efficient strokes. "We image the checks nowadays. It looks like it was made payable to your father. Would you like a copy?"

He nodded. He left the bank and examined the copy on his way to the drug store. His heart skipped a little as he studied the bold handwriting. It sure looked like his daddy's. The back of the check had a number of stamps on it, but it was clear that it had been negotiated at a bank in Henderson, Nevada. Why would his daddy be there? Or was it someone pretending to be his daddy? And how was the check negotiated if his daddy didn't have his identification?

He folded the paper and stuck it in his pocket, determined to get back to the psychic. Right after he bought some water to cure Ms. Devine's thirst, he'd find out what she knew about all of this. He only wished it would be as easy to cure what ailed him. What he thirsted for couldn't be satisfied by water—or by having a few questions answered.

Inside the store, he walked to the refrigerated section and bought a six-pack of bottled water and a single 20-ounce Coke. He broke one of the crisp twenties he'd gotten at the bank then walked back toward *Deja's View*.

Hennessy drank the Coke on the way back, enjoying the sting of the cold liquid as it slid down the back of his throat. It was the next best thing to drinking liquor, he'd decided long ago. But as he came nearer to the psychic's door, he wished he had a shot of rum to mix with the remaining soda. He slugged back the last drops of Coke and tossed the bottle in a trashcan along the sidewalk.

He was ready now—to face her, to ask about the house she co-owned with his daddy and to force his desire for her out of his system.

He pushed through the door. Deja watched with amusement as Hennessy took in the sight of Rayne lying on the floor on a long red mat.

Her eyes closed, her body still, her shoes off. Deja sat on the floor beside her, replacing her crystals into a foam-lined box.

Deja held a finger to her lips to keep him from asking the question he was about to voice: "What's going on?"

Hennessy held up the bottled water and pointed.

He was so damned cute it made Deja smile. She put a lid on her box, set it on the floor carefully then rose to her feet. She took the water from his hands and motioned him to follow her to the back room.

Ray Ray still slept peacefully in the chair.

Deja pulled a bottle from the pack and placed the remaining bottles in her refrigerator alongside the bottles of green tea, peach tea and several types of soda.

"What's all this?" Hennessy obviously couldn't remain quiet any longer. "You've got a refrigerator full of drinks. I went to the store for nothing?"

She closed the door and drank deeply of the bottle in her hand. "I had everything but water." Deja noticed he looked at her with a mix of exasperation—and something else. Something she couldn't quite read. "Thanks."

She walked to the doorway and peered in on Rayne. "I think she got a lot out of her reading," she whispered. "Look how peaceful she is."

Hennessy looked around the brown curls that were loose atop Deja's head at his sister. "She looks comatose," he announced.

Deja frowned. "I gave her a crystal cleansing. It clears the mind, helps open up the body's chakras."

"Whatever," he said. He took a step back and looked at her with a curious expression. "I went to the bank while I was out."

"The one down the street? It's great that they're open again," she said, giving him a quizzical look.

"My daddy has a safe deposit box there. Guess what I found?"

"What? We're playing games now?" she asked. She crossed her arms and shifted her weight on her right leg. "I give. What?"

"I found a deed to a house. One in Jefferson Parish," he said slowly. "One he co-owns with you." There was a look of accusation in his eyes and a little bit of anger.

Deja didn't understand these emotions on his part. There was a perfectly logical explanation for them co-owning the house. "Yeah, I know all about it," she teased. "I owe your father a lot for that. He bought the note to keep it from going into foreclosure. I couldn't afford the house payments at the time."

"You know what?" Hennessy was holding up his hands and shaking his head like he was trying to keep something offensive from getting closer. "It's okay, you don't have to explain. I understand what was going on."

Deja laughed at his bold statement. "No, you don't."

"Maybe not exactly," he clarified. "But I have a pretty good idea."

Crossing her arms, she looked at him with amusement. "You're just like your father, aren't you? Both of you think you know everything there is to know."

"Come on, Deja. There's no mystery here," he spoke to her like she was a child. "A man, especially my dad, doesn't buy a house for a woman unless he loves her."

"That's true enough. But there's a lot more to the story."

Again, he was shaking his head. "I really don't want to hear the details."

"All right then." Deja sighed and walked into her "Reading" room and sank gently onto the pillows. "Sit down."

"I told you, I didn't come here for that."

"Go ahead, Hen. She won't bite." Rayne was sitting up on the red mat smiling.

"Look who it is," he smiled devilishly. "Sleeping Beauty."

"Mmmmaaa-maaa," a tiny hoarse voice drifted from the back room.

"And her little dwarf, Sleepy."

Before he could turn around, Rayne was on her feet.

"I'll get him," she said sending a quick look in Deja's direction.

Good, Deja thought. She'd made her decision. But it would be a long, hard battle to break free of the Devil's chains. She hoped with all her heart Rayne had the stamina to go the distance.

Rayne quickly returned with her son, Teray in her arms. "He's hungry. I think I'll take him home for some dinner and come back for you, okay, Hen?"

"I'm not stayin'," he protested.

Deja stopped shuffling her Tarot cards to study him. He was a cocky, stubborn, pig-headed mule and she couldn't for the life of her figure out what made him so enticing.

"No offense," he looked her way. "But I don't need what you're sellin'. I already found out what I needed to know."

"Are you sure?" she let her words hang in the air like an invisible lifeline. Either he took it or he didn't. The choice was always the individual's to make.

For a moment, he looked as though he was actually re-considering. His gorgeous gold-ringed brown eyes held hers in a gaze of careful caress. Quickly his look turned into a hungry, predatory sort of wildness.

Deja warmed in response to his unspoken desires, wanting to unleash her own. "Are you sure?" she repeated. This time, her tone held more temptation than salvation.

Hennessy swallowed hard. The floor was doing that crazy shifting thing again and he wanted so bad to throw her down on those pillows, rip off the bright satin bustier, push up the folds of her white skirt and take her right there on the floor. Preferably, they could make love where the orange and gold streams of sun formed a spotlight in the room.

He closed his eyes tightly to break the growing pull of lust and desire. His daddy was going to marry this woman, he reminded himself. He repeated this over and over in his head quickly. To want her this badly was sick and twisted in a *Twilight Zone* kind of way and he had to stop.

"You all right?" Deja asked.

Opening his eyes, he saw the tiniest hint of a smile lift the corner of her exquisite mouth. She wasn't asking out of concern. She knew exactly what was bothering him.

Realizing this changed his mood. Hennessy grew irritated. Why was she acting like this? Why was she tempting him? With the good possibility of his daddy being out of the way, was she looking for her next Sugar Daddy? Well, he wasn't the one. "I'm fine," he said quickly. Then to his sister, "Let's go."

Deja watched as they left her shop. At the window, she moved aside the sheers to see them climb into the car and take off down the street. She bit her bottom lip and moved a hand over her pelvis to the place where desire continued to stir. The desire he'd conjured with his long, hot gaze.

Turning away from the window, she crossed the room to the mat and eased herself into a resting position. She had to think and she couldn't do it back in her FEMA trailer. She'd parked the trailer in the driveway of her mamma's house in order to get electricity and water. But during the day, the contractors were hammering and sawing and making too much noise to give her the quiet needed for mediation.

So she lay here in her shop, hoping for paying customers, but not expecting them. People appeared to have stopped wondering about their futures. Maybe they thought the worst had already come and thinking beyond today was too much to handle, and not worthy of the cost no matter how discounted.

But Deja was willing to look past today and into the future. The near future, at least. She'd played along with Hennessy today letting him believe he had all the answers. She'd allowed him to continue to think his daddy bought her a house because they'd been having an affair. She'd let him think that because he'd refused to listen to the real story. But next time she wouldn't be so playful, because this couldn't happen again. She laid both hands across her pelvis this time, willing the wildness of her desire to still to something calm and tame.

The next time they met in the real world, she refused to be left with this burning inside, this wanting. A woman could only take so much.

So, she lay on her mat and asked a simple question, "How do I make sure there *is* a next time?" Quietly she waited, knowing the answer would surely come.

Chapter Six

The next few days were agonizingly boring. Hennessy wished he had something more to do than sit around waiting for answers. He'd called Christine the teller to find out if any more checks had been negotiated on his daddy's checking account—she'd reported that none had. His calls to Jack and Johnnie were quick because they had to be squeezed into the brief hours of daylight when they were both awake and not yet onstage or in the arms of the next nameless honey. Worst of all, he had to live with the never-ending bickering between Rayne and their mamma.

He sat on the front porch and fingered chords on his guitar, though without electricity, he couldn't hope to drown out the sounds coming from inside the house. Ray Ray played in the yard with one of the neighborhood boys and Antoine was leaving for yet another one of his trips to the grocery store. Hennessy suspected the man used the trips simply as an excuse to escape the rage of estrogen that was nearly palpable inside.

Teardrop pulled up to the house just as Antoine reached his car.

"Mr. Marshall," Antoine said formally.

"Mr. Ellis," Teardrop responded in kind.

"I was just on my way out," Antoine said opening his car door.

"Oh, I was just stopping by to see Hennessy," Teardrop said casually.

A smile slid across Antoine's lips—the second in as many days, Hennessy noted.

"Nice uniform," Antoine said sarcastically, his narrow eyes roaming up and down Teardrop's McDonald's shirt.

Ray Ray, on the other hand, was thrilled. "You work at Mac Donnell's, Uncah Drop?" he asked, running to greet the old man.

"Yes, I do, Ray." He rewarded the boy's enthusiasm with a box of cookies. "Make sure you share with your friend, now."

"I will," Ray Ray tore at the box while his friend looked on with anxious round eyes.

"What's going on, Drop?" Hennessy laid his guitar carefully across the seat of the porch bench and greeted the old man.

"I'm awright, doin' awright." Teardrop moved up the stairs and took a seat on the rocker. "Just got offa work. Who'd a thought a man could get a job at McDonald's for twelve dollars an hour, huh? Life shore has changed."

"It sure has," Hennessy placed his guitar back in its case, wanting to give the man his full attention. "Fast food is a lot different than carpentry, huh?"

"Yeah, you right," he said, scratching his thinning white hair. "I never thought I'd make twelve dollars an hour, let alone at a McDonalds. It ain't that hard, just dropping a rack of fries in some hot oil. The machine buzzes when its time to take 'em out. All you gotta do is push a button. I done much harder work'n that before."

"Why ain't you tryin' to get on with one of the construction company's then?"

"Did," he acknowledged. "They said I was too slow,"

Hennessy shook his head. "You'd think they'd be happy to have all the help they could get."

"They more interested in quantity than quality." Teardrop shook his head. "My daddy always tole me anything wurth doin' is wurth doin' right."

Hennessy nodded. "My daddy told me the same thing."

"But your daddy didn't beat you near 'bout to death to prove it." Teardrop said flatly.

Hennessy looked over at him, a frown bending his sweaty brown forehead. "That happen to you?"

The old man gave a slow nod. "Yo' daddy jumped in to help me that night. That's how he came to be my best friend. And when my daddy died a few years later he was by my side at the services." He stared straight ahead for a moment. "Boozie's the one nicknamed me. Said he ain't never saw nobody cry just one tear before. But, I swear that's all I could muster for that man."

"And you've been Teardrop ever since," Hennessy deduced.

"That's right," he nodded. "So, about yo' daddy—heard back on them tests yet?"

"Naw," Hennessy said. "Should get something today or tomorrow, though. That's what the website said."

Rayne rushed out of the house at that moment. "Mamma's absolutely impossible. I swear to God if I made more money I'd move outta this damn house."

"Good day to you, too, Miss Rayne," Teardrop chuckled.

Rayne didn't even crack a smile at his tease. "Oh. Hi, Teardop."

"I was just tellin' your brother what good money I'm makin' under the golden arches. I can put in a good word, if you like."

That made her smile. "Are you kiddin' me? I'd spend my whole paycheck keeping Ray Ray in french fries and cookies."

"All right. Don't say I didn't offer." He rose to his feet and groaned. "Ooh. All that standing has put a hurtin on my dogs. My bunions are barkin'." He held tight to the rail as he walked down the porch steps. "You should prob'ly think seriously 'bout movin' out this house, Rayne," he threw over his shoulder. "Your step-daddy ain't got the best reputation, you know?"

"What do you mean by that?" Rayne asked.

Hennessy stood beside her, anxious to hear what the old man had to say about the mysterious Antoine Ellis.

"I'm just sayin' he ain't always at the grocery store when he say he is. I hear tell he's into some pretty shady business."

"How do you know that?" Hennessy asked.

"Got ears. Got eyes. Only good news is the hurricane purdy much run all his customers outta town for now. Bad news is men like him don't like it when their funds dry up."

"Are you saying my mamma's in danger?" The thought bothered Hennessy.

"Naw. Ain't sayin' that. I'd just hate to see your sister get all wound up in that junk again, that's all. I come around just to remind him I'm pay'n' attention."

"I thought it was just to eat Mamma's food," Hennessy teased.

"That's a perk, son. That's what that is. I gotta soak these feet. I'll see you around, children."

Hennessy looked over at her sister. She stared unseeing into the distance, her arms crossed.

"What's the matter?" he asked.

"I'm gettin' awful tired of everyone spending time worrying about me and drugs."

Hennessy noticed that for the past few days, she seemed angrier, but less panicked. Her hands weren't shaking anymore. He wondered if Deja Devine had given her some kind of strange herbs. "People care about you, Rayne, that's all. But, I notice you seem…calmer the last few days. What happened? The psychic tell your future?" he asked, only half-teasing.

Rayne looked over at him. "Wouldn't you like to know?"

"Yeah, actually I would. How does that reading stuff work?"

"You coulda found out first hand," she peered over her sunglasses at him. "But you ran outta there like the place was on fire."

"I didn't need to stay. I found out what I needed to know when I went to the bank and got into Daddy's safe deposit box."

"You had a key to his safe deposit box?" Her thin eyebrows shot up.

"Yeah," he shot back and gave her a straight look to stop further questions. "I found a deed to a house in Jefferson Parish with his and Deja Devine's name on it."

Rayne sucked in a huge breath of air and her eyes widened. "You mean he really was havin' an affair with her? I thought Mamma was just doin' her jealousy thing. She thinks half the women in New Orleans slept with Daddy."

"This time, it looks like Mamma is right," Hennessy said.

Too Much Hennessy

Rayne turned her attention back to the road and a moment later, a wicked look stole across her face. "I guess that puts a little crimp in your style, doesn't it?"

"What're you talking about?"

"I saw how you was lookin' at her when we walked in that place — tongue all hangin' out — drool slidin' down your chin."

"I did not." Hennessy tried to sound cool, but the truth was he was a little irritated his attraction for her had been so transparent.

"Did so. I had to push to get you outta my way. The way you was stumbling, I thought you were gonna drop my baby." By now, Rayne was laughing like crazy.

Hennessy was more than irritated. "Stop playin'."

"Serves you right, Mr. I'm-God's-gift-to-women." She swiped at the tears rolling down her cheeks.

"I never said I was God's gift to anybody," he argued. "All I did was look at the woman — all men look at attractive women. It didn't mean I was tryin' to get with her."

"'Course not," Rayne said sarcastically. "You couldn't 'cause your daddy beat you to her."

"You're sick, you know that?" Hennessy slumped on the bench.

"Mamma, if you sick, you shud take sum med'sin," Ray Ray said running up the stairs to the porch. Apparently, his little friend had gone home.

Rayne laughed more. "Mamma's not sick, baby. But, I think your Uncle Hennessy needs some help. I recommend two cold showers," she said, pretending to hand her brother a prescription. "And call me in the morning," she finished in a clinical tone.

It was so crazy Hennessy laughed, feeling his irritation melt away.

Ray Ray giggled and kicked his feet joyfully as he sat on the top step. "Do it again, Mamma. Do it again," he pleaded.

Rayne obliged her son and kept him laughing until his grandmother poked her head out the screen door.

"Ya'll better get dressed in a hurry." She was referring to church services that didn't start until six. She seemed to think that because it took her a few hours to get ready the same was true for everybody else. "What's that you eatin', Ray Ray?"

"Mack Donnels!" He smiled and chomped on the last of his cookies.

"Lord, God what you be feedin' that child?" she asked, but Rayne and Hennessy could tell she wasn't expectin' an answer. "Well? You check the mail yet today?"

Hennessy nodded. "Left all your bills on the table beside the couch. No results yet."

"I 'spose we're not havin' his funeral anytime soon then." She seemed distracted and agitated.

"I told the funeral director we'd let him know when we knew."

"Well, we still got church today." Lila sped off toward her bedroom. "Antoine better get back here soon for he makes us late."

"I guess we'd better act like we're getting ready before she drives us all nuts," Rayne said. "Ray Ray take that McDonald's box and throw it away. Hen, why don't you try calling the 800 number and see if they've even started that DNA test?" She was starting to get bossy again.

Hennessy was glad to see the return of the old Rayne. She'd come out for an appearance like he and his band did when playing a set of songs for an audience. But, he knew she'd disappear again into the frail, messy woman whose hands shook with the agony of withdrawal. If only she could get her sets of normalcy to last longer and longer…maybe the other woman would disappear altogether.

He took a piece of paper from his pocket and called the number that had been on the kit. The phone rang four times and Hennessy grew impatient. On the seventh ring a woman answered with a nearly hostile, "Hello?"

Identifying himself, Hennessy requested status on the test. It seemed like he was on hold for an hour, waiting for the representative to get back on the line. "Mr. Walker, you're from New Orleans?" she asked, her tone much kinder.

"Yes."

"Well, the results of your kit were mailed out yesterday. We try to expedite anything that comes from your area. You should have it anytime now."

"Do you have any idea what the results showed?" Hennessy pressed.

"We don't have access to that information, Mr. Walker. Sorry." She paused. "I'm showing we Fed Ex'd your package to arrive by ten tomorrow morning, though."

"All right. Thanks." Hennessy shook his head at Rayne. "The package is supposed to be here in the morning."

"I think that DNA stuff is for the birds," Lila said, adjusting her dress as she came down the hallway. "Ya'll seen your stepfather?"

Hennessy saw the man's car coming down the street. He looked at Rayne. He could tell by the look she gave him she didn't think they wanted to witness the tongue-lashing the man was about to get.

"At least she'll be pickin' at someone else besides me for a while," Rayne said under breath as they went inside the house to change.

The package arrived at exactly nine forty-six the next morning. Hennessy sat it on the kitchen table and wondered if he should wake his sister or open the envelope and get it over with.

As is turned out, he didn't have to make the decision. Rayne walked into the kitchen and made a beeline for the coffee maker. "Is that it?"

"Yeah. You ready?" Too anxious to wait for her answer, Hennessy ripped the envelope open.

"What's it say?" Rayne walked up to the table.

"Good news," Hennessy scanned the document looking for the information he needed. He couldn't believe it. "The man in the casket doesn't have any DNA in common with us. It's not Daddy."

Rayne squealed and jumped up and down. "I knew it! I knew it!"

Lila and Antoine came down the hallway in a rush. "What's goin' on?" Lila asked. "What happened?"

"It's not Daddy," Rayne squealed and grabbed up the paper to read it herself. Deja Devine was right. "That dead man isn't Daddy."

Ray Ray ran out of his bedroom and seeing his mamma so happy made him start jumping up and down.

Lila looked dumbstruck. "I guess I gotta tell folks there ain't gonna be no funeral," she said flatly.

Hennessy stared at his mamma then like it was the first time he'd ever saw her. If he didn't know better, he'd swear she was happier when she'd thought her ex-husband was dead.

"Mamma," he said, stopping her from leaving the living room.

"What baby?" she asked..

"Aren't you happy about the news?"

"Of course. But I can't believe Boozie put me through all this trouble for nothing."

"Mamma how could he have known?" Hennessy asked.

"Oh my God," Rayne interrupted. She put a hand on Ray Ray to stop his jumping.

"What?" Hennessy asked.

"Oh my God," she said again, the papers in her hand were shaking. "This says you and I only have one parent in common, Hennessy. Did you see that?"

He hadn't. He'd skimmed the information so fast he hadn't noticed anything except the fact that the dead man didn't match his and Rayne's DNA at all. He took the paper from her hand. "Where does it say that?"

She pointed and then stared at Lila. "Mamma is this true?"

At first Lila looked startled, then she regained her composure. "I'm sure they made some kinda mistake. 'Course ya'll got the same parents," she said dismissing the matter.

"They claim these tests are over 90 percent accurate," Rayne challenged. "It says my daddy isn't really my daddy."

Hennessy studied his mamma closely. Was that the barest glint of guilt he saw in her eyes?

"You might as well tell 'em the truth, Lila," it was Antoine who spoke. He stood just behind his wife, arms folded across his skinny chest. As usual, his expression was unreadable.

Lila gave her husband an exasperated glare then turned back to face Rayne. She looked to be making some decision—not whether or not to tell her, but how to tell her, Hennessy guessed. As she moved to sit in the chair next to him, she motioned for Rayne to sit on the other side. She took both of her hands.

"You're mine. Make no mistake about that," she said with emphasis. "But Rayne, your daddy ain't Boozie Walker." She said quietly like an apology.

"Your daddy's name is Charles Flowers."

Rayne's eyes glazed over with tears. "What? Why didn't you ever tell me?"

Lila's eyes grew full as she turned all her attention to Rayne. "I didn't mean to keep you in the dark, baby. It's jus that Boozie married me while I was pregnant with you."

"Does he even know I'm not his?" Rayne asked clearly struggling to take it all in.

"'Course he knows. He's known all along and it didn't matter to him one bit," Lila continued. "He loved you from the minute he saw you and never once treated you like anything but his own flesh and blood, now did he?"

Rayne was sobbing now as she shook her head.

"It doesn't change anything, baby. Can't you see that?" Lila lifted Rayne's chin to look into her eyes. "You see that don't you?"

"You know what?" Rayne pulled her hands from her mother's and pushed herself to standing. "Just leave me alone, all right? I just…just leave me alone."

A door slammed, but Hennessy could still hear his sister's muffled sobs as they traveled down the hallway. He looked at his mamma then. Lifting a hand, he cupped her soft, creamy brown cheek and wiped away a tear with his thumb. "You're wrong, Mamma. This does change everything," he said softly.

He kissed her gently on her forehead, walked past a cross-armed Antoine who actually seemed happy all this was happening, then went to get Ray Ray who was knocking on Rayne's bedroom door begging to get in.

"Come on, little man." He picked up the three year old.

"Mamma's cwyin," he said, his bottom lip trembled slightly.

For a moment, Hennessy thought he should go in and try to console his sister, but he knew she'd have to work this out on her own. If the situation had been reversed, he would definitely need some time alone. "She'll be all right," Hennessy patted the boy and forced a smile. "Let's go get us some ice cream, okay?"

"Can we bwing some for Mamma?" he asked.

"You bet," Hennessy answered. "I know just the kind she likes." A string of curses played in his mind as he collected the keys to his sister's car and headed out. Talk about your good news and bad news, he thought. Today, they wouldn't be paying respects to his dearly departed father. Instead, he'd found out that, though Boozie Walker had departed, he might still be alive somewhere. Then again, what if his daddy really was dead, but the authorities hadn't found him yet? And what if some other family had buried him weeks ago, thinking he was their father?

Just thinking about the possibilities was making Hennessy's head hurt. He had no idea what he should do next. He supposed he could go back to California, except he'd already changed his ticket. He had an additional week to be stuck here in New Orleans unless he wanted to spend another hundred bucks to change it again. Or, maybe he could fly standby.

He looked over at his nephew. He'd moved the car seat to the front so he could reach him better. Ray Ray smiled at him and giggled the way kids do for no reason.

Hennessy smiled back. He didn't have to make up his mind today.

Too Much Hennessy

Deja dreamed of Rayne Walker. Dreamed she was in the midst of a field of flowers—dozens of them in vivid reds, pinks and yellows. She'd scooped up armfuls smiled happily as she walked along a path.

Deja saw the horrible black whirl of wind coming up behind the woman and wanted to warn her, but couldn't. But Rayne sensed something and looked behind her.

Too late. The horrible wind had come, quick and black, ripping the bundles out of flowers from her arms and throwing her to the ground. She'd screamed at the wind, but the wind's voice was louder and carried her tiny voice off into the distance along with the entire field of flowers.

The black wind stopped as suddenly as it started, leaving behind a scraped gray sky. Deja watched with concern as Rayne managed to rise unsteadily to her feet.

Her arms and legs were marred with bruises and cuts. And all around her was nothing but the shriveling brown remains of flower petals.

The dream ended and the connection was broken.

Deja stared at the dark ceiling of her room and tried to catch her breath. Something awful had happened to Rayne. Something was threatening to break her spirit and send her back to the chains of her addictions. Rayne had revealed to her during her Tarot reading she was feeling weak and vulnerable. Deja had asked her to think about the true joys in her life and how important it was to hold on to them.

Perhaps that's what the flowers symbolized in Rayne's dream—her few joys being ripped out of her arms by some horrible wind.

Deja threw off the covers and headed for her closet. She couldn't sleep anymore. She wasn't quite sure if she could do anything, but she felt a need to be close to the woman. To watch over her, just for the night.

Rayne awoke with a start. Her bedroom was dark and quiet. For a moment, she thought she was still dreaming, and that the horrible, black wind had scraped the sun from the sky as it had the flowers from the earth. But seeing the red numbers of her clock let her know it was simply the middle of the night. She'd fallen asleep in her clothes after crying every tear she had. Even now, tears threatened, but could not come.

How could her Daddy not be her daddy?

Rayne sat up and immediately regretted it. Her head pounded like the morning after an all-night drinking binge. Unfortunately, she knew the feeling too well.

As quietly as she could, she left her room and went to check on her son. Ray Ray was sprawled all over the place, one leg on top of his Uncle Hennessy and one chubby hand over the man's face. Rayne thought about covering the boy, but knew in minutes he'd just wriggle his way out again.

Pain bounced in her head like a muffled gong. Her stomach felt queasy. Rayne felt her way across the hall into the bathroom. She studied herself in the medicine cabinet mirror. She looked terrible. And it was her mamma's fault.

Flowers. She'd said her real daddy's name was Charles Flowers. No wonder she'd had a nightmare about plants.

For a brief moment, it occurred to her she might be related to Pam, her best friend, whose last name was also Flowers. She wondered if Sister Alveta, Pam's grandmother, also knew the truth.

So many lies, she thought, growing angry and agitated. Who gave people the right to lie about this kind of thing? And not just any people, her mamma and—

She stopped and braced herself before the word hit her mind like a bullet. *Daddy*.

Karlem Walker. Boozie. A man who'd only pretended to be her daddy for all these years. Her head pounded harder as though trying to force the new reality into the tiniest crevices of her brain. Her hands started shaking as a familiar need clawed at her gut and crawled along her skin. She needed a fix. She needed…

No.

She clenched her teeth, her fists, her eyes. No drugs, dammit! Panicked, she splashed water in her face and popped a couple of Tylenol.

Too Much Hennessy

Maybe if her head stopped hurting she could fight this thing. She'd fought the need at least a dozen times today, at the park with Hennessy and Ray Ray, at the *Deja View* and first thing that morning when she'd been with Earl.

She looked up, breathing faster. Earl. She fumbled around to find her makeup and put on a fresh face. She rushed into her bedroom to find something less rumpled to wear and spritzed on perfume.

A few moments later, she was feeling around for her purse and keys on the small table by the living room door and, not long after, she was on her way to Elysian Fields and the Blues 'N Booze.

She'd found the pack of cigarettes she kept in case of emergency in her glove compartment and smoked two of them on the way. Smoking helped…but only a little. She pulled into the alley alongside the dark building. It reminded her of the haunted houses in movies the way the breeze blew straight in through the dark, vacant windows.

Rayne shivered and dropped the cigarette to the ground and twisted it beneath her shoe. She straightened her blouse and pulled her fingers through her spikes of hair as she rounded the corner where the trailer was parked. No lights were on. He must be sleeping.

It occurred to Rayne she was simply trading one addiction for another, but right now that didn't matter. The only thing she needed right now was for the crawling and clawing to stop. That, and the damned pounding in her head.

She placed a foot on the bottom step and stopped. She'd heard something behind her. It was probably a rat, but she moved her right hand to her purse, unzipped it and put a hand on her pistol. She removed the safety like she'd practiced a thousand times, though never with her head pounding in pain and her heart thumping with fear.

Rayne took another step up. She heard the sound of a shoe grinding pebbles into concrete a second time. Without thinking, she turned, pointed and shot.

Earl cursed loudly as he hit the concrete.

"Earl?" It was Rayne.

He moved his hand to his head where he'd felt the bullet hit. His temple was warm, wet and sticky. Earl's stomach turned violently at the feel of his own blood, but he managed to hold back the stinging bile. If he was going to die, he didn't want to be covered in vomit.

He looked up to see smoke curling lazily from the barrel of the small gun in her shaking hand. "What the f—, Rayne?" Though it was dark, he could see her clearly in the light of the full moon.

"I'm sorry…I thought you were a mugger or something." She put the gun inside her purse and pulled out a pack of cigarettes. "Sorry," she said again. She turned on wobbly legs and lit the cigarette.

Earl got a strange feeling just then. He knew Rayne had had problems. Lord knows he'd seen the condition she'd been in when she was high on crack. She'd like to tore up the bar that last time, except her daddy got a hold of her and took her to the detox.

It suddenly didn't seem like such a good idea, his getting with her. The pain in his head intensified and his stomach lurched. "Damn." He lay back down. "I know this is my own fault, Lord," he stared at the stars twinkling low in the ink black sky. "But, if you let me live, I'll make it up to you."

He'd been in worse places, but dying in a foul smelling alley outside of the most legendary Blues club in all New Orleans wasn't right. Not for the man who was going to own the place one day.

Just then the back door to the club opened and Teardrop stuck his head out. "Earl!" The man ran over to where Earl lay. "You all right, boy? What happened?"

"Rayne shot me."

"What the…?" Teardrop looked quickly at Rayne. She was just a dark silhouette in the near distance. She was staring at the two of them, the red tip of her cigarette wriggling in the dark. "I'm sorry," she apologized again.

The old man turned Earl's head to the side roughly then sat back with a sigh. "You all right, son," he stated firmly after his quick examination. "It's just a flesh wound."

Teardrop was hardly a medical provider and was probably drunk from all the whiskey sours he'd been drinking all night so Earl wasn't sure he believed the man's quick diagnosis. "I don't know, man. I can't feel my legs and my head feels like it's splitting wide open."

"I could call a ambulance, but it'd be a waste of your damn money. Get up, son. Ain't nothing wrong with you a couple a Tylenol can't cure," Teardrop insisted as he rose from the pavement. "Take my hand."

Earl obeyed. Miraculously, his legs held when he stood, but the effort made his head pound angrily.

"Get inside your trailer 'fore she decides to really shoot you," Teardrop said with a laugh.

"She *did* shoot me," Earl argued, wiping the blood from his temple with his hand.

"I'm really sorry, Earl," Rayne repeated, following behind the men. It seemed to be the only thing she was capable of saying.

Teardrop laughed as he pulled open the door to the trailer for Earl. "You know Rayne has fierce aim with that gun a hers. Treats it like a pet...cleans it...oils it...takes it out for practice. If she'd meant to kill you, you'd be dead."

Earl eyed him with a frown. "You're drunker'n I thought, old man." Earl went into the small bathroom. He hadn't thought to buy any first aid items so he wet one of the washcloths he'd taken from the Embassy Suites and placed it on his scraped skull.

When he entered the living room, Earl found Teardrop and Rayne sitting on his new furniture drinking his beers. "Make yourselves at home," he said, dropping onto the couch beside Rayne. He eyed her suspiciously. "You didn't know it was me when you were shootin', right?"

"Of course not. Here." She offered him a can, then tilted her head and drained another.

"Dang. You thirsty, girl?" he asked. He'd never seen any woman drink a can of beer so fast.

Rayne had her eyes closed and took a deep breath before a relaxed smile took over her face. "I'm fine." She nodded.

Earl wasn't convinced.

"Let me look at that." She moved to take the washcloth out of his hand.

"Naw. That's all right," Earl felt the need to protect himself.

Rayne frowned. "Stop being a baby. " She took the cloth then and proceeded to look at his wound. "It's not too bad," she assured him.

She was angled across him. Her perfume filled his nose and he thought how easy it would be to kiss the part of her breasts spilling out of her lacey black bra. But, he remembered he was supposed to be scared of her. She'd just shot him after all. Plus, it'd be hard to bust a move with Teardrop sitting there looking.

"So, if you didn't come over here just to shoot me," he began, "what did you come here for?"

"I thought you'd be in bed." She sat back and gave him a sexy smile.

He couldn't stop the feeling rising anymore than he could stop the sun from setting. "Is that right?" He put a hand to her soft thigh.

"I should ask you, where ya'll were coming from," she added, running a hand down his chest.

"We were inside the B&B," Earl said with a smile. "Plannin' on how to rebuild the place. Teardrop says he can make a new bar if we get him the right wood."

"Didn't Mamma call you?" Rayne asked. "Dad…Daddy might still be alive." She felt funny calling him Daddy when he wasn't anymore, but old habits died hard.

"Yeah, we hurd all right," Teardrop confirmed. "But the way we figure it, Boozie'll still want to see the place gets up and runnin' again when he shows up. We jus tryin' to get a jump on it."

Rayne frowned. "I don't get why ya'll are doin' all this planning in the middle of the night. Seems like it'd be easier in the day time."

"Well, we started out at a poker game up to Drop's house," Earl explained. "We walked back here once we got talking about rebuilding, just to see what we're up against."

"Brung my flashlight along." Teardrop tapped the object that hung from a ring on his workpants. "It's a right mess in there. It'll take months to get it back in shape."

Rayne nodded. "I guess that makes sense."

Earl gave Teardrop a look and a nod. Immediately the old man rose to his feet. "I best be on my way. The missus'll be missin' me." He slammed back the last of his beer, made a satisfied noise and headed out of the trailer.

When the door closed behind him, Earl wasted no time, sinking his face into the soft skin of Rayne's breasts. "I'm so glad you decided to bring the girls over for a visit," he said between hard, hungry kisses. " 'Cause the boys can't wait to come out and play." Rayne lifted her tiny skirt and straddled him. She let her head fall back and allowed herself to get lost in the feel of his lips and hands as he worked to grope and suckle every part of her. "That's it, Earl. That's it baby," she moaned and ground her hips into his lap.

She needed to get lost for a little while. To have something stop the other need, the other hunger. She knew she could count on Earl to always be ready for her, but for a moment she wondered if it was wrong to use him. *Use him? Right.* She chided the little voice of her subconscious. The way he was moaning and carrying on it was pretty clear she was causing him no pain.

She was too late. Deja parked across the street and stared at the house where Boozie Walker's ex-wife lived. Rayne had mentioned she and her son lived with her mother, but there was no sight of the little car she'd seen Rayne drive off in that afternoon.

She drummed the steering wheel with her fingers and tried to think what to do next. Something had happened to Rayne—she could tell by her dream. But, even Deja knew she'd look more like a psycho than a psychic if she went pounding on the door at three in the morning asking questions.

And then she felt it. A little breeze of serendipity went past and a light went on in the front of the little house. In a matter of seconds, the front door opened. Deja could feel the concern and panic as Hennessy came out of the house shirtless, looking left and right down the street.

He was looking for her, too.

Deja got out of her car. "Hennessy," she called to him.

He stood completely still as she crossed the street. "What are you doing here?"

What else could she tell him but the truth? "I thought your sister was in trouble. I came to see if I could help."

"Did she call you?"

"No. I just felt it."

Hennessy planted his legs a little further apart and crossed his arms over a sleek, muscled chest. His biceps bulged slightly and Deja couldn't help but stare. Moonlight spilled over the hard lines of his physique, giving him the look of a Michelangelo statue. She wanted desperately to feel his skin beneath her hand, and would have, except she saw the forbidding look on his face. "You felt it?" he repeated her words back to her. "Look, Deja, I don't have time for games right now. I need to find Rayne."

"She's not in danger," Deja offered quickly. "I'm pretty sure she's all right for now."

"I'm afraid she's not all right mentally," Hennessy spat back irritably. His eyes scanned the darkened street. Nothing moved except the two of them. "There's no telling where she went. Maybe to her friend Pam's house…"

"What do flowers have to do with anything?" Deja asked, interrupting his stream of consciousness babbling.

His eyes widened with either fear or wonder. Maybe a bit of both, Deja decided. She was on to something.

"I thought the flowers had something to do with the joys in her life, but now that I'm closer, it seems like they have another meaning too."

She walked past him to the front door of the house. The images and impressions grew stronger. She turned to look at him. "The word flowers isn't about anything happy at all, is it?"

Hennessy shook his head slowly. "How did you know that? Are you and Rayne playing a joke on me?"

"I don't sense she's in the mood for joking right now." Deja sighed and shifted her weight to one foot. "I'm just here to help if you'll let me. Why is it so hard for you to believe that I might be extra intuitive?"

"Intuitive?" Hennessy gave a joyless laugh. "You're a damn witch, woman."

Deja was irritated. "I thought you'd be a bit more open-minded, given you're a creative person. Now, are you going to invite me in to talk about this or not?"

"All right, all right." He moved past her and held the door open for her to enter. "Come on in."

Deja had pulled her clothes on quickly and remembered as she walked past Hennessy that she hadn't bothered with a bra. She could tell by the way he stared her breasts this little detail hadn't escaped his attention.

The thought made her smile. No sense in her being the only one burning with lust tonight. He escorted her quietly down a darkened hallway until they reached the kitchen in the back of the house. He turned on the lights and started moving around the room like he was lost.

"I'm not sure where Mamma keeps the coffee, but it's around here somewhere," he said absently, pulling open cabinets and drawers.

"I don't drink coffee this late at night," Rayne said quickly, leaning across the counter to look at him.

Hennessy's eyes went to the top of her blouse again, then quickly away. "I do," he countered.

"I'll have some tea, though. If you have tea."

"Sure you wouldn't rather have water?" he asked, a devilish smile lifted the corner of his mouth as he tossed his dreads back off his face.

Rayne gave him a wicked look then took a seat on one of the stools at the counter. She watched him as he found the coffee, made a mess of spilled water and coffee grounds on the counter, push the mess with the side of his hand into the sink and rinse it away.

He swiped his wet hands on his jeans a few times to dry them and surveyed the cabinets once again. "Tea, huh?"

Deja could tell he was talking to himself so didn't bother to answer. Instead, she studied him with hungry eyes, enjoying the way he moved, the way his jeans hung low on his hips, revealing the very top of his navy blue underwear. And most of all, she enjoyed the way he got so caught up in what he was doing that he began humming and singing the tune of some Jazz song, as if he'd forgotten she was there at all.

A few minutes later, he slid a cup with a tea bag in it across the counter at her. "Here you are. Tea."

"Thank you," Deja said, now so completely under his spell she felt a little drunk.

"You need sugar?" he asked, dumping two huge spoonfuls into his cup of coffee.

"No, thanks."

"Cream?" he asked holding out the container.

"No." She said simply, dipping the bag until the water turned a deep brown. "I'm good."

He held his hand out for the tea bag when she squeezed the excess water from it. He tossed it into the trashcan beside the counter. Pouring cream into his cup, he stirred until it turned a pretty creamy brown color. Seeming satisfied, he sipped from his cup. "Perfect."

Images of them kissing, of his fingers playing along her spine came back to Deja like ocean waves spilling onto the shore. "Yeah," she sipped from her cup and drew his eyes into hers. "It sure is."

Chapter Seven

Hennessy knew he would never forget the way Deja Devine looked that night. Her loose, unruly curls were pulled carelessly back into a ponytail and the sheer print blouse she wore did nothing to contain the free sway and bounce of her breasts. The way she looked at him, with lowered lids and dark, mysterious eyes made him shiver. Really shiver, like she'd blown a cool wind down his back.

He closed his eyes and thought of even colder things, ice cubes, Chicago snow, Antarctica...anything but how hot Deja Devine was making him feel right now.

"You all right?" she asked.

Hennessy opened his eyes and sank right back into the dark depths of her sexy eyes. "I'm fine," he answered. He placed both palms on the counter—maybe to keep his balance, maybe to keep from reaching for a delectable looking breast. He had to give it to his daddy; he sure knew how to pick 'em.

"So you were going to tell me about flowers," Deja said taking her mug of tea in both hands. "And, what it has to do with your sister."

Blowing a long breath, Hennessy stared down at his coffee, trying to figure out how to start. He told Deja what his mamma had told him and Rayne. That the man they'd believed was their father all their lives wasn't Rayne's after all. "Turns out some man named Charles Flowers is her real dad," he finished.

Deja nodded. "That makes sense."

"What makes sense?" Hennessy challenged. "None of this makes any sense to me. My daddy is missing, but not dead—I think. And my sister has a father we've never even heard of."

"It explains her dream."

"She told you about her dreams?"

"Not exactly. I sort of eavesdropped on one she had tonight. It woke me up." She took a sip of her tea like she'd said something completely normal.

"What do you mean 'eavesdropped'?" he asked, feeling goosebumps travel up his arms.

"Sometimes, after a reading, I'm so in sync with a person, I can see inside their dreams. It usually goes away after a few nights."

He shook his head. "You know you're askin' a lot if you expect me to believe this stuff?"

Deja smiled. "I'm not asking you to believe anything. It is what it is — whether you believe or not."

"Okay." Hennessy had a feeling arguing would do no good at this point. "All right so tell me what you think you saw in her dream?"

"I saw her standing in a field of flowers, holding a hand-picked bouquet in her arms. Then a dark wind came up behind her and stripped the flowers from her hand, knocked her to the ground and destroyed the field. She was left in the middle of nothing. She looked completely distraught. That's when she woke up. That's when I woke up."

"What time was that?"

"About two-thirty. I threw on some clothes and came over."

"To do what?"

Deja looked at him with an empty expression. "I don't know, Hennessy. I just thought she needed someone to talk to. I thought I could help."

"You know about her drug and alcohol problem?" Hennessy asked carefully.

Deja nodded.

"Did she tell you or did you see that in her dreams too?" His tone held a hint of wariness.

"She told me when we did her reading," she answered dryly. "She wants to break free, but she's feeling weak. Your dad was helping her, talking with her, trying to keep her clean. He's made a sacrifice for her — a big one."

"Do you know what sacrifice he made?"

"No. She didn't tell me that part." She looked at him then as she took a sip of tea, "I just feel it."

How weird. She kept saying things it seemed she couldn't know, but Hennessy wasn't ready to believe in all this psychic nonsense just yet. A rational explanation existed for her knowing or "feeling" so much. "Rayne said Daddy told her before the hurricane he'd made sacrifices twice in his life to keep the bar. But, she didn't say anything about him making a sacrifice for her. Do you know or 'feel' what other sacrifice he might've made?"

Deja suspected she might know, but not because she'd divined it. Karlem had alluded to something he'd been fighting for when she'd seen him last. He'd probably said as much to his son. "I can't say I know what the sacrifice was. But maybe you do."

"Sure I do," his tone dripped with sarcasm. "That's why I'm asking you."

Deja gave him a wincing look. "A reading will help you think through all this."

"I don't believe in that stuff."

She gave him a cutting glance. "Do you wanna figure out what's going on or not? If you do, you've gotta have a little faith, all right?"

Hennessy just stood there looking conflicted.

Deja took that as a positive sign. "I've got my cards in the car. I'll be right back."

"Wait, wait, wait," he said in an urgent whisper as he followed her down the hall. "If you're going to do that wacko stuff on me, we ain't doin' it here. Let me get a shirt and shoes on. We'll go to your place."

"You're right," Deja said inspired by the thought. "The aura is much better there."

"Yeah…okay. Whatever," he said before disappearing into a bedroom.

Deja noticed he didn't bother with a light and that he was out of the room fairly quickly. He took a seat on the living room couch and pulled on socks, shoes and finally, his shirt.

"Ray Ray's in there sleeping," he said as if she'd asked for an explanation. "Don't wanna wake that kid up, he'll be playing till sun up." He turned off the lamp and they left the house.

Deja started up her car and headed toward the Quarter. "You're good with your nephew," she said, just as an observation. "Ever think about having kids yourself?"

"Me? Naw. I'm on the road too much." He grunted and settled his large frame into the seat of her Mini Cooper. "Makes it hard to settle down."

"You like it that way?"

"Yeah." Most of the time, he wanted to say but didn't. Coming home this time was harder than usual. The devastation of the city, the Blues 'N Booze without music and his daddy's presence completely missing from all of it was taking a toll on him. Hennessy was feeling unsure of heading back to California, but he wasn't sure why. "I like seeing different cities, playing Jazz with my buddies way into the night, sittin' around shooting the breeze afterward…it's fun," he said, maybe to remind himself why he'd made the choice to leave in the first place. "I don't know what I'd do if I couldn't play Jazz. Something about the music gets into your soul." He'd gotten more personal than he'd meant to. He quickly switched gears. "How about you? You think about kids?"

"Sometimes," she answered honestly. "But I've got my hands full with my mamma right now."

"How so?"

"She's got liver disease. We managed to get her on a transplant list, but she'll be taken off if I can't get her covered under health insurance." She was silent for a moment. "The thing is, I know I can't get her covered. No insurance company in the world will take her now."

"That's too bad," Hennessy said sincerely. He didn't know how he would react if his mamma ever had such a problem. His heart felt a ping of panic just for thinking such a thought.

"Heaven knows I haven't got the money for the operation. The psychic business doesn't pay all that well, especially lately," Deja said with a hollow laugh.

"She stays with you?"

"Well, more like I stay with her. That was before the hurricane. Katrina made a huge mess of her house and so I left Mamma with her sister in Tennessee and came back to make repairs."

"The house is in Jefferson Parish," she said turning to look at him in the dim interior. "Your dad helped me save it from foreclosure. It took all my savings and a little of his. That's why both our names are on the deed."

A big empty moment opened in his mind before he realized the meaning of what she was saying. Finally, it hit him like a hammer. He'd made a huge mistake. "Oh."

"That's it? That's all you have to say—'Oh'?"

Of course she was right. He'd assumed she was gold digging, dating his daddy for his money, having him buy her a house. When he was wrong, he was really wrong. "I'm sorry I jumped to conclusions. Okay? You happy now?" he spat out quickly, hoping it would ease his embarrassment.

Deja smiled as she turned her attention back to the road. "Since you're apology was so sincere…" she teased. "I'll accept it."

"There's still something I don't understand," he sat up straight in the seat. "Why did he help you? People don't usually bail complete strangers out like that."

He'd just asked the million-dollar question. Deja was sure Hennessy and his sister deserved to know the truth about Boozie Walker, but she could tell only so much. "I've known your daddy the better part of my life. We're hardly strangers."

"How do you know him?" The question came quietly, hesitantly. "Why didn't I ever see you with him?"

Deja didn't blame him. After what he'd just found out, he was probably terrified to find out what other skeletons his daddy had packed away in a closet. Unfortunately, she and her mamma were just two of many. "Mamma used to love going to the Blues 'N Booze," she stared straight ahead through the windshield as the memories came back to her. "I'm pretty sure she loved that place more than she loved me." It was a tough admission, but one she'd come to grips with years ago though she still hurt.

Hennessy remained quiet.

"One night…I must've been about five or six at the time…your daddy brought my mamma home from the bar. I ran out of my room to see what all the noise was. Mamma was crying and fall-down drunk. I remember being afraid of him at first. But then he talked so calm and sweet to Mamma the whole time. He even talked to me and asked my name. Somehow, he got Mamma into bed, but he didn't leave after that."

Deja paused, trying to swallow down the lump of emotion rising in her throat. "He…he asked me if I'd had any supper and I just shook my head. I told him sometimes Mamma forgot…about supper. Truth was, she forgot about a lot of things back then. Everything except drinking."

"Geez. That must've been tough." Hennessy said softly from across the darkness.

"I didn't see your daddy for a long time after that, but I knew he stopped by every once in a while. Some mornings there would be food in the refrigerator and cereal and canned goods in the cabinets that hadn't been there the night before. And Mamma would be in her bed, fully clothed, the smell of old alcohol and cigarettes filling the room. I used to think your daddy was our own personal guardian angel. Every night when I said my prayers, I'd thank God for sending him to take care of Mamma and me."

"But you saw him again later, right?" Hennessy asked. "When'd you run into him again?"

"When I was about thirteen or so. Mamma made a habit of going to the bar after work everyday, so I made a habit of stopping by the B&B after I'd finished with my homework. Your daddy had started watering down her drinks then. I'd go in and talk Mamma into coming home for supper. I'd started paying the bills back then…your daddy told me I should. Anyway, I'd go by the bar to get Mamma and try to get her out of there quietly, but that hardly ever happened. She'd get all loud and tell everybody how smart I was. She'd brag to anybody who'd listen how I paid the bills and not once had the lights and water been cut off. It embarrassed me. And the thing was, I wasn't sure if she was happy about me taking over that responsibility or if she hated me for it."

"Maybe she was both," Hennessy offered. "It can't be easy for a mother to admit to herself, or anyone else, she can't take care of her own house and her child has to do it for her."

"Yeah, I'd considered that." Deja had thought about that a long time ago. "Your daddy helped me help myself and Mamma. I got good grades in school and won a scholarship to Texas Southern. When I left for college though, Mamma went from bad to worse.

"By the time I graduated, Mamma had lost her job and her house was in foreclosure. I turned down a job offer I'd gotten in Houston so I could move home and take care of things. I hated to do it, but I had no choice. I asked your daddy to help me save the house. That was some six years ago."

"A few days before the hurricane hit, your daddy and I were having lunch—just catching up, you know? And I was telling him how well I was doing. The business degree had come in handy when I'd decided to become a card-carrying psychic and I set up my shop here in The Quarter." She pulled her car to a stop in one of many open parking spaces in front of *Deja's View*.

"But I told him about how sick Mamma was. How all those years of drinking had damaged her liver and now, she couldn't drink anymore, but her health was going downhill fast. I needed money for the operation. He'd agreed to let me take out a second mortgage and I was thrilled. I'd been hugging and kissing on him when your mamma walked up on us."

"Oh, that explains why—"

"Why she thinks your daddy and I were having an affair," she finished for him.

Deja pulled the keys from the ignition and exited the car.

Hennessy quickly followed. Inside, he watched how confidently she moved about the room, turning on a lamp, placing her keys inside a drawer in her office, lighting the candles around the room, kicking off her shoes and sitting on the cushions behind the table. Suddenly he could see Deja Devine, the kid who'd had to grow up too fast. Deja, the competent business owner. Not Deja, the divine kook. It was all very deliberate, all very normal.

"Come on," she waved him over to the table. "Have a seat."

Well, *mostly* normal. He looked at her warily. "Is this really necessary?"

She smiled in that wicked way of hers as candlelight danced in her dark eyes. "Don't be scared."

Because she shifted on the cushions causing her breasts to sway in a lovely way, he decided he could endure the weird stuff for a little while. "Okay, fine."

She talked him out of his tennis shoes and he sat opposite the table from her. She closed her eyes and took several deep breaths before unwrapping the large cards from their cover of blue silk and separated them into two stacks. She took the stack with fewer cards and spread them out, face down, in front of him. "Choose any three," she instructed him in a quiet, hushed voice.

He did as she said. Each card he handed to her, she laid face down in a row before him.

"This is a three-card spread," she said quietly, not looking at him. "It gives an initial indication of your situation. The first card represents your recent past." She turned the card face up. "The Moon."

Hennessy studied the picture on the card. It showed a moon with a half moon inside it. There was a landscape where a wolf stood at the edge of a river baying at the moon. An image of the moon was also reflected in the water of the river. "What does it mean?"

"Generally, it means you've recently experienced a time of uncertainty and fluctuation. You've felt slightly out of control of your life and a little confused about something. Does anything in particular come to mind?"

"In my past?" he asked, thinking. "Before coming here, I was a little confused about signing a contract to go touring in California."

"Why was that such a hard decision?" she asked, her dark eyes were probing, caring.

Hennessy shifted and tried to think. "I dunno. I think it seemed like such a binding thing, restrictive."

"Why did that bother you?"

"I'm not sure," he said honestly. "But, I think it has something to do with being tied down. I like to go with the flow most of the time, you know? But, really, I can't put my finger on a specific reason."

She nodded, but made no judgment about what he said. Hennessy found that nice. It put him more at ease.

Deja pointed to the card. "The pool of water here indicates the part of us that is intuitive. If you allow yourself to work through the feelings of confusion, the answer will come to you. You'll understand your hesitancy better."

The words seemed wise, but Hennessy realized she hadn't told him anything really. She was making him draw his own conclusions. So that's how this worked. Settling into his pillows, he relaxed even more. This wasn't so weird after all. "Okay. What's the next card?"

She turned it over carefully. "The Hanged Man."

The image alarmed Hennessy at first. Then, he realized the man in the picture was hanging upside down from the gallows by one ankle. He seemed to be quite content and there was a circle of light around his head. "What's this about?"

"The Hanged Man represents your Present. It suggests the time has come for you to sacrifice something in order to improve your chances of getting something better. The man is serene because he's made the sacrifice willingly and knows he will be better off in the end."

Frowning, Hennessy asked, "What am I supposed to be sacrificing?"

"You tell me," she folded her hands in her lap and waited for his answer.

"The only thing I've been thinking about is when to go back to California. Things seem so unsettled here with my dad missing and my sister having problems. I just don't feel right about going back."

Deja sat quietly, not interrupting.

"But then I think I'd be letting the guys down if I don't go back. I mean we've got the contract for all those gigs and I…I just don't know."

"Which is the sacrifice that will get you something better?"

"I *am* my music," he said pointing to his chest. "I'd die without Jazz, without the feeling of playing in front of an audience, the thrill of improvising and having something wonderful come out—something I didn't know was in me. And New Orleans…well, I've been gone for such a long time I think I've lost my connection to the place…to my family. I'm feeling the need to stay, to reconnect. But everything is so crazy now. I don't know if my staying would make a difference."

"This is a decision you'll be making very soon. You'll have to sort it out."

"Great. I thought this was going to be easy."

Deja sighed. "Life is never easy, Hennessy. Even for people you think have it all." She looked tired just then, as if all the years of hearing other people's problems and taking care of her alcoholic mother had taken their toll.

"I bet you've heard a lot of sob stories, huh?"

"Some you could hardly call problems and some that would just break your heart," she admitted. The light from the candles made the space between them small and intimate. Hennessy had the urge to reach across to touch her cheek, to kiss her lips and wipe away the tiny frown on her lips. "And a lot of them look at me like I've got all the answers to life, you know?" Her eyes were pleading for understanding. "Like I can make a difference in whether someone defeats cancer and lives or whether or not their son or daughter comes home from Iraq."

"Really? They take this stuff pretty seriously, don't they?"

"You'd be surprised," she said. "I think that was the hardest thing for me to get used to when I started this. How much people—need."

"Why did you decide to be a psychic?" he asked. "It's not what most kids grow up wanting to do."

She laughed. "No. I wanted to be an actress, to be anybody else but me. I was pretty good at it I guess. I got to play some lead roles at school. One day I was playing a psychic in a comedy. I pulled it off pretty well, because I've always had this sort of gift of intuition. I see things sometimes others can't and that day, I let them know what I saw in each of them. Of course, they all thought it was a great trick and asked how I did it. I made something up that sounded plausible. But that's when I started thinking, I could really do this."

"What kinds of things do you see?" Hennessy was genuinely interested now. "Besides dreams."

Her face shifted into amusement. "I saw you," she said. "The day before we met."

He could tell by the way she waited she didn't expect him to believe her, but somehow he did. "You saw me on the street?" he asked hopefully.

"In another realm. Another world."

Hennessy shook his head. "Now you're back to talking crazy."

"You remember it too," she said, leaning over to whisper it. "You were playing Jazz with your band and I was winding my way through the crowd just to get a look at you. Remember?" It was more a challenge than a question.

Hennessy had a flash back to the dream he'd had the night before his father's Visitation. He'd remembered dreaming about her. "In my dream?" he asked.

She shook her head. Her curls swayed in the romantic lighting. "That was no dream. I didn't know your name and you didn't know mine, but you recognized me the next day, didn't you?"

"Yeah, but...I don't see things like that."

"You're a Traveler," she said simply. "You remember flying sometimes? At night? You rise out of yourself when you're sleeping and can see yourself lying in the bed, can't you?"

He could. He remembered having those feelings many nights. Goosebumps rose along his arms and the back of his neck. "I thought those were dreams."

"You knew they weren't. You told your conscious self that, because the only thing that made sense was a dream. Otherwise, you'd have no choice but to believe you're crazy."

"I'm not crazy?"

"No," she whispered. She was leaning completely over the table now, her cheek touching his cheek. Hennessy was deeply aroused by the connection and the feel of her warm breath on his ear. "You were traveling the night we found one another. You held me to your lips and played music along my bare spine. You breathed your music into me, Hennessy, and I was lost in you." She eased back on her cushion. Her eyes full of candle fire, her breasts heaving with each breath she took. "Remember?"

"Hell yeah, I remember," he admitted. He climbed over the table, desperate to reach her—to hold her in his arms. Her sweet, soft lips responded to his kiss, anxious to feed his hungry mouth the way it had the day he dreamed her...the day he traveled to see her.

The heavy weight of her breast in his hand, made him moan in ecstasy. Oh, how he wanted her. He played with the nipple through the coarse, sheer material of her blouse, and moved his mouth to cover one then the other. She moaned his name in response and it nearly drove Hennessy out of his levelheaded mind. He couldn't get enough of her. He wanted to breathe her, to touch her, to take her right now.

Lifting himself, he pulled his shirt off and writhed out of his jeans and briefs. To his delight, she did the same and lay naked in the soft light of the candles. His arousal peaked, hard and fast. He wanted to go slow, to enjoy every second of what they were about to do, but the moment he was inside her, he knew he couldn't. Nothing had ever felt this good. No woman had ever commanded every part of his lust like this one.

Deja cried out as he moved faster and faster inside of her. She held tight to his back, then his arms, as he worked his way deeper with each push. And he heard it then, the music inside his head, that frenzy of staccato beats and strong melody that pulsed within his blood—fast, furious and as wild and untamed as his lovemaking.

Deja moved with him, matching his rhythm, Hennessy was sure he felt their souls unite. Finally, together they hit a long high note that seemed to lift them from time and space and suspend them, cradled in completion, before dropping them back to earth in tiny jerky spasms.

"Lord, have mercy," Hennessy panted as he rolled off her hot slick body onto the cool wood floor. "That was…that was…"

"Magnificent," Deja panted. "If I had the strength, I'd climb on top of you right here and now and do it all over again."

"Amen to that," he agreed.

They lay for a while, catching their breath. Deja closed her eyes to make the feeling of complete ecstasy last as long as possible.

After a while, Hennessy rolled to his side and threw an arm around her bare waist. As he sat up, Deja noticed a card sticking to his back.

"What's this?" She pulled it from his skin.

"What?" he asked, twisting to get a look.

"It's your future card." She turned it over so he could see the picture. "The Fool."

"He looks like he's about to walk off a cliff," Hennessy said examining the card.

"He is, but in a good way," Deja assured him. She seemed completely at ease sitting there naked, not at all self-conscious. "The Fool indicates new beginnings. It means you'll start a new venture, one others may think is foolish. One even you might think is foolish, but worth the risk."

"What venture would that be?" he asked pulling her into his arms again, wanting her to be close.

"You tell me," she smiled and gave him a long, slow, mind-blowing kiss.

"You're not full of answers at all, are you?"

"No. My job is to help people find the answers within themselves. To find their own strength and courage."

"I know what you can help me find," he teased, cupping her behind in his hands and kissing each breast in turn.

"You don't have to tell me," she said, kissing him again. "I can see it in your eyes."

"Then you're looking too high, sweet thang. You're looking way too high."

Deja felt desire returning. For a moment she wondered if she weren't the one who was being The Fool—falling for Hennessy James Walker. Loving him was like walking off a cliff—a very tall, handsome one. Once a man started wandering the way he did, getting him settled in one place would be hard. But the thought began slipping from her mind as his hands and mouth worked their magic on her flesh.

She'd worry about tomorrow tomorrow, she decided. For now, she wanted to be lost in the feel of Hennessy's music once more.

Chapter Eight

Rayne awoke on the floor of Earl's trailer, twisted in a sheet, and feeling like ten miles of bad road. Earl sprawled nearby, half covered, half not, snoring.

Why wouldn't he be content, she thought. He knew who his parents were and any secrets they'd forgotten to share with him had been buried along with them years ago. They'd died in a car crash she remembered Earl telling her. He hadn't seemed too unhappy at the time. He'd acted like they were a mere annoyance he no longer had to deal with. She remembered thinking how horrible it must've been for him not feeling close to them the way she was to her daddy and mamma—the two people she trusted most in the world.

The two people who'd told her the biggest lie, she corrected. Boozie Walker wasn't her daddy. In a way, it explained why she didn't have the easy way with people he did—like Hennessy did. And why she didn't have an ounce of creativity while her mamma could make clothes, her daddy could make up songs and Hennessy could play music. She couldn't do any of those things and all her life she'd wondered why.

"You jus has to find the thing you good at," her daddy had told her. "That's all that matters." How many times had she struggled through things and he'd given her that answer? All along he'd known the truth, that she wasn't his child. Why didn't he tell her?

Rayne rolled off the floor and staggered groggily to the bathroom. She noticed fresh bruises on her hip and arm. They'd played a bit rough last night, she and Earl. She'd wanted to make sure she felt something other than the need for drugs. Earl had been more than happy to help her into and out of any position she'd wanted. She was sure he'd invented a few new ones last night. He was a flat-out pervert, she decided.

But, who was she to be calling people names? He probably thought she was a freak the way she'd jumped him. The truth was, she wasn't a freak and there was a time where she wouldn't have even thought about playing sex games with Earl. But that person was long gone now.

She stared at the woman in the mirror. The makeup had slid off her face and she looked like a sad, down-and-out clown. "Who *are* you?" she asked.

She found no answer, only a slight twitching of an eyelid.

The twitching spread quickly to the rest of her face then turned into full body shakes and spasms. Finally, a craving as intense as the desert heat attacked her, doubling her over. Rayne slid to the floor and wrapped her arms around herself tight, wondering if, this time, she would shake herself completely apart.

Earl walked in. The sleepy look on his face turned to shock and he quickly pulled his hand out of his briefs. "Rayne. You all right?"

She couldn't talk, her teeth were chattering and cold chill had seeped into the very marrow of her bones. She shook her head and closed her eyes.

"You want me to call 9-1-1?" he asked.

Again, she shook her head. "C…c…call m…my…brother," she finally managed.

Earl cursed and fled from the room.

Rayne could hear him ask how to use her cell phone, but he must've figured it out. She heard him talking but couldn't make out what he was saying. Soon she was unable to focus on anything but the feel of her bones rattling around as she shook. She thought about dying. It would be such a relief, she thought. Death would be so much easier than having to deal with all this pain. Then she heard Deja Devine's voice in her head. She'd asked her, "Don't you have anything worth fighting for?" And Rayne had said: "All I've got is Ray Ray. And I'm not sure he deserves a mamma like me."

The psychic had tried to assure her that her son needed her and wanted her. Rayne remembered feeling stronger after the session, more focused. But today, the strength was all gone and she couldn't find her focus anymore. It was buried under the pain, under the need crawling through her veins and pounding in her head. She needed the drugs to make her feel…Feel what? Better? No. Not anymore. All they did was make her feel helpless and needy. But not better.

Rayne cried a little. She wanted her daddy, but she didn't know who that was anymore. She wanted to feel the comfort of his arms, to hear his voice telling her she could kick this habit, that she was stronger than she gave herself credit for.

But Earl had called Hennessy. He'd be there soon. He wasn't Daddy, but he was her brother. At least that hadn't changed.

Content wasn't a word that applied much to Hennessy's life and the fact he was feeling it now was a little strange. But here he was, wrapped in some satiny black and red robe Deja had pulled out of her messy closet, watching her make breakfast for them feeling more content than he had in years. "You sure you know what you're doing?" he teased. He rested his chin on his hand as he sat on a barstool at her short counter.

"Absolutely. Veggie omelets are my specialty." She was bent over, getting vegetables from the refrigerator. She wore a sheer, pink and purple nightshirt that made it possible for him to glimpse her soft curves and impossible for him to stop smiling about it.

Dumping the vegetables on the counter, she went to make coffee.

"I thought you didn't drink coffee," he said, thinking how grateful he was she was making it. He couldn't remember a single morning where he hadn't had a cup of coffee to get him going. He was definitely not a morning person.

"I don't drink it late at night," she corrected. "You've got to start listening better." She pulled out a large knife and began hacking at a bell pepper; it could hardly be called slicing.

"I'd be happy to help," he offered. "You're killing that thing."

She lifted an eyebrow and glared at him for a second. "I like big chunks. I like to see what I'm eating."

"You could see those bad boys from Mars, sweet dahlin," he teased.

She gave a long-suffering sigh, but couldn't hide her smile. "Fine, you do it." She handed him the knife. "I'll mix the eggs."

Hennessy jumped off the barstool and clapped his hands eagerly. "Watch the Master, kid and don't forget to take notes."

Deja rolled her eyes and kept cracking eggs into a bowl. "You can't be a master of *everything*, can you?"

The question caught his attention. "Are you saying I'm already a master of something?"

He saw the gleam of mischief in her dark eyes. "Pretty much the best I've ever seen," she said suggestively, biting her bottom lip. He loved when she did that.

Hennessy could feel his ego inflating in his chest. He moved closer to her, putting a hand around her small waist. "Tell me more," he urged her and placed a tender kiss on her lips. "Am I the master of The Kiss?"

She placed his hands on her soft bottom then put her arms around his neck. He felt her warmth seeping through the robe.

"Well," she said sensuously, "You're pretty good at The Kiss…but you're thinking too high, Mr. Walker. Way too high."

"Have mercy," he said, completely taken with her. He pulled her tight against him and filled his mouth with the sweet taste of her. He wanted to eat breakfast and was craving caffeine, but he was ready to sacrifice those little comforts to have one more round of lovemaking with Deja. "I believe you're going to be the death of me, woman."

"I believe in dying happy." A brilliant smile broke out on her face and Hennessy felt something—maybe his heart—flip in his chest. "Come with me," she commanded. "I have to show you something." She walked toward the bathroom, pulling the sheer pink and purple nothing over her head.

Hennessy followed, knowing that even if she were about to lead him over a cliff like The Fool on her Tarot card, he'd still follow her. Today, he was choosing the happy death. The moment he stepped into the bedroom, his cell phone rang. He hesitated.

Deja frowned. "I think you'd better get that. It's about your sister."

The door opened and Hennessy pushed through in a rush. "Where is she?" he asked an unkempt Earl. Hennessy noticed a large cut on the man's temple near his hairline, but dismissed it.

"In the bathroom. She looks bad, man. Real bad." Earl walked quickly to the bathroom and opened the door.

Hennessy saw his sister lying on the floor, arms wrapped around herself and shaking like she was freezing. A whole ton of emotions welled inside him, panic, anger, concern. "How long has she been like this?" he shot at Earl. Why had the man left her on the damned floor?

"I dunno." Earl pushed a hand over his short, wavy hair. "I woke up and found her like this, man. I called you right after."

Hennessy cursed then sank to his knees to tend to Rayne. "Come on, Sis," he said softly as he re-arranged the sheet around her and lifted her from the floor. "Let's get you out of here."

"Okay," she pushed the word past her ashen lips.

"You wanna go to the hospital?" he asked, not sure where to take her.

"N…no." she said. "It…it'll pass."

"You sure?" He had to ask because she looked real bad, just like Earl had said.

"S…sure," she said with a jerky nod.

Hennessy lifted her from the floor. "Where are her clothes?" he asked Earl.

The other man had to stop his pacing to answer the question. "In the bedroom, I think." He looked around as if he wasn't really sure.

"I'll take her in the bedroom. Find her clothes and help her into them." Hennessy wasn't nice about issuing the instructions. He hated finding his sister this way and hated even more that Earl didn't seem to have the faintest idea how to take care of her.

"Help her? I…I…"

"For God's sake, man." Hennessy was careful as he laid Rayne on the bed that his frustration wasn't taken out on her. From the clothing and bedding scattered around the trailer, they hadn't ever made it to the bed last night. "You've seen her naked, what's the big deal?"

Earl hesitated, then began picking up her clothes, jeans, shirt, panties, bra.

Hennessy stroked her arm. "Get your clothes on and we'll get out of here," he said, wanting nothing more than be gone already. He noticed the bruises on her arm then. "How did this happen?" he asked her. "Did Earl do it?"

She didn't answer, but her mouth moved as if she started to say something.

Fury made the blood rush in his head like ocean waves. Hennessy caught Earl by the neck as the man tried to explain. "Did you put your hands on my sister, you sonofa—"

"No!" Rayne shouted and managed to sit up slightly. "He didn't. L…let him go Hen."

"You're lying, Rayne. He ain't worth protectin'."

Earl pushed away from him. The clothing he'd gathered was once again on the floor. Gagging, he stumbled backwards against the wall. "She likes it rough, man," he panted. "I didn't beat her. I promise, I didn't beat her." He bent over and struggled to catch his breath.

Hennessy didn't know what was worse, thinking his sister had let another man beat her or knowing she liked having rough sex. "You know what?" he said walking out of the bedroom. "I don't need to hear anymore. Help her into her clothes, man, and let me know when you're done."

In the living room, he walked to the window and stared out at the waste behind his daddy's bar. He was sorry he'd told Deja it was all right to leave when they'd gotten to the B&B. How had a day that had started out to be so perfect turn out to be this messed up?

Too Much Hennessy

Of course, Deja had her own problems to deal with. When she'd dropped him off, she'd been trying to call the contractors she'd hired to fix her mamma's house. They hadn't shown up that morning and she didn't know why. She'd paid them in advance.

The bedroom door opened and Earl pushed Rayne's purse into Hennessy's hands. "Here. She's all yours, man. And you ain't got to worry about me touchin' her ever again," he said like it was the furthest thing from his mind. "Ain't no woman worth all this damn drama."

Hennessy punched him the gut just for saying it. "That felt good," he said with a smile. He stepped over Earl now doubled over on the floor. He helped Rayne off the bed and out to her car. He wanted to chide her for making yet another bad choice sleeping with Earl, but thought now wasn't the right time for the fight. She was shaking less now and was at least able to walk on her own. He opened her purse to find her keys. He saw the gun then. "What's this?"

"Protection," she said with a bit of challenge in her tone.

He wanted to tell her she didn't need that kind of protection if she would just stay away from scrubs and derelicts. Instead he pressed his lips tight and said nothing. He found her keys and started the car. "I'll have you home in a few minutes."

"No, Hen." She reached for his arm. It shook a little and her grip was weak. "Ray Ray can't see me like this."

"We'll just tell him you're sick," he told her. "No big deal."

"It is to me, Hennessy," she cried a little then. "What am I gonna do for him? How am I gonna take care of him when I can't take care of myself, huh?"

Her eyes were tortured and teary.

Briefly, Hennessy wondered if this was how Deja's mother had felt when she realized her daughter was better able to pay the house bills than she was. It broke his heart. "Is that why you're always leaving him with other people?" he asked.

She looked wounded and deflated. "Hennessy, please don't start on me."

"I'm not picking a fight," he assured her honestly. He put the car back in Park and turned to his sister. "I'm just trying to understand. You love him a lot, don't you?"

"More than anything," she said wiping her wet face. "I can't stand for him to see me looking like this. He deserves better."

"Maybe he does," Hennessy took her hand. "But you're his mamma and always will be. The question is how are you gonna get better for him? He needs you, Rayne."

She didn't say anything, just dropped her head against the headrest and closed her eyes. "I wish he didn't," she said. "I know that's a terrible thing to say. But, I really wish he didn't." She started shaking again.

"I think you should see a doctor," he insisted. He put the car in Drive and backed his way out of the long alley beside the bar.

"Take me to Pam's. She'll know what to do." She fell asleep a few minutes later.

Hennessy had seen his share of people who'd been high on drugs, but he'd never seen withdrawal before—not in real life. Seeing Rayne on the bathroom floor, covered only with a sheet, shaking like she was freezing to death hadn't been like watching a movie or a documentary on television. In those situations, he'd had some ability to detach from the person going through withdrawal. But this was different. This was his sister, his flesh and blood and he hurt like hell to see her so messed up.

Twenty minutes later, they reached Pam's trailer. Unfortunately, Hennessy hadn't thought to bring a cup of coffee with him as a peace offering. And when she answered the door the adorable Ms. Flowers wasn't in the mood for company.

"You can come in, but I can't promise I'll be nice," Pam yawned in greeting as she hung on the doorknob. She was still dressed in the casual top and bottoms characteristic of on-duty nurses. Hers was pale blue with balloons all over it.

"Actually, Pam, I was wondering if you would take a look at Rayne. I think she's going through withdrawal. She was shaking a lot this morning."

"Where is she?" Pam looked past him with concern.

127

"In the car. I'll go get her." In moments, he'd carried his sister from the car and laid her on Pam's couch.

"I'm not a doctor," Pam offered a disclaimer even as she took the tiny space next to Rayne and began checking her pulse and raising her eyelids. "Was she vomiting?" she asked.

"Not that I could tell," Hennessy answered.

"She complain of thirst?"

"No. She didn't say much at all," he said.

"I can't check her pressure, but her pulse seems okay. So do her eyes," Pam said sitting back and sighing. "If it is withdrawal, I'd recommend we try doing what they do at Narcanon."

"What's that?" Hennessy moved closer and took a seat in the chair next to the couch.

"It has a lot to do with her diet, exercise and getting enough sleep." She rose and moved toward her table. "I can look it up online. The program also has to do with giving her vitamins and oil supplements." She took a seat at the table and turned on the PC sitting there. As the machine booted up, she leaned back and mussed her brown hair. "She's addicted to Methamphetamines, you know?"

Hennessy nodded.

"It's tough to detox from whiz—that's just one of its many street names. At first you become dependent upon the drug to feel good, and then you need it just to feel normal. It takes a lot of effort to change the patterns of the mind once you get hooked. Rayne was doing real good though…before the hurricane. Your dad was helping her a lot."

Blowing a long sigh, Hennessy sank back into the chair. "That's not good."

"I know. It's tough with him being dead and all."

"Turns out, my dad isn't dead…at least he's not the one in the casket." It felt funny saying "my" instead of "our" dad.

"That's good, isn't it?" Pam perked up.

"You would think," Hennessy sighed.

"She should be happy with that news, not trippin' out like this."

"Yeah," Hennessy said quietly. He knew what was bothering Rayne.

"Do you know a Charles Flowers?" Hennessy asked, hoping to jog her memory.

She shrugged. "Fraid not. It's a pretty common name here in the South, though. Why?"

"No reason. Just ran into someone by that name the other day…thought you might be related."

"Oh." Pam turned back to the PC, clicked around a bit then printed out a page of information. "Here you go." He handed Hennessy the paper.

"Thanks," he said, walking over. He read it quickly. "Exercise, sauna, Niacin and oil supplements? What kind of treatment is this?"

"Holistic. Tries to get the person into a healthier lifestyle," Pam said, giving another yawn. "It works wonders if the person stays on the program and gets eight hours sleep regularly. Speaking of sleep…" She stood and stretched. "Sorry to be rude, but…"

It didn't take Deja's psychic powers to get the hint. "Okay," Hennessy said. "We're outta here. Thanks, Pam."

"You can leave Rayne if you want," Pam offered when Hennessy moved to lift his sister from the couch. "She won't bother me."

"Mamma'll have a fit if she isn't home to take care of Ray Ray. Probably fussin' about it right now." Hennessy lifted his sister. She was lighter than a bag of cotton. It worried Hennessy. Maybe the holistic detox thing had something going for it. His sister was in need of a good meal—a heck of a lot of them.

Rayne slept all the way back to their mamma's house. He knew she didn't want her son to see her like this, but he really didn't see a choice. She'd have to stop running from her problems some time. Maybe Ray Ray would be the only person who could help her find the strength to kick the need for drugs once and for all. Lucky for her, her son was not around to see him carry her inside. He was off with Antoine doing some shopping according to his mamma.

Lila muttered under her breath, following Hennessy into Rayne's bedroom. "Lord, what am I gonna do with this chile?" she asked more to herself than him.

Rayne barely moved when he settled her on her bed. Hennessy had never seen anyone sleep so deeply. It worried him.

And worried his mamma more. "You sure she's all right?" She hovered over her daughter's bed.

"I had her friend Pam take a look at her. She's a nurse."

"I know Pam," Lila said irritably. "But what does she know about this?"

"She seemed to know what she was doing. Here. She gave me this." He offered his mother the information Pam gave him. "We have to help her take care of herself."

"Too much coddlin'. It's all your daddy's fault," Lila insisted. "If he hadn't been so soft on her, she woulda been more responsible like you."

"Don't say that, Mamma." Hennessy walked out of the bedroom, not wanting Rayne to hear her, even in her sleep.

Lila followed behind him. "Why not? It's true."

He reeled on her when he reached the living room. "It's not true, but she thinks it is because you've been sayin' that since we were kids. She thinks you love me more than her."

"That's just crazy," Lila insisted, crossing her arms across her ample bosom. "How that child come up with something stupid like that?"

"Well, for one, you talk different to us."

"What?" Lila reared back in disbelief.

Though he'd not put much thought into it, Hennessy just realized it was the truth. "The second she walks in the room, you're all over her, criticizing what she wears, how she doesn't take care of Ray Ray, her choice in men. It got to be such a habit, I picked up on it and started to do the same thing."

"Well, she hasn't made good decisions, Hennessy. You can't fault me for tryin' to help her see that."

"I know you think you're helping, Mamma, but you're not. Rayne gave me crap about that yesterday. Now I know she's right."

"And you?" Lila took a seat on the couch. A deep frown wrinkled the pale brown of her forehead. "How do I talk to you, Hennessy?"

Walking over, he sat next to her and looked into her lovely brown eyes. "Like you love me," he said simply. "Your eyes light up when you see me, you hug me and kiss me. Just to have you look at me like that makes me feel—I dunno—it feels real good, Mamma."

"I think that's how Daddy always made Rayne feel. And now, she doesn't have him anymore. When you told her he wasn't really her daddy last night, it was like telling her he died all over again."

The front door opened. Antoine and a beaming Ray Ray walked inside.

"Bout time you showed up this morning, Hennessy," Antoine said, carrying his bags down the hallway. "Had yo mamma worried."

A look passed between Hennessy and his mamma. He could tell she was disturbed by what he'd told her, but he was glad he'd said it. Maybe his words would make a difference. Maybe she and Rayne could work through this mess together. They'd have to when he went back to California.

"I went shopping!" Ray Ray beamed, lifting a small plastic bag clutched in his fist.

"Good, baby." Lila smiled and kissed her grandson. "Go take that in the kitchen with Papa 'Twon." She watched him as he ran down the hall to catch up with his Grandpa.

"I had no idea," she said quietly. When she turned back around he could see tears glazing her eyes. "I didn't know I was doin' that to Rayne."

"I know, Mamma. But now that you do, maybe you can change it."

"Maybe," she whispered. "I'ma go lay down, baby."

"All right, Mamma." He watched her go, quite a bit slower than usual, down the hallway. She stopped just outside Rayne's door. She placed a hand to the wood for a moment then crossed the hall to her own room.

Hennessy sat staring at the wall for a moment. The wall that used to be an eggshell white was now a dull, tan color. A distinct line traveled through the entire house, marking the place where the water had stayed for several long days before receding. He could tell by the less distinct lines below it.

"What the hell am I doing here?" he asked the empty room. This trip home had gone from bad to worse, with the only good news being his daddy might still be alive. But, Hennessy had had enough. Enough of this harsh, colorless, lifeless place. Enough looking at the broken shell of a once beautiful, active city. Enough twisting in the winds of broken lives and broken hearts. He needed to get back to what was good, what was real. His music.

Flipping open his cell, he called the airlines. He'd made his choice. He was going back to California on the first flight he could get. Once the arrangements were made and he'd authorized another hundred-dollar fee on his credit card, Hennessy knew what he had to do next and that would be the only part about leaving he would regret.

Deja's muscles screamed as she lifted the heavy sledgehammer for what seemed the thousandth time. Grunting, she sent it smashing through the wall. Sweat streamed down her face and soaked her back. She wore the mask and suit one of the contractors had left behind. It was supposed to protect her from all the mold eating at the walls of her mamma's house. The walls had to come down, she'd been told. She'd been paying people to do this. *They* were supposed to be sweating and tearing down the walls, not her. *They* were supposed to be putting up new ones in their place.

"We'll be back," the foreman had told her when she'd finally reached him by phone. He said they'd been offered a job paying a lot of money if they dropped what they were doing to go right away.

"Money," Deja said between clenched teeth. She lifted the sledge-hammer again and brought it down just beside the last hole she'd made. Why did money, or the lack thereof, have to be the basis of all her problems? She swung the hammer again and it nearly toppled her with its weight.

Defeated, Deja sank to the floor and tried to breathe through the mask. It was so hot.

"What're you doing?"

He was like a shimmering oasis, appearing through the haze of her exhaustion. "Hennessy." She felt good just saying his name and even better to look at his gorgeous brown face.

He squatted in front of her. "That is you in there, right Deja?" He tapped the nose of the mask with his finger.

"Yeah. Help me up. You can't stay in here without a mask," she told him.

He stood and offered a hand, which Deja gladly accepted. She led him to the driveway. "Oh, that feels good," she said pulling off the mask. The breeze was cool as it moved across her overheated skin. Lifting her hair off her neck, she allowed the air to circle her neck. "That thing is so hot, I could hardly breathe there at the end."

"I take it you couldn't find your contractors?" Hennessy asked, watching as she shed the rest of the protective suit.

"No, I found them. They took another job paying lots more money. They told me they'd be back in a few weeks."

"Then why don't you wait for them to do this?" He pointed at the house she'd been demolishing.

"Because my mamma doesn't have that long." She said it quickly, but not fast enough for him to miss the hitch in her voice.

"What do you mean? Has something happened to her?"

Deja nodded and stared at the ground. "She passed out today. My auntie called 9-1-1 and they took her to the emergency room."

"Is she still in the hospital?"

"No. They released her." Deja looked at him then. Her eyes were dark with dread. "They couldn't do anything for her. They said she's got a couple of months, but that's it."

"Then why are you here?" Hennessy gestured at the house and trailer. "Pack up. Go to Tennessee and be with her."

"When I go to Tennessee it'll be to bring her back. She wants to die in her own house in New Orleans. Not in a strange place with a sister who can't find two kind words to say to her." She stormed up the stairs and flung open the door of the trailer.

Hennessy followed her inside. "That house won't be done in time, especially if you have to do it yourself. Why not let her stay in here?"

Deja sighed. "I might have to." She sat on her couch, put her face in her hands and cried. For the first time in a very long time she allowed herself the luxury of tears. She didn't have time to feel sorry for herself, she always had so much to do.

Even now she wasn't crying for herself. She was crying for her mamma and how awful she must feel to be dying around people who didn't love her.

Hennessy was next to her in an instant, pulling her into his arms. He kissed her forehead and stroked her back soothingly. He said nothing, just allowed her to cry all the sadness out of her body.

"I've made such a mess of things," she finally confessed. "I haven't helped her a bit. I left her with people who don't give a damn about her."

"You left her because she needed someone to take care of her. I'm sure she knows that."

"Yeah, but you're right. I've got to go back to get her." Deja relaxed against him. He smelled wonderful, like expensive cologne. She could feel his warmth beneath the soft material of his shirt. Coupled with the soothing rhythm of his hand moving up and down her back she was able to relax and let exhaustion take her.

"You going to sleep on me?" he asked.

"Um, hm," she hummed.

He buried his face in her hair. She realized faintly that it must be a mess and smell like sweat, but she couldn't do a thing about it now.

"I have something to tell you," he said quietly. Too quietly.

A twitter of panic skittered up Deja's spine. She looked up at him. "What?"

She could see the unspoken apology in his eyes and knew exactly what he was going to say. She held two fingers to his lips. "Don't," she pleaded. "You don't have to say anything."

He kissed her fingers then moved them aside. He bent his head to kiss her lips—a long, slow kiss full of good-bye.

Forgetting her exhaustion, Deja returned the kiss. She let her tongue roll around his, and grew excited by the taste of him. She was going to miss kissing him when he was gone. Honestly, she would miss everything about him, which was silly considering she'd just met him. But something—"Oohhh," she sighed as he slid his tongue down the center of her breasts while he made her nipples hard with the pad of his thumbs. When had he unbuttoned her blouse? She had no idea.

His hands moved up and down her back, but no longer were they soothing. Instead, they were moving quickly, urgently up her sides, stopping only to cup her breasts. His tongue was now suckling a breast and all Deja could do was hold on for the ride. Normally, she hated good-byes, but she had a feeling this one would be the exception.

Chapter Nine

"Hennessy." Deja breathed as she drifted off to sleep.

For the first time he, hated the sound of his own name. Deep down, he knew this would be the last time she'd ever say it. He was leaving for California tomorrow and he didn't plan on coming back to New Orleans for a very, very long time.

Hennessy lay in the darkness of her room, listening to the sound of her breathing. He could leave now and save the awkwardness of good-byes in the morning, but he didn't want to. He wanted to lay here and listen to her breathe a while longer. Turning onto his side, he watched as she slept.

Deja Devine was easily the most beautiful woman he'd ever laid eyes on…and he'd laid his eyes—and hands—on quite a few. Running a finger along her cheek, he marveled at how soft her skin was. Letting his gaze fall lower, he felt the hunger return. He wanted to throw back the blankets and see the rest of her, but he fought the urge. Instead, he remembered the look of her all bouncy breasted and round-hipped.

Hennessy smiled just remembering. He didn't know how long he watched her, but after a while he decided he had to go. Staying longer would only make leaving harder. He'd tried staying with other women— tried having real relationships, but they had never worked. They'd all told him the same thing; he didn't pay enough attention to them. But, he couldn't help it. The music pulled at him, called him back night after night. And it was calling him now.

Rising, he found his briefs on the floor and tiptoed into the living room to find the rest of his clothes. He dressed slowly in the dark. The sudden heaviness in his arms and legs made it difficult to move any faster. Finally, he slid on his tennis shoes and wandered back to the doorway of her bedroom. "So long, Deja," he whispered. He closed the door and left the trailer, not daring to look back, fearing he might change his mind.

Deja heard the front door close. She slid her hand along the sheet where Hennessy had been. The scent of his cologne lingered and she breathed it in deeply. "See you later, Hennessy," she said, meaning every word.

Hennessy landed in Oakland just late enough to miss Jack and Johnnie. They'd checked out of the hotel. He figured they were on their way across the Bay to San Francisco. Hennessy rented a car and requested a map to where he knew they would be playing.

The plane ride had been miserable. He'd tried to sleep, but all he could do was remember the tears his mamma and Rayne had cried before he left for the airport. His stepfather Antoine seemed happy to see him go, however. That was saying something for a man who didn't seem to have any emotion except when it came to his wife. Hennessy hadn't been able to find Teardrop, so he'd left without telling the old man good-bye.

He'd felt strange leaving New Orleans, as if he'd left things unfinished. But he didn't have a clue how to solve all the problems simmering there. All he knew was that he had to get out. He needed to play tonight, to breathe the soul in a darkened room and feel the burn of hard liquor on his tongue. He couldn't wait to blow his horn, play his guitar and have the past few days erased from his memory—at least for a little while.

When he arrived at the Savanna Jazz club, he could feel his spirits lift. The warm colors and soft lighting made a cozy backdrop to the music. He recognized the group on stage as the Warner Baily Quartet. They played a catchy melody and his boys, Jack and Johnnie, sat at a back table, entertaining a couple of fine ladies. *Ah, yeah.* It was starting to feel like home.

"What up, *boyyz?*" Hennessy greeted them.

Jack and Johnnie got loud when they saw their trumpet player and greeted him with back slaps and homeboy hand slaps. "Sit down, man. Join the party," Jack said, pulling a chair from a nearby table. "What you drinkin' tonight? A little of your namesake?" When he smiled, his gold tooth glinted in the soft lights.

"That sounds good. A little Hennessy on ice," Hennessy told the waitress when she stopped by. "And, is there some place I can put my instruments?"

She told him he could put them in the back room whenever he was ready and pointed at a door down a long hall.

Hennessy decided they were all right by his side for the moment. "What's that in your mouth, Jack?" He noticed the gold tooth had a J carved out of the center.

"That's my new grille, man. Got it custom made over in the flea market down in Alameda. Women go crazy over it. Ain't that right, baby?" He winked at the pretty, scantily clad woman at his side.

He was rewarded with a sexy, "That's right, sugah" from the light brown woman of indiscernible ethnicity.

Jack was the showy one of the group, always in something flashy like his black shirt sparkling with silver threads and his diamond pinky ring that was making his current companion love him more by the minute. One thing about Jack, he didn't have nothing against gold diggers.

"How you been, Johnnie?" He slapped the large man on a huge shoulder. Johnnie was their bassist. He was a dark man with carefully cut hair and goatee. He was six-foot three and weighed about three hundred pounds, a weight he needed when he'd played Linebacker for LSU...and it helped keep him from getting lost behind the large instrument he played. The Chinese woman he was with also believed in showing off what nature gave her, but she was quieter than her friend, preferring to nuzzle Johnnie's neck and whisper things in his ear.

Whatever she'd just said had him grinning ear to ear. "I'm doin' all right, Hen. We missed you," Johnnie said quiet and slow, the opposite of Jack who talked a mile a minute.

"Good to hear," Hennessy laughed. "I had to come back and make sure Terry didn't get too comfortable."

"Yeah, well, Terry's been doin' all right for us, man," Jack jumped in. "Since we weren't expectin' you back, what say you let him sit in tonight? It'll be his last gig."

Hennessy couldn't see any harm in allowing Terry one last gig and happily agreed. When the waitress returned they all ordered dinner. They had to start playing in an hour and he'd gone all day without a meal. He ordered the Yassa, a sort of African lemon chicken over rice. The delicious food and warm liquor put him in the right mood for music.

After his meal he strapped on his guitar and strummed the fevered chords of their signature tune, *Quick Liquor*, then put his horn to his mouth and played the long, lazy notes of *Whiskey River*. As they played song after song the joy returned in waves of excitement. Terry, who'd arrived just before they went on stage, seemed relieved to be allowed to play that night and his keyboard added a nice layer to their trio. Hennessy was in such a good mood he let the man share the vocals, surprised at how fresh they sounded when Terry added his own flavor and style.

Hennessy had worked up a nice sweat by the time their first set ended, but wasn't ready to take the fifteen minute break. But, because the others were, he had no choice but to vacate the stage. He placed his horn on the stand and headed toward the bar.

"I forgot how well you play, son."

Hennessy froze for a moment certain he was imagining the familiarity of the voice. A warm hand on his arm forced him to turn around. "Daddy?" he said not able to believe his eyes.

Boozie Walker pulled his son into a long, hard embrace. "I missed you, Hennessy. I really missed you."

Too Much Hennessy

Burying his face in the man's shoulder to hide the tears, Hennessy held tight to his father, clutching fistfuls of sweater. He couldn't trust his voice, couldn't trust himself to hold on to all the emotions swimming through him; relief, happiness, love, so he just kept holding on.

"All right. All right," his Dad said patting him on the back. "It's all right, son."

Finally, Hennessy regained control and felt strong enough to release his grip. "We thought you were dead," was the only thing he could think to say. His old man didn't look any worse for the wear. Except for the extra gray in his short shaven hair and mustache, he seemed just the same, strong and self-assured. "We were planning your funeral."

Boozie nodded. "I know. Saw the obituary on the 'Net yesterday." He led his son to the table he'd been occupying and told him to have a seat.

"Why didn't you call us?" Hennessy asked feeling irritated. "Why'd you let us worry like that?"

"I got a good reason for ever'thing I do, son. Remember that." His tone said *tread carefully*. "So, how'd the funeral go?"

"It didn't." Thirsty, Hennessy pulled the full glass of ice water from its place and took a long sip. "To make sure we were burying the right person, we had a DNA test done on the body of the corpse they found at the B&B."

"What the hell you go and do a fool thing like that for?" His dark face folded in irritation.

"A psychic told us it wasn't you in the casket." Hennessy wondered if his dad thought it sounded as crazy as he did.

"Psychic?" Boozie frowned. "You mean Deja?"

"The one and only," Hennessy confirmed. The thought of her made him warm. He drank more water. "Rayne insisted we check it out." He paused and wondered if now was the time to tell him they'd found out he wasn't Rayne's father. There'd be time later, he thought. "When we found out the dead man wasn't you, we called off the funeral."

Boozie leaned back in his chair and laughed. "Bet that gave ole Six Foot a conniption, huh? Man loves his money."

Hennessy assumed Six Foot was the funeral director and laughed along. "Yeah, he's on the police to find the man's family so he can get paid for embalming and visitation services."

"Don't blame him, don't blame him," the old man said soberly. "It must be hard to make a livin' after all this mess."

Images of debris and destruction flashed through Hennessy's brain. The despair he'd felt while in New Orleans came back to him full force. "Honest, Daddy. I don't know why they try. They should all move out while they've got the chance."

The frown returned to his dad's face. "Is that what you think? New Orleans ain't worth savin'?"

"What's the use?" he answered honestly. "They don't have any real plans to reinforce the levees to the point where they can withstand these kinds of storms in the future. In a few months another hurricane could come along and destroy the city all over again."

"And maybe it won't." Boozie leaned his arms on the table and directed a hard look into his son's eyes. "New Orleans is our city. We built The French Quarter with all those fancy buildings. We built Jackson Square in all its majesty. We invented Jazz and Cajun cookin' and we're known the world over for it. And now, 'cause we hit on by hard times we 'spose to just give up and move on? That ain't even American. And that ain't who I am. I'm goin' home. I'm goin' home soon." His finger stabbed at the table to punctuate his words.

"All right, Daddy. Do what you want." Hennessy could tell he'd never talk the man out of it. But it did raise some questions in his mind. "If you feel that way, why did you leave in the first place? Why haven't you gone back before now? And, why are you in California?"

Boozie blew a long breath and looked past Hennessy. "That's a long story, son. And it don't look like you got time enough for me to tell it right now."

Hennessy followed his daddy's eyes. The band was going back onstage. Jack motioned for him to join them. "You're right. After we're done then." He rose from the table and pointed at his father. "Don't go runnin' off before I'm through."

His daddy sat back with his arms wide open as he smiled. "Wouldn't miss it for the world, son. 'Sides, I ain't got nuttin' but time."

The second set was better than the first in Hennessy's opinion. He'd played with more feeling and joy, maybe because he was thrilled to finally know his father was alive and well. Maybe it was to show off in front of the old man. *I forgot how well you play, son*, his dad had said. The words filled Hennessy with pride and made his fingers fly along the chords of his guitar. It seemed like he never got too old to want his daddy's approval.

The Whiskey Sins Trio, plus Terry Pryce, ended the night at eleven thirty. Jack and Johnnie had wrapped their honeys around their arms and escorted them to the hotel. Terry said he was meeting friends. Hennessy and his father checked into a room with double beds.

By the time Hennessy showered and pulled on pajama bottoms, his father was on his second bottle from the mini bar. He never touched liquor when he was working at the B&B. "Better slow down, old man. That stuff costs nearly ten bucks a bottle."

Boozie squinted at the dark liquid in the glass. "Really?" He rolled to his side on the bed and pulled out a money clip full of twenties from his back pocket. He tossed it carelessly onto the other bed. "That oughtta cover what I plan on drinkin' tonight. You know I don't like to overindulge."

"Damn," Hennessy said, picking up the wad of cash and sitting. "Don't you believe in credit cards?"

"Too easy to trace. Dontcha watch Court TV?"

Carefully, Hennessy placed the cash on the table between the headboards just beneath the lamp. "Seriously, man. What's going on? Why do you all the sudden care about your credit cards being traced?"

His dad stared at the glass and puckered and un-puckered his lips a few times before answering. "Bought myself a little trouble 'for I left the city, son."

Hennessy didn't like the sound of that. "What kind of trouble?"

"You remember DeTron, right?"

"Rayne's husband? Of course." The man who had beat his sister to a pulp too many times to count was kind of hard to forget. The thought had Hennessy making fists. "What about him?"

"You know he started your sister on drugs?"

"No. I didn't," he admitted. Like many things that had happened in the past five or six years, he'd been on the road and only caught the bits his mamma had fed him.

"Well, he did," Boozie said draining his glass. "Her and half the city from what I found out."

"He was a dealer?"

His dad nodded and reached for another tiny bottle. "Prob'ly still is. Folks like him don't get swept away in floodwaters like they 'spose to…like they do in the Bible."

"What do you know about the Bible, old man?" Hennessy teased.

"I read it once." Boozie gave him a crooked smile and winked at him. "Shore did. I learned enough to find fault with the Father durin' one of his sermons one Sunday, too. He got the scripture wrong see? So since I'd remembered it fine, it bein' so fresh in my mind and all, I thought it was my duty to stand up and correct him right then and right there." His smile grew wider at the memory. "Yo mamma never did make me go back to church after that." His daddy laughed his full-bodied, no holds barred laugh that had filled their house for so many years.

"I'll bet she didn't." Hennessy joined along and let the sound wrap him in warmth and make him feel whole again. He hadn't felt that way since the hurricane had ripped the Gulf Coast apart. He realized his daddy still hadn't answered his question. "But what about DeTron? What kind of trouble did you get in with him?"

"Shot a man who worked for him." He downed the scotch he'd poured.

"That was the man we found in the back room, wasn't it? The man we almost buried?"

Boozie nodded.

"Did you plant your wallet on him on purpose?"

"Hell naw. I must'a laid it down somewhere and he picked it up. I couldn't find it 'fore I left the bar, so I left without it."

"Why'd you shoot him?"

"He shot at me first." His daddy reared up indignantly. "I knew some damn punk would try and break in to get at my likker, so I put it all in the back room and was just about to lock it when I heard 'em bust in the front door."

"I turned around and one was runnin' into the room after me. I pointed my gun at him and told him he'd better stop and he did, but...I had no choice, son. I had to shoot him. He had one of them automatic weapons and when he lifted it to point it at me..."

The look of horror in his daddy's eyes told Hennessy all he needed to know to fill in the rest. His daddy had shot and killed the man...just like Deja had said. "How do you know he worked for DeTron?"

"Cause I seen him 'fore. He came ever' week with another one to collect DeTron's money. I been payin' him off for months."

"I can't believe you gave in to those thugs, Daddy. Why didn't you call the police?"

"Payin' him off was my idea." He turned his brown eyes in Hennessy's direction. "It was all I could think to do to get him away from Rayne. To get him to divorce her. I knew I couldn't get her to rehab as long as she was with him."

"Unbelievable," Hennessy said, pulling a hand over his damp dreads. This was the sacrifice he'd told Rayne about. He'd taken money from his precious Blues 'N Booze club to pay her ex-husband off. "This is unreal, Daddy. You know that, right?"

"Real life's stranger than fiction, son. That's what they say." Boozie laid his glass on the side table next to his money and leaned back against the over plump bed pillows. He sighed an old man's sigh. "I gotta go back, Hennessy. But I'm afraid DeTron'll find out I'm back when I start rebuilding the bar. I don't know what he's like to do when he finds out I ain't dead."

"Call the police," Hennessy insisted.

"For what?" he said scoffing. "Once a man shoots ya, it's pretty much too late for the police."

"Well, stay with me then. Have Teardrop and Earl start rebuilding the bar."

"I don't trust nobody but family, son. You know that."

He knew. Hennessy's stomach clenched tight when he realized why his daddy had traveled all the way to California. He wanted Hennessy to go back and help rebuild the B&B. But going back to New Orleans was the absolute last thing Hennessy wanted to do. "Of course it's darned near impossible to find a contractor out there," he tried to redirect the conversation. "Deja lost hers because they found a better paying job."

"There's plenty more where that come from." Boozie gave a nod at the money clip. "I learned a long time ago that money can't buy ya happiness, but it can buy whole lotta other things."

Hennessy was at a loss for words. He didn't know what more he could say except, "Don't ask me to go back, Daddy. Please."

"Wouldn't want you to do nothin' out of your nature, son. I know how important your music is to ya. Lord knows I believe a man should follah his dreams."

And just like that, he'd been excused. Hennessy should've been relieved, and he was a little, but he couldn't help feeling he'd let his old man down in some way. "Thanks," he said, but it didn't seem to be enough.

"Guess we should get a little shut eye, huh?" his daddy said, rising up to remove his clothes. He belched as he tossed his sweater onto a chair by the little table across the room.

Hennessy shook his head. *Family*.

Boozie pulled off his pants and reached inside a pocket. He pulled out a piece of paper and handed it to Hennessy before tossing his pants over his sweater. "Here you go, son. I wrote this and was wonderin' if you could put it to music for me."

Curious, Hennessy unfolded apiece of paper from a spiral notebook. He had a little difficulty getting the circled edges from catching on one another. He read it:

Too Much Hennessy

Livin' Wrong
Your eyes held my future and I tried/
To be the man you saw inside.
Didn't know that the path I chose/
Would force the door on our love to close.
I loved you hard, but I did you wrong/
Couldn't stay in one place too long.
I wandered away when I shoulda stayed/
And losing you was the price I paid.
Oh, Lord what a price I paid.
Don't know why I couldn't make it good.
Thought the rapture of your sweet arms could/
Turn the false in me to true/
'Cause my world rocked, baby, when I made love to you.
I loved you hard, but I did you wrong/
Couldn't stay in one place too long.
I wandered away when I shoulda stayed/
And losing you was the price I paid.
Oh, Lord what a price I paid.

"Reads like a Blues song," Hennessy observed, touched by the sentiment in his fathers' words.

"Yeah you right," his daddy said as he crawled under the covers. "I figure if you can write Jazz, you can write Blues."

"I'd be happy to. It's about a woman, huh?" His mamma if he guessed right.

"I'd 'preciate it if you start on it soon, son," he said, ignoring the question. "I don't know how long I have 'til I'ma need it."

"Sure, Daddy." Hennessy read the words a second time and a tune started to form in his head. Sinking against his pillows, he placed the paper on top of his chest and he listened to the music in his head. Nothing solid, nothing concrete, just bits and pieces of a tune formed, but he knew the rest would come in time. It always did.

His daddy's heavy snores interrupted his composition. He rolled to his side and turned off the lamp over the little table. The room fell into darkness, but he could still hear the sounds of San Francisco outside the window of his second story hotel room. With his father and the streets as his lullaby, Hennessy closed his eyes and let the tune roll around in his head. He saw her face then, the lovely Deja Devine, just as he'd left her—sleeping soundly, looking beautiful. He longed for her as the tune in his mind grew stronger and stronger. He let the memory of her capture his soul as he fell asleep.

It was quiet in the car. Deja had long ago lost the signals of the decent radio stations, but that didn't bother her. She preferred silence and she rather enjoyed the feel of solitude that came from driving in the middle of the night. The streaks of headlights in the black night were few and far between and the rhythm of the car's tires on the road made it increasingly difficult for her to stay awake.

Deja arched her back against the car seat, trying to ease the discomfort of sitting in the same position for over three hours. She'd been driving all day and couldn't wait to get into bed.

"How much longer, baby?" her mamma's hoarse voice drifted across the dark space of the Mini Cooper, startling Deja.

"About an hour. You need a rest stop? There's one coming up."

"Not just yet." Ivalou Devine raised her seat to a more upright position. Her sigh filled the interior. "I bet you wished you were never born."

"Of course I don't," Deja answered honestly, wishing her mamma would stop saying things like that.

"Bet you wish you didn't haveta keep takin' care of your mamma. If I'da known I was gonna be such a burden on you, Deja, I swear I woulda took my life a long time ago."

"Stop it, Mamma," it bothered Deja to hear her mother speak that way. "You're no burden. Sometimes in life, we just have to take care of one another, that's all. Let's just be thankful for the time you have left and have some fun."

"Fun," she gave a humorless laugh sounding more like a cackle. "I forgot a long time ago what that was like."

But she hadn't completely and Deja knew it. She could see it in the long, faraway looks her mamma got sometimes when she didn't think anyone was looking. There'd be light in her eyes and hint of laughter on her lips. She looked that way anytime Boozie Walker was around. Always had.

Not for the first time, Deja thought if maybe Boozie was the one who insisted Ivalou return to New Orleans. Maybe it wasn't her house she longed for at all. When Deja had told her about the house not being ready to live in, she'd just kept insisting she wanted to go home to die. Of course, Deja could hardly blame her. Her Aunt Billie had a sharp tongue and hateful eyes and hadn't done anything but criticize her younger sister from the time she'd arrived in Tennessee until the very moment they got inside the car. With surprise and delight Deja had watched her mamma give her sister the bird as they pulled away. "I bet you thought flippin' off Auntie Billie was fun," she reminded her, wanting to lighten the mood. "Even though you always told me that kind of thing was beneath Uptown ladies."

"It was lewd, crude and socially unacceptable, " Her mamma laughed. "Oh, but she deserved it. My sister is a hateful woman. She's never approved of me. All she did while I was there was talk bad about me. She'd be on the phone telling Mamma I'd finally got what I deserved from living in sin all my life."

"That must've been hard," Deja said feeling guilty for leaving her alone.

"No harder than it ever was, I suppose. Besides, she's probably right. I did have a knack for the scandalous," she said with a hint of pride mixed with regret. "But there was a time when I could walk away and do what I pleased. Now I'm so helpless and needy I can't stand it."

Because she could hear the frustrated tears in her voice, Deja tried again to change the subject. "I told you what happened at Boozie Walker's visitation, didn't I?"

"About you sensing he wasn't dead?"

"Yeah. Turns out I was right."

"You always are, baby." There was no mistaking the pride in her tone. "But how'd you find out?"

"The family did a DNA test and found out the dead man is somebody else. They don't know who yet."

"Isn't that something? Where do you suppose Boozie is if he isn't dead?" Interest and enthusiasm were obvious in her tone, furthering Deja's theory.

"Haven't figured that out yet." Deja bit her bottom lip. She'd been trying to get a sense of where he could be, but had received no signals. "Sad thing was the DNA test proved he wasn't the father of his daughter, Rayne."

"Oh," her mamma said simply. "So now she knows."

"Yeah. She's pretty upset about it."

Her mamma stared straight ahead into the darkness. "I can imagine how she must feel."

Deja didn't know when she was first told that Boozie Walker had left her mamma for Lila Walker Ellis, but she knew it had happened nine months before she was born. Ivalou, in a drunken fury, had taken a butcher knife over to Boozie and Lila's wedding reception and had tried to plunge it into Lila's pregnant womb. Of course, Boozie had stopped her and taken her home.

"Boozie was hell-and-damned-well determined to make sure that child, Rayne was born." Her mamma said bitterly, obviously the scene was replaying in her head. "I used to think she was the only reason why he hadn't married me instead of that woman."

"It wasn't?" Deja was confused. She'd heard stories about what happened many times as a child at her grandparents' house—before she and her mamma had been banned from ever stepping foot inside the place again. The conclusion was always the same—Boozie Walker married Lila to save the unborn child from abortion. Apparently Lila's father, an up-and-coming pastor, had been insistent that she wasn't bringing an illegitimate child into their family to shame him.

"No." Her mamma sighed. "It was because of that damned bar."

"The Blues 'N Booze?"

"Of course," her mamma shot back quickly. "He wanted to buy it so badly. It was his dream, his destiny he'd said. He'd make me sit outside the vacant building with him and pretend to hear the music and laughter that would come out of the building one day. Because I was mad about him, I indulged him. Besides it usually led to us making out in his old jalopy of a car. Good, God, but that man had great hands."

The thought of Boozie and her mamma making out in a car made Deja uncomfortable, but she said nothing.

"But, I swear, Deja. Most of the time he had me convinced I could see and hear the whole thing before it ever came to be," she said with just a hint of wonder.

The thought wasn't such a stretch for Deja as it might be for most. "I don't understand," she said. "What did that have to do with you getting married—or not?"

"He couldn't get a loan and didn't have but a few hundred dollars in his savings. My daddy offered to give him the money. Boozie accepted it happily and promised to pay Daddy back. He started to put the place in order and after a couple of months he opened the Blues 'N Booze. And oh, what a night it was. He'd brought in local bands and singers, folks no one had ever heard of except him. They tore that place up with their music. We danced until dawn. And I mean that literally," she emphasized. "We danced until the sun started to peek in through those stained glass windows on the door."

Deja didn't say a word, hoping her silence would encourage her mamma to finish the story.

"After everybody else went home, he told me he loved me. He said as soon as he started to make some money and could afford a wedding ring and a nice house he would ask me to marry him. I was so excited I started looking at patterns for wedding dresses the next day." She fell silent for a moment. "Mamma and Daddy pretended to be happy for me, but a couple of months later my daddy told Boozie he was going to call in the loan if he ever thought to marry me. Of course, Boozie didn't have the money to pay him back. Back then if you went in debt like that you could go to jail, let alone lose what you'd bought."

"What?" Deja was alarmed. "Granddaddy was going to take the bar and send him to jail. Why would he do that?"

"Because he was a hateful man, Deja. Boozie was too dark-skinned and had nappy hair in his opinion. He came from a poor family so my daddy figured he wasn't good enough for me. His offer to give Boozie the loan was like a chunk of cheese on a mousetrap. As soon as Boozie took it, he was pinned in and couldn't get out."

"That's so shallow and…and…insensitive," Deja sputtered angrily. She was constantly amazed at how cruel people could be to one another—especially family. "I'm glad they disowned us."

"Me too," Ivalou said with conviction. "Of course I thought they would've done it earlier—when I got pregnant with you."

"Right," Deja acknowledged. "The tale of the unknown sailor."

"But you know all about that…what there is to tell."

Yes, she knew. Her mamma had told her about her father a long time ago. He was a Navy pilot, a White man, who Mamma had seduced the night after all the commotion. He went back out to sea the day after. To this day, Deja had never laid eyes on the man—probably because Ivalou had never bothered to ask his name.

Deja's mamma came from a well-to-do family with a lot of pride. They'd been immensely embarrassed by their drunken, promiscuous daughter and had spent the balance of the past twenty years pretending neither Ivalou nor Deja existed.

She supposed she could be bitter and angry about it. But Deja had witnessed what those emotions had done to her mamma over the years and she didn't want any part of it.

As if reading her mind, Ivalou asked Deja to drive by her parents' house before they headed for home. "What's the point, Mamma?" Deja protested. The house was out of the way and they wouldn't be able to see much in the dark.

"Indulge your old mamma," she said softly.

Too Much Hennessy

At this point, there wasn't a wish Deja wouldn't grant her mamma. The woman had lost the love of her life, been disowned by her family, been addicted to alcohol for the past twenty years and was now dying of cirrhosis of the liver. A woman who'd led such a hard life deserved some kindnesses in the end. The least Deja could do was grant her last wishes.

They drove up the street full of big plantation-style houses. Her grandparents' house looked the same as she remembered: majestic, with shuttered windows and white columns on the first and second floors supporting a large porch and a wraparound balcony on the second floor. The usually manicured yard was growing long and wild and as they drove by, they saw the huge pile of broken furniture on the side of the house.

"My how the mighty have fallen," her mamma said quietly. "But it looks like they survived the storm." She seemed relieved by that fact—despite everything. "Let's go home, baby. I'm tired."

Chapter Ten

Deja and Ivalou finally arrived home at two o'clock in the morning. Even in the dark of night, the toll Hurricane Katrina had taken on the little house in Jefferson Parish was easily seen.

"Lord have mercy," Ivalou said, putting a shaking hand over her mouth. "My house, Deja. Look at it."

Deja patted her mamma's leg then ran a soothing hand along her arm. She'd been looking at the hollowed-out house with tattered ceilings and broken walls for over a month now. She'd felt the same horrible shock her mamma must be feeling seeing it for the first time.

After opening the car door, Ivalou walked slowly toward the house. Deja quickly joined her, helping her navigate around the mounds of debris piled carelessly about the yard. The low hanging half moon was bright, making it possible to distinguish the dismembered picture frames, broken dishes, and twisted bed frames—the tattered pieces of what had been Ivalou's life.

The scene appeared surreal to Deja, like some distorted reel of a horror film. She knew she was seeing it the way her mamma was—as the worst possible nightmare.

Ivalou reached the space where her front door hung from its frame at an odd angle. She just stood in the opening staring.

Deja heard her take a huge inward breath. "We don't have to do this now, Mamma." She tried to turn her around, but the older woman wouldn't be moved.

"It's all gone," Ivalou wailed, her voice bordering on hysteria. "Everything I ever had is gone." Her anguish and pain rang pitifully through the dark void of what used to be her living room. She bolted from her spot in the doorway and began wandering like a crazed woman through the rooms of her house. "Noooo," her wails filled the air, forcing their way through the ragged roof into the night sky. "Dear God, no."

"Oh, Mamma. I'm so sorry," Deja cried, watching helplessly. She wanted to go to her mother, to put her arms around her and pull her away, but knew her grief could not be comforted. Not yet. The pain was too great to be restrained and would only do harm if her mamma tried to hold it inside.

Deja sank to a squat and covered her face with her hands. Soon the wails lessened and she could no longer hear her mamma's footsteps echoing through the hallway. When she looked up she saw her, standing in the middle of the front room, looking bewildered and unsteady. "Mamma?"

In an instant, she was up and running toward her. She reached her just as the older woman's legs buckled. Ivalou was hardly a large woman, being only five foot three and weighing just over a hundred pounds, but Deja struggled to keep her upright. "Come on, Mamma. Stay on your feet. Let's get you to the trailer." She threw the woman's arm around her neck and grabbed her around her tiny waist. The feel of bones beneath her hand alarmed Deja.

"You a good daughter, Desha," Ivalou slurred the words as she stumbled out of the house reminding Deja of the times her mamma had been drunk. She talked and walked exactly this way. How ironic, now that she was completely alcohol free, the cirrhosis had exactly the same affect. Clearly her toxin levels were up and it was time to flush them out of her system. She seemed to be having these episodes more and more frequently, which saddened Deja. "Thank you," she answered, struggling to keep the woman on course as they walked across the yard. "You're a good mamma too."

"No. No, I'm not." Ivalou hung her head and wept softly. "I'm sho shorry, baby."

Deja finally shepherded Ivalou up the stairs and into the trailer. Propping her on the couch, she rushed back to the car to get her medicine and one of her bags of clothes. After taking the prescription diuretics, it took twenty minutes for her mamma to go to the restroom.

Almost immediately afterward, the disorientation and confusion disappeared. Once she had her mamma tucked into her double bed, Deja made her own bed on the couch. She threw a sheet over the cushions and wrapped herself in a blanket. Though bone tired, she tossed and turned for what seemed hours. She suspected the whole experience of watching her mamma grieve had muddied her chakras and now they needed cleansing. But, she was too tired to go through that exercise. Plus, all of her crystals were at the shop.

Deja rolled to another position and closed her eyes. After a while, she felt that wonderful light feeling in her head, her arms and legs. A second later, she was looking down at herself asleep on the couch. So. She was to travel tonight.

She heard the faint notes of a Blues tune in the air and, in the blink of an eye, she felt herself flying outside the house. She flew across the once great city of New Orleans and took note of how drastically it had changed since she'd first flown across it as a child. Most of the power had been restored, but no longer did the city lights twinkle like millions of earth-bound stars. Instead there were only pockets of lights, then huge dark areas where Katrina had scarred the land.

Another blink and she found herself entering the other plane…the other reality. She heard the music playing more loudly and knew in an instant it was Hennessy. Anxiously, she turned her head left and right to find the origin of the sounds. Suddenly, the notes his horn was playing appeared like a flowing silvered path to guide her. Deja followed the twists and turns until she arrived at the club. It looked exactly like the old Blues 'N Booze and Hennessy had taken center stage.

Her eyes sought and found his.

He let his horn drop to his side and let his mouth gape open. "I'm dreaming again," his thoughts pushed inside Deja's head.

She drifted softly to the floor and smiled. It was so good to see him after the long night she'd had. All of the sadness within her melted away. "You called me with your music," she sent her thoughts in his direction. "You can't live without me."

"You're tryin' to freak me out again, aren't you?" he answered as his eyebrows lifted.

"Oh, no, boo." Waves of lust and desire warmed Deja from head to foot. She wanted to touch him, to feel the warmth of his solid chest under her hand, to feel his soft, wet mouth over hers. "I'm trying to seduce you. I'm a little disappointed that you can't tell the difference," she teased.

He stared at her hotly, desire lighting up the gold around his irises like fire. He grabbed the microphone, opened his gorgeous mouth and sang to her. "Your eyes held my future, *baaaby*. And Lord *knows* I tried…to be your future, *hoooney*. To be the man *you* saw inside."

Deja was awed by his voice. The strong, raspy baritone mesmerized her and sent everything feminine within her humming like a taut guitar string.

"I loved you hard, sweet baby," his brow wrinkled as he felt the words he sang, "but I did you wrong. I tried and tried, my honey. But couldn't stay in one place too long. I *wandered* away when I *shoulda* stayed and *looosing* you was the price I paid. Oooh, *Lord*! What a price I paid."

Deja knew then he regretted leaving her and New Orleans. She could tell from the words of his song that he missed her as much as she was missing him. His writing a song for her was beyond romantic. It was soul shaking.

"I love you, Hennessy James Walker," the words sprang from her heart to her mind before she could stop them, but Deja didn't care. Just seeing the look of surprised shock on his face made her love him more. She wanted him. She wanted him now.

The music from the band got louder and Hennessy's hand trembled slightly as he placed his trumpet to his lips. Deja closed her eyes and willed herself to become the instrument. She cried out when his hot hands touched her bare back as they had the first time they'd met. His soft lips pressed urgently against hers and he filled her with his music. Filled her with his need. Filled her beyond all reason.

Again, the silvery notes appeared, but this time they wrapped around the two of them until they were pressed tight against each other, cocooned in Blues and desire. They were moving through time and space in rhythm to the stars and the brightly shining moon. If this was heaven, Deja never wanted to drop back to earth. But like before, the feeling grew too intense to bear. "Hennessy!" she cried out as a brilliant light shattered her from within until she shone as bright as any other star in the night sky.

Breathlessly, she awoke and squinted against the bright morning streaming through the window. Her cat, Jazmeen lay on her feet, staring at her with her green eyes. She wasn't mewling so her mamma must've fed her.

Her mamma sat in the chair opposite her, sipping coffee and smiling. "Morning, baby. Good dream?"

Embarrassment flushed Deja hotly. She covered her head with the sheet, but didn't know why. She doubted her mamma knew what she'd been doing just moments ago and, eventually, she'd have to come out. "Why're you up so early?" she asked irritably.

"Never did like sleeping," Ivalou said matter-of-factly. "Always seemed like such a huge waste of time. Even more so now."

Deja could understand that sentiment given her mamma's current state of health.

"Now, come out of there and tell me about this Hennessy," her mamma insisted. "That's Boozie's son isn't it?"

Geez, she must've said his name out loud. Sighing, Deja pushed the covers off her head, knowing she couldn't lie. "Yes," she admitted, eyeing her mother's coffee enviously. She got up and walked to the kitchenette to pour herself a cup. "What else do you want to know?"

"Well," her mamma pulled her robe around her and took a seat on a barstool to better talk with her daughter. "With all the moaning and such you were doing a while ago, I'd say he's made quite the impression."

Deja wished she had darker skin. The flush crawling up her neck and into her cheeks must be obvious to her mamma. She tried to hide her growing embarrassment by being as cool about the topic as the older woman. "I met him at his father's visitation. I told him he was burying the wrong man. I told him his father killed the man in the casket."

"And?"

"And, he thought I was a nut. No surprise there."

"Yet the two of you had a connection?" her mamma pressed.

"Yeah." Deja leaned her arms on the counter and sipped her hot coffee. The liquid felt good going down her throat. "I'd met him traveling just the night before. I was drawn by his music. He plays a mean trumpet." Deja couldn't stop the smile. "We recognized one another that day. It's kind of weird to meet Boozie's son after all these years. I'm surprised we never ran into them before."

"Boozie was always careful to keep his family away from us and the other way around."

"You didn't like that, did you?"

"Resented the hell out of him for it," her mamma admitted. "'Course most folks didn't blame him a bit, considering…"

Considering you'd tried to cut a child from his mamma's womb, Deja quietly finished the thought. "But, he was always kind to us."

Ivalou's eyes softened and she placed a hand over her daughter's. "He took care of you especially. Lord knows how you'd of turned out if he'd left it up to me."

"Hey," Deja stopped her. "You were a great mamma—when you were sober," she teased.

"Yeah. And you're a great daughter—when you're asleep," she teased back. They fell into a companionable silence for long moments.

Finally, Deja asked the question that had been pressing in the back of her mind for a long time. "Why didn't you and Boozie get married after he divorced Lila fifteen years ago?" she asked cautiously.

"I was a mess, you know that," Ivalou answered brutally. "I wasn't fit to be any man's wife and he knew it."

Deja stared into the dark brown depths of her coffee cup, again disturbed by how little happiness her mamma had been afforded in her life.

"But he asked me anyway." Ivalou said it so softly, so sadly that it nearly broke Deja's heart.

"You refused?" she asked.

"I not only refused, but I cursed at him, threw things at him, called him every name but the Lamb of God." Tears appeared in her eyes. Ivalou swallowed hard and forced the rest out with a trembling voice. "I was too proud by then to marry him—too indignant. He'd ripped my heart out when he'd married Lila and I was going to do the same to him. I wanted him to suffer. But in the end I was the one who suffered most."

Deja moved around the counter to hug her mamma, but the woman waved her off.

"I don't need anyone's pity, Dejanette." She wiped angrily at the tears streaking her sallow cheeks. "I made my bed. It's high time I stopped crying about having to lie in it."

Surprised, but glad for this small burst of bravado, Deja let her hands fall to her sides. "Good for you, Mamma," she said. "'Cause we've got things to do today. We have to figure out what I'm going to do for a job until the tourists come back to the French Quarter. And, we've got to figure out what we're gonna do about your house. I didn't save it only to turn around and lose it to a darned hurricane."

"Amen to that," Ivalou said. "And, we need to check into hospice care."

"What?"

"I'm getting worse, Deja. I know it and you know it. You can't be takin' care of me all the time. I need a nurse to come to the house so you can get out and work."

Hospice wasn't a contingency Deja had planned for, but of course, her mamma was right. She couldn't be left alone when she was subject to such swings in mood and orientation. "I'll look into it," she said quietly.

"Now." Ivalou pushed her cup across the counter and signaled to her daughter to refill it. "How's about you stop changing the subject and tell me about this Hennessy."

Too Much Hennessy

"You're in San Francisco, Daddy. The city with some of the finest restaurants in the world and you wanna come to the IHOP for breakfast?" Hennessy lifted his eyebrows as he eyed his father who sat across the booth making short work of his stack of pancakes. In an hour, he'd be taking him to the airport and the old man would be flying back to New Orleans. His two days with him had been too brief. "You sure you wanna go back? What if DeTron *is* looking for you?"

Boozie shrugged. "Man's gotta do what a man's gotta do, son. You know that."

"Yeah. Well I thought I'd lost you once," he rolled his warm coffee cup between his palms. "I didn't like it much."

Boozie set down his fork and took a sip of coffee. Sitting back, he eyed his son fondly. "I have to say, I'm mighty glad to hear that, son." He let a wide grin spread across his dark, handsome face. "Mighty glad."

Hennessy grinned, but avoided looking at his daddy. "I learned a lot about you while I was home."

"Like what?"

"Things I didn't know. Like how many people you helped. I had no idea the number of lives you touched."

"Is that right?" Boozie leaned across the table, pushing his plate to the side. "You mean folks actually had good things to say 'bout me?"

Hennessy laughed. "Yeah. A lot of 'em."

The old man waved off the sentiment. "Folks'll say anything when they think you dead. Wait'll they get a load of me walkin' down the street later today. They'll think I'm a dadgum ghost, won't they?" He laughed his big laugh.

The sound warmed Hennessy through and through. More than anything he wanted to keep his daddy with him. "You sure you don't wanna hang around California a while longer? We're heading for San Jose next. I hear it's a great place."

"Naw, naw." Boozie ran a hand over his thick tuft of graying hair. "You move around too much for your old daddy. I likes to stay in one place. Besides, I got important things to do when I get back. I told you that already, son."

160

"I know, I know," Hennessy backed off. He eyed the man and tried to decide whether or not to tell him what they'd found out about him and Rayne. Finally, he decided the man needed fair warning before heading back home. "We learned something else, too."

"What's that, son?"

"We found out you're not Rayne's daddy."

His daddy sat silently staring him in the eyes. "How'd she take the news?" he finally asked.

"She's real tore up about it," Hennessy said honestly. "I'm scared for her. She seems a little out of control, you know? And Mamma…well let's just say she isn't helping the situation any."

"Hmmm." The old man nodded. "What else?"

Sighing, Hennessy leaned his arms on the table. "I just have questions, Daddy. None of this makes any sense. Why'd you marry Mamma if she was pregnant with somebody else's child? Who was this Charles Flowers anyway?"

"Charles Flowers is a made up name. He never existed." Boozie poured more coffee into both their cups. "Your granddaddy, the Reverend Edward Crumbie, had a perverted younger brother who couldn't keep his hands off young girls."

Hennessy felt his heart sink.

"Least of all his own daughters and nieces. It was easy pickin's see? They'd be at his house stayin' over. He'd wait for his wife to go to sleep and—"

"That's all right. I don't need the details." Hennessy waved away the thoughts turning his stomach topsy-turvy.

"Anyways, your mamma got pregnant. She wanted to keep the baby. Said despite the fact her uncle raped her it was still her flesh and blood. Her daddy wanted to get rid of it so's nobody would question the integrity of his Christian household." Pausing, Boozie studied his coffee cup for a moment. "I'd had other plans 'fore that, but they'd fallen to hell in a hand basket. So, when Lila asked me to marry her and get her away from her daddy…I obliged."

"Another good deed?" Hennessy asked.

Boozie nodded. "Seems like I'm just full of 'em," he agreed but there was no pride in his voice, only humility. "All the more reason I gotta get back home. Got to set stuff straight."

"I understand," Hennessy agreed.

"You got something back home tuggin' on you, too."

Frowning, Hennessy asked, "What're you talking about?"

"You was talking in your sleep, son. Saying 'Deja' over and over again." His daddy gave him a telling look. "You take a likin' to that girl, Hennessy?"

The old man's tone was serious, not teasing and Hennessy knew he needed to take care how he answered the question. Given what Deja had told him about the way his daddy had taken care of her and her mamma, giving a flip answer didn't seem like a good idea. "Yeah. She was very nice." So nice he'd had wet dreams over her. Last night's was the second since puberty, but he decided to leave that part out.

"Very nice, huh?" His daddy gave him a measured look.

"Crazy too—all that psychic business—but nice," Hennessy amended. Hoping to end the inquiry he added, "She was on her way to get her mamma from Tennessee when I left."

"What was Ivalou doin' in Tennessee?" Boozie asked.

The renewed interest in his voice didn't escape Hennessy's attention. "She said her mamma was miserable stayin' with her sister. Deja was bringin' her home to..." he stopped himself short.

"To what?" Boozie pressed.

"To die." Hennessy watched his daddy's face fall and his shoulders sag. The news seemed to take the light right out of his eyes. "You were fond of her, weren't you, Daddy?"

Boozie reached behind him to pull out his wallet.

"I got this," Hennessy held up a hand to stop him. "Don't worry about it."

"I'll meet ya outside, son." The shimmer of tears brimmed in the old man's eyes. He wiped them away briskly and headed for the door.

Hennessy paid for breakfast, met his daddy outside and they took a taxi to the airport. They didn't talk much on the way, but Hennessy made sure to give him a long, hard hug before he let him go.

As Hennessy headed back to his hotel, he had an overwhelming feeling of loneliness. For the first time since he'd left New Orleans, he felt empty and hollow. A part of him wanted to head back to the airport, buy a plane ticket and head back to the city where he'd been born, but that wouldn't be fair. He and Jack and Johnnie had commitments and Hennessy wasn't about to let his career go into the toilet for a lame excuse like loneliness. Besides, when he started playing tonight, the feeling would go away and he'd be right as rain again.

He no sooner reached the hotel than it was time to pack up and move on to San Jose. Jack and Johnnie were dragging, which was no surprise given that it was only eleven o'clock in the morning. The two of them partied hard nightly and it wasn't unusual for them to stay up until six in the morning.

"You sure we gotta leave this early, man?" Jack asked adjusting his sunglasses as he sank into the rented van. "My head hurts like hell."

The smell of digested liquor drifted across the car. Hennessy opened the sunroof for air drawing more moans and groans from his hung over partners. "I'm sure. We got a meeting with the manager of the club and I don't wanna be late. What happened to your pinkie ring, J?" The flashy bauble was noticeably absent.

Jack checked his hand quickly. "That witch!" he shouted, shooting straight up in his seat. "Turn around, Hen. I gotta go find that girl. What was her name, Johnnie?"

"Trisha something, wasn't it?" The larger man said groggily. He leaned against the door, his hand cupping his oversized head.

"That's it. Trisha. Turn around, man, I ain't playin'."

"How you gonna find her if that's all you know? You have her address?" Hennessy challenged, knowing the answer.

"No."

"You know where her friend lives?"

"Dadgum it! No."

"Then how you gonna find her?" Hennessy asked again.

"I told you to put that thing in the hotel safe," Johnnie said from the back.

"Shut up ya mammoth-sized excuse of a bass player. Shut up both of ya." Jack crossed his arms and sank lower in the front seat. He mumbled a string of curses for the next five minutes. Typically Jack was surly and irritable in between moments of real highs, but today his surliness wore on Hennessy's nerves. By the time they reached The Improv an hour later, he wanted to pound the man into unconsciousness to put them both out of their misery.

"Why don't ya'll check into your rooms while I talk to the manager," Hennessy suggested. Grateful to be rid of the bad-tempered Jack, Hennessy felt he could now focus on the job at hand. He had to have his wits about him when negotiating with the club owner. They were always trying to take advantage of bands without agent representation. But he couldn't see giving up any percentage of their profit to someone just because they could talk fast and read a contract. He went to college. He could do that.

Hennessy exited the manager's office bouncing along like John Travolta in *Saturday Night Fever*. He'd needed all of ten minutes to get their contract in order and to find out some television talent scouts would be in the audience that night. Of course they were there to find the next Eddie Murphy or Dave Chappelle, but that didn't mean the Whiskey Sins Trio shouldn't give them a show they wouldn't forget. And that was exactly what he told Jack and Johnnie.

The couple of hours' sleep they'd managed seemed to have put Jack in a much better mood. And Johnnie...well it was pretty hard to tell what mood the man was in most of the time. His demeanor was like stone until he started playing his bass. Then a look of pure joy would ease the lines of his forehead and the music would send his fingers popping along the strings of his instrument.

"Say listen," Hennessy said to the guys as they set up on stage. "After we play our normal sets, I got a head arrangement I need to work out. I need you to lay down a four beat, Jack, and we'll jam from there."

"All right, man. You got it." Jack did a test round on his drums as he looked around the room. "I hate this kind of set up. When the lights hit us I won't be able to scope out the honeys."

"You got a learnin' disability, Jack?" Hennessy stopped tuning his Ibanez guitar to stare at the man. "Didn't that woman—"

"Trisha," Johnnie offered.

"Yeah. Trisha. Didn't she teach you anything?"

"I learned something all right," he said laughing. "I learned to look for a lady of charity. Someone who likes to give of herself to others." He smiled and did a quick round on his drums. His gold tooth flashed in the light.

"Well, don't sleep with your mouth open," Hennessy cautioned, wondering how a man could live without taking anything seriously. All he did was play music, get drunk and lay women wherever they went.

The thought gave him pause. Who was he to criticize? For the past several years he'd done pretty much the same thing. Except he'd been more discriminate about the women he'd slept with—slightly. And, he was a lot more serious about their music. He'd written all of their songs, gotten them into a studio to make a CD, and he was the one lining up all their gigs. Still, it was getting more and more difficult to know if their little trio was moving forward or just moving around.

Hennessy played with all his heart that night and at the end, he sang his father's song. "*I loved you hard, sweet baby. But I did you wrong. I tried and tried, my honey…*" He half expected to see Deja walk through the crowd as he sang, smiling that sexy smile of hers like she had the night before. But this was the real world, not a dream world where the two of them could read one another's minds and wrap themselves with music and desire.

The memory of her, of the way her voice whispered softly in his head made him want her more than he wanted air to breathe. The words became real to Hennessy, as if he could feel the pain in his daddy's heart—the pain that had made him write these words. "*I wandered away when I shoulda stayed and looosing you was the price I paid. Oooh, Lord! What a price I paid.*"

Jack and Johnnie did a great job of improvising. What could've easily been a train wreck was a thing of beauty. Hennessy got lost in the music, in the memory of Deja and didn't open his eyes until the last note had silenced. He opened his eyes to a roomful of standing people, enthusiastically applauding their performance.

"Looka there, Hen," Jack yelled from behind him. "We got us a standin' ovation over that there song. What you call it?"

"'Lovin' Hard,'" he said, pushing his dreads away from his heated face. "My daddy wrote it."

"We addin' that bad boy to our play list. Look at this!" He stood up and held his sticks out wide. "Yeah, baby. I know for sure I'm getting laid tonight."

The applause was unexpected and made Hennessy a little light-headed. The doubts he'd had before they took the stage disappeared. When one of the agents in the audience came forward asking to speak to him, he knew for a fact they were moving in the right direction. What was more, he was sure it was going to be a smokin' ride.

He thought about Deja for a moment—thought about how she'd told him he had to make a choice to give up something to get something better. If the choice was between New Orleans and California, it looked like he'd made the right choice after all.

Chapter Eleven

Deja stared out the window of her shop and scowled. It was late December and Mardi Gras posters were going up all over Bourbon Street. The "krewes" that put the event together were emphatic about making this New Orleans tradition happen despite the city's continuing recovery from Hurricane Katrina.

On Twelfth Night, January 6, the day tradition held the three wise men visited the newborn baby Jesus was to be the first night of Carnival, the 'Farewell to the Flesh.' From that day until Fat Tuesday in February it was the time of year when people were supposed to get all the vices out of their system before the forty days of fasting for Lent. In Deja's humble opinion, the Carnival was simply an excuse for people to behave badly with a lot of other people who get their freak on while they do it.

She started closing her shop the year she saw a drunken young woman walking down the street, showing off her breasts to any man who cared to ogle and photograph them, while her six-year-old daughter stood by watching.

Deja checked the wall clock for the time. Two o'clock. She'd have to be headed home soon to check on her mamma. The interview she'd just had at the bank had been a complete waste of time—as had every other interview. She'd heard that New Orleans employers were so desperate for labor they were offering nearly double the wages they were pre-hurricane Katrina. Deja scoffed. None of them had offered her a single job, saying her psychic abilities wasn't the experience they were looking for. The sad part was it wouldn't have mattered if they had. Her attempts to find hospice care for her mamma had also dead-ended. Few hospices remained and those were so short-handed they couldn't accept additional patients. As a last ditch effort, Deja attempted to leverage her radio notoriety to get a job with the *Times-Picayune*. After several attempts, she'd gained an interview with the editor and asked him to look at an article she wrote entitled—what else? *Deja's View*. She'd dropped a little nugget about the upcoming faux pas of a prominent city official that had to do with chocolate. She'd received images of the event and told the editor if it came to pass he'd be short sighted to pass on her as a regular columnist.

Deja sighed and turned away from the plate-glass window. She retrieved her keys and was about to leave when her front door opened. The sight of Boozie Walker nearly floored her. "Hey!" she screamed and ran into his open arms. "Where've you been? When did you get back?"

Laughing his big laugh, Boozie squeezed her tight before letting her go. "One question at a time, girl. How's my little Dejanette, huh?"

"Full of piss and vinegar, to tell you the truth. Until you walked in. I'm so happy to see you." All the kindnesses he'd done for her in the past rolled quickly through her mind to warm her heart.

"You a sight for sore eyes yourself, sugah. You lookin' real good."

"Thanks, Boozie." Deja wanted to return the compliment, but she noticed the strain around his mouth and the tired lines around his eyes. "You came here for my help, didn't you?" she asked, searching his face.

"Yeah, baby. I did." Boozie sighed and moved toward her back room and the round chair. He grunted a little as he sat and suddenly he looked like an old man.

When had that happened, Deja wondered. He'd always been larger than life to her, but now he seemed all too human. "What's wrong?" she asked.

Boozie gestured toward her desk chair and she sat obediently. "It's Rayne…I…" His voice choked and he struggled for composure. "I…lost her. She's gone."

A cold grip took hold of Deja's heart. Something in the way he said it made her think he meant it more than literally. She rolled the chair closer to her friend and took his hands. They were calloused and rough as if he'd been working with them. "What happened?"

"I came back to town 'bout three weeks ago after visitin' with Hennessy out there in Californy." Telling the story seemed to help him maintain his composure. "He tole me they found out I wasn't that chile's daddy so I was prepared for that. What I weren't prepared for was how hurt she was gon' be about it." His eyes brimmed as he sought Deja's eyes. "She was downright nasty, accusing her mamma and me of bein' liars right in front of her baby. She tole me she hated me. It cut deep, Deja." He pounded a fist into his chest. "Lord knows I couldn't love that chile any more'n if she was mine." He buried his hands in his face.

Deja sat on the edge of the round chair next to him and held him tight. In the past, he had always held her, letting her cry whatever hurt her mamma had caused right out of her soul. As she held him, she closed her eyes and thought about Rayne. The connection she'd felt with the woman after her reading had long since dissipated, so she tried to connect through Boozie while she held him. She sensed nothing.

"Right 'fore Christmas," Boozie said, his voice muffled by his hands, "she left her mamma's house. I looked ever'where I could think to look since then. I can't find her." He looked at Deja, his watery eyes desperate. "I need your help, baby."

No way could she, or would she refuse. Though Deja didn't have the faintest idea of how to go about looking for Rayne, she agreed. "I'll do what I can, Boozie. I promise." He patted her leg as he'd always done. "That's all I ask. Thank you."

"Oh!" Deja cried, realizing she'd forgotten why she was on her way out. "I need to get home. I gotta check on Mamma."

His eyes widened. "I'd like to tag along," he said. "It's been a while since I seen yo mamma."

"She would love that," Deja said, grabbing his hand and pulling him out the door.

Boozie drove a pickup truck—not his Cadillac. Deja figured it had been totaled, like so many others, and he'd had to buy a new vehicle. He followed her the short distance back to the FEMA trailer she was still forced to call home. The contractors had never returned and, though she'd filed a police report, she had yet to have a single penny of her deposit money returned. Her bad mood was slowly returning.

"It ain't much, but it's home," she said dryly, climbing the few stairs to the door. "Mamma," she called out as they entered the living area. "I have a surprise for you."

"Deja?" her mamma's voice called from the bedroom. A moment later, Ivalou was swaying in the doorway of the bedroom. She steadied herself with one hand on the doorjamb while she thrust an orange medicine bottle in her daughter's direction. "I can't open dish thing. How'm I sshposed to take 'em?" she slurred her words, which bothered Deja, but not nearly as much as the fact she was completely wet and naked.

Deja's embarrassment and irritation for her mamma flushed hotly on her cheeks. She rushed over to help her back into the bedroom. "Mamma, good grief. We've got company." A detail the woman had apparently missed altogether until that very moment.

"Boozie?" Ivalou said, staring at him in wonder—or maybe a stupor. Deja couldn't tell the difference when she was like this.

"You came back for me?" Ivalou asked dreamily, holding her arms out to him. The medicine bottle fell from her open hand to the linoleum floor.

Deja put an arm around her mamma's non-existent waist and tried to move her into the bedroom. "Come on, Mamma. Let's get some clothes on, then you can take your medicine and talk to Boozie." Deja struggled to sound comforting and not put out, but the truth was, taking care of her mamma was taking an extreme toll on her patience.

"'Course I came for ya, Ivalou." Boozie put a hand on Deja's shoulder, gently moving her aside. "You're lookin' good, dahlin." With that he gave her the tenderest of kisses on her lips.

Deja stepped back, recognizing the steps to their familiar dance. Back in the days when her mamma had been drunk nearly every day, he'd always come just in time to relieve Deja when she'd tired of taking care of her. Today would be no different.

Boozie put an arm around her mamma, whispered something in her ear that made her chuckle then reached down to pick up the medicine bottle. He rose just in time to catch Ivalou by the waist as she swayed once more. He turned, gave Deja his it's-gonna-be-all-right look then closed the door behind them.

Deja sank to the chair in her tiny living room and stared at the door for long moments. Tears burned the backs of her eyes, so she closed them tight. At first, she tried to tell herself her tears were because she was tired and irritated because nothing seemed to be working out, but she knew that wasn't it.

The truth was, she wanted Boozie Walker—not the man, but a man like him. A man who loved a woman no matter what, forgave her everything, and loved her without condition. A man who came back for her time and again.

The moment she'd met Hennessy in the other plane, she knew she wanted him to love her in that way. She'd thought serendipity had led her to find the magnificent man, but now she believed she'd found him specifically because he was Boozie Walker's son.

But Hennessy James Walker wasn't anything like his father. Boozie was kind, caring, patient and as loyal as the day was long. Hennessy, on the other hand, was charming, creative—kind, but incredibly self-centered. He wasn't a man built for coming back and he'd tried to tell her that. He'd tried to tell her that night they'd spent together before he left for California, but Deja's stubborn heart had refused to listen. When they'd found each other *traveling* over a month ago, she thought he'd be back and that would be the beginning of their lives together. But, he didn't come back. He disappeared. He'd laid no musical paths to guide her to him since that night.

"Some psychic I am," Deja sighed, remembering the song he'd sang "...*I loved you hard, but did you wrong. Couldn't stay in one place too long*..." Her heart had soared when he sang it to her. She'd thought the words meant he was coming back, when obviously he'd meant it as a good-bye. The realization was breaking her heart a little bit more each day.

Deja wiped the melancholy from her eyes a moment before the bedroom door opened. "How's she doing?" she asked Boozie who was closing the door softly behind him.

"She doin' all right," he said quietly. "Sleepin'. She lost a lot of weight, huh?" His forehead wrinkled with concern as he took a seat on the couch.

"Quite a bit," Deja acknowledged, sitting upright in her chair.

"Them spells of hers are g'tting' worse, ain't they?" he asked.

Deja nodded. "And they come more often. The medicine isn't helping as much as it used to."

They sat in silence for a moment before Deja remembered her manners. "Can I get you anything? A drink or a sandwich?"

"Naw, baby," he said, waving off the question. "I gotta be goin'. I'm rebuildin' the Blues 'N Booze, you know?"

"Really?" Deja perked up. "I didn't know. How'd you get a contractor? I've been having a terrible time."

"I knows a fella does contractin'. I got ahold of him," Boozie said, rubbing a hand over his thick salt and pepper hair. "Then I got some of the folks in the neighborhood to come out and help. Folks wanted to get focused on doin' something. They's tired of waitin' on the government to help 'em out, so we got together and planned how we was gonna rebuild businesses and then some of the homes they got red-flagged."

"The homes they want to demolish?" Deja had heard about that. "I'm afraid of that happening to Mamma's house since we haven't been able to make repairs."

"Jefferson Parish is a little out the way, but you know I'll do what I can, sugah." He gave her a steady look. "Other than that, how you doin', chile?"

Deja shrugged. "Tryin' to find a job. You know the government money won't last forever. And if I find a job, I have to find someone to look after Mamma. As you can see, I can't leave her alone too long during the day."

"Tell you what," Boozie said rising. "When we finish up the B&B, why don't you manage the place for me? That'll put a little change in your pocket. Least till you start getting' some bizness back at your place."

A night job would allow her to at least be around during the day for her mamma. "What about Earl? He's back in town, you know? You don't want to give him back his job?" she asked, trying to make sure there weren't any loopholes to ruin this beautiful plan.

"Let's jest say me and Earl got us a little understandin' these days," he said, a wide grin spreading across his strong, dark features. "He understands if he sets foot back my bar, I'll beat him within a inch of his life."

Though his voice sounded teasing, Deja knew the man was serious as a heart attack. Boozie Walker had always protected what was his and apparently, Earl had done something to put himself out of Boozie's good graces. She didn't know what, but she was happy to take advantage of this turn of good luck. "You've got a deal, Boozie." She stood and offered her hand.

"Don't insult me, girl." He ignored her hand and gave her a tight hug. "We's family. We ain't got no need for handshakes."

"All right," Deja smiled. Somehow she knew everything was going to be better now with Boozie back. "I'll give you a call if I figure out anything on Rayne," she added as he opened the front door.

"Do that, baby." A brief moment of sadness filled his eyes and then he was gone.

"Who the hell is Deja?"

The question woke Hennessy from a deep sleep. His heart pounded in panic as he tried to get his bearings. The orange-red rays of morning sun slipped through the slit in the hotel room drapes and a moderately pretty black woman, hair mussed from sleep, glared accusingly at him. "What?" he asked, trying to shake loose the cobwebs created by a late night jam session and too much after party from his brain.

"I said, who the hell is Day Zha?" Her head moved from side-to-side as she emphasized each word.

The question irritated Hennessy. He barely knew this woman—was struggling to remember her name—and here she was demanding to know who Deja was? He didn't think so. "She's a friend of mine," he answered, giving her a glare. "If it's any of your business."

She backed off immediately in response to his anger. Like flicking a switch, her demeanor went from Angry Man-Hater to Playful Sex Kitten. "I'm sorry," she said in a childish tone, dropping her eyes and drawing circles on his chest with a red-manicured nail. "You were saying her name in your sleep and I thought I was your best girl." She pushed the sheet away then to expose her naked breasts.

Well, now he knew why he'd brought her back to his room.

The woman—Casey—that was her name—leaned over and whispered, "I bet I can make you forget you ever knew her." Her breath was foul and her makeup had moved all over her face, distorting it like a crazy clown. When she moved to straddle him, Hennessy grabbed her at the waist, barely able to contain his disgust.

"I've got some things to do this morning," he lied. "I need for you to leave."

Again, her mood shifted. She cursed him and rolled off the bed in a huff. "All ya'll musicians are alike," she spat as she forced her legs into her thong panties, "thinking you all that. Well you ain't! Ain't a damned thing more special about you than anybody else."

She was right and Hennessy felt as low as the names she called him as she moved around the room gathering up her clothes and putting them on. Ordinarily, he wouldn't treat a woman so badly. Usually, he'd have a nice cordial conversation about how this wasn't going to be a long-term thing, just a night in their lives they could hold on to and cherish. Most women went for it based on the Secret Romance factor and left happy in the morning—and so had he. But not last night. He'd done everything is his power to make this woman feel like he worshiped the ground she walked on—as if he'd been waiting for her all his life. Hell, he might've even said as much. Geez, what had he been thinking? "I'm sorry, Casey."

"Cassie, you pig!" she reeled on him. "How many times do I have to tell you? My name is CASSIE!" She slammed the door and left.

Groaning, Hennessy rubbed his face in his hands. "Dammit, Deja," he said letting his hands fall to the bed at his sides. The memory of her, the wanting of her had made him go after Cassie last night. He'd wanted to get his mind off of Deja, but, obviously, distraction hadn't worked. Here he was still saying her name in his sleep, even though he'd stopped seeing her in his dreams. He missed her—was lonely without her, but he didn't know what to do about it.

Things were going so great for the Trio. Now in Los Angeles, they'd signed on with a recording label and cut a CD that was getting decent airtime on Jazz stations in the area. He'd called his daddy to get permission to include "Lovin' Hard," which was still bringing down the house with live audiences every night. But Hennessy was no longer walking away from their performances with the same high as he had in the past. Jack and Johnnie noticed it, asked why he'd been so down, but he'd made like it wasn't anything. "Just need to get laid, I guess," he'd joked. It was all the explanation they needed, especially Jack, who thought getting laid was the answer to nearly everything.

Hennessy had lied to Cassie—heaven knew he'd never forget her name again—about having to do anything that morning, but he was wide awake now and decided he may as well get out of bed. He could get into the recording studio anytime he wanted, he figured he'd go in and see who might show up. Being around other people who were all about Jazz was cool. It inspired him.

He stopped for breakfast at the hotel restaurant, picking up a *USA Today* to read while he waited on his meal. Halfway through, he saw the articles on New Orleans. A large one detailed efforts to move forward with Mardi Gras and a smaller one declaring "The First Family of Jazz Returns to New Orleans." The article was about how Jazz trumpeter extraordinaire, Wynton Marsalis, was returning home to New Orleans to help his father, the legendary pianist and teacher, Ellis Marsalis, in bringing music back to the city.

Hennessy folded the paper and put it to the side when his food arrived, ashamed of the fact that he wasn't doing the same thing as Wynton. His own daddy was spearheading an effort to build businesses and homes and here he was, eating scrambled eggs in a decent hotel, after having used a woman like a dog. He was lonesome and feeling sorry for himself and for what? For not figuring out how to have Deja and his music, too? Well, he could definitely do something about that.

Newly inspired, he stabbed at his food with his fork. By the time he finished, he'd made up his mind—he was going home to New Orleans. He was going to help his daddy rebuild the B&B. And he was going to make love to Deja long and hard. He threw money on the table and rushed out of the little restaurant. He had tell Jack and Johnnie he was going home.

"Why you do this to us, Hennessy?" Johnnie asked with disgust. He scratched at the mass of bare brown chest between his unbuttoned pajama top. Hennessy had dragged Jack, almost literally, from his room next door to Johnnie's. "Things're going good, man. Why're you leavin'?"

"I told you," Hennessy sat in the other chair in the room, leaning his arms on his thighs, "my family needs me. I gotta go back."

Jack had his head buried beneath a pillow on the bed. "It's wrong how you do us, Hen," his voice was muffled. "You just drop us when the mood strikes ya."

"I thought my daddy was dead the last time, fellas. Have a damn heart."

"Yeah, but he isn't dead, is he?" Jack challenged, sitting up. "And now he needs you so you go running back? You made a commitment to this band, Hennessy, man. Our songs are getting played. We're on the damn radio. We all know its time to get aggressive and get in front of folks while the iron is hot."

"We have plenty of time for that," Hennessy argued, feeling ambivalent because he knew Jack was right. "I'll only be gone a few months. We can get back to it then."

"You're the one signing contracts and getting us gigs, man," it was Johnnie arguing now. "You can't just grow a damned conscience about New Orleans all of the sudden and leave us. Where's your loyalty, man?"

Hennessy had never seen Johnnie so irritated before. How could he justify this decision to him, to both of them, when they were right? Now was the time to really push if they wanted their career to take off. "Tell you what, fellas. What if I promise to get some publicity out of going home for the Trio?"

They eyed him skeptically.

"Look. Wynton Marsalis did it." He pulled the rolled up article out of his back pocket and showed it to them. "I could get us some gigs out that way—maybe even play at my daddy's club once it's open. The Blues 'N Booze has hosted some of the hottest Jazz and Blues bands in the country. We could get large over it." He waited in anticipation, hoping his argument would win them over.

"Aw'ight." Jack scooted to the edge of the bed. "Say we go for this bull. What do we do about the third man for our Trio until you get us set up?"

"You still got Terry Pryce's number? Ya'll did all right with him before," he offered.

Jack looked at Johnnie. "Whadd'ya think, man?"

Johnnie shook his head and sighed. "Whatever, man. We gotta do what we gotta do."

Hennessy left the room knowing he was walking a tight line with his friends. But they'd forgive him if he actually pulled off the plan he'd just concocted. Hell, making it work was the only way he'd be able to live with himself.

A week later, Hennessy's plane approached the New Orleans airport and his confidence waned. As he flew over the city, he could tell the recovery wasn't nearly as far along as he'd hoped. For the hundredth time that day, he wondered if he'd made the right decision. "This is what you get for thinking with the wrong head, you idiot," he whispered to himself. How in the world could he help his band get exposure in a city that was gasping for every breath?

His disappointment must've showed. Once he'd retrieved his baggage, his daddy asked, "Was your flight bumpy, son?" Boozie asked. "Your lookin' a little peak-ed."

"I'm all right." Hennessy pretended a smile. His daddy picked up more gray hair since he'd seen him last. And his broad shoulders slumped like he was carrying a heavy load. The sight of him worried Hennessy. "How're you doin'? You look a little tired."

"Been puttin' in long hours is all, son." He slapped Hennessy's shoulder heartily. "Now you're here, maybe I can take a day off."

"Sounds good," Hennessy laughed.

They talked about the progress on the B&B and the other neighborhood projects on the way to his mamma's house. His daddy had apologized for not being able to put him up, but explained his nearly rebuilt house wasn't quite ready for company. It didn't matter much to Hennessy.

"There is one other thing, son."

"What?"

"Your sister—she's gone missing."

Alarmed, Hennessy stared at his daddy. "For how long?"

"A few weeks."

"Why didn't you tell me? Why didn't Mamma call me?" Hennessy couldn't believe it. His sister was missing and no one thought to let him know.

"Didn't wanna worry you—it's not the first time she's done this," Boozie added.

"Then why're you so worried?" Hennessy challenged. More than hard work had his daddy looking so tired.

"Gotta bad feelin' this time, son. Gotta bad feelin'. This time she left Ray Ray behind." And that was all his daddy would say. They drove the rest of the way to his Mamma's house in silence. "Hey, Baby," Lila greeted him at the door with a kiss when he arrived, but there was no bounce in her steps this time. "Boozie," she acknowledged her ex-husband coolly as he followed Hennessy into the house.

"Hello, Lila. You lookin' good today." His greeting was warm and held no underlying hostility. "How's Antoine?"

"Wonderful," Lila said with emphasis, as if she were trying to make a point. "He's at the store. Took Ray Ray with him."

Hennessy was a little disappointed, he'd been anxious to see the little boy. Lila instructed him to put his bags in Rayne's room. Hennessy felt strange as he looked around. The room was neat and tidy. A sure sign Rayne hadn't been there and his mamma had. His parents were arguing when he got back to the living room.

"Look, Lila. Alls I want is a piece of clothing or her handbag. Why's that askin' too much?"

"Because I don't want that little witch touchin' my baby's things," Lila shot back. "First you mess around with Ivalou and then you mess around with her little ho brat. You took better care of them than your real family. If you think I'm given either one of them anything of my child's you've lost your ever lovin' mind."

"Lila I never had an affair with Deja. When you saw us in the restaurant, she was just thanking me for a gift I gave her. That little kiss on the cheek was innocent. As for Ivalou—well let's just leave the past in the past." Boozie pleaded.

"Why?" she insisted. "'Cause you can't stand the sound of the truth?"

"Because it won't help us find Rayne."

Lila's lips quivered as she glared at her ex-husband "I don't believe in that psychic stuff," She finally managed to say.

"It don't matter what you believe if it works." Boozie insisted, holding her arms. "We runnin' outta choices, Lila!"

The desperation in his voice hung in the dense silence. Finally, Lila sank to the couch letting her anger give way to tears. "This is my fault, isn't it? I ran her off once and for all. This is all my fault."

"It ain't nobody's fault, Lila. How was you 'spose to know she'd take it this hard?"

"I picked at her. Even after she told me to stop, even after Hennessy told me to stop, I kept at it," Lila whined. "I ran my baby off and now she's probably laying dead in a back alley somewhere."

"She's not dead," Hennessy said, drawing his mamma and daddy's attention. He moved further into the room. "I know my sister. She may be drunk or stoned, but she's not dead," he insisted. Few women knew how to protect themselves as well as Rayne. She'd been able to hold her own with any girl, or boy, who'd crossed her when they were kids. He also remembered the little pink handled gun she'd had in her purse the last

179

time he'd been with her. He was pretty sure she didn't carry it for decoration.

"What are you asking for, Daddy?" he asked. "What do you think we need to do?"

"I need take something of Rayne's over to Deja. She said she might get a read if she had something that belonged to Rayne."

The thought of seeing Deja again had Hennessy's heart skipping despite his concern for his sister.

"Seems like a big waste of time," Lila complained as her crying eased.

"Well, I don't know I believe in all this psychic stuff either, Mamma. But Daddy's right," Hennessy offered honestly. "It can't hurt anything."

"Fine. Fine. Just don't take her hairbrush or comb. Folks'll use that and put a voodoo spell on her."

"I'll just get a jacket or something from her closet, how's that?" Hennessy was gone before she could answer. He noticed no comb or hairbrush was on her dresser or nightstand, nor were they in the drawers. When he opened the closet door, he noticed a gap that looked like some clothes had once been there. So she hadn't just wandered off like he'd assumed. She'd left on purpose. He didn't know why, but the thought made him feel better.

He pulled a light blue jacket made of sweat suit material from the closet. He'd remembered her wearing it when he'd been home the last time. He and his daddy were on their way moments later.

"So, how's Deja doing?" Hennessy asked casually.

"She's doin' all right," his daddy answered. "Comes by the B&B every once in a while to see how it's goin'. I'ma let her run the place once it re-opens."

"You are?" Hennessy was surprised. "I thought you said not to trust anybody but family."

"Did." Boozie gave a quick nod. "Known that girl all her life. Practically raised her like I did you'n Rayne. She's like family," he assured his son.

Hennessy really didn't like the sound of that. If his daddy thought of her like his daughter, then that would make her his sister and something was not right about having the hots for his own sister. "Did she say anything about me," he asked, again trying to sound casual.

"Naw," Boozie lifted an eyebrow and looked sideways at his son. "Why? Is there something she shoulda told me?"

"Nothing important," Hennessy answered, not sure if he was bothered by the fact she'd said nothing about him to his daddy or if he was relieved. What he really wanted to know was if she would be happy to see him. It looked like he'd have to wait for that answer.

When they arrived at the trailer, Hennessy was disappointed to see Deja's mamma's house still in shambles. She hadn't caught up to her contractors. *The crooks*. People who took advantage of someone who had already lost so much angered him.

His daddy was out of the truck quickly, as was Hennessy.

"Don't forget that jacket," his daddy reminded.

Hennessy reached back into the cab to pull it out. He caught up to his daddy, just as he was tapping on the door. "It's Boozie, Deja," he called out.

A few seconds later the door opened. Hennessy couldn't see her at first, his daddy was blocking the way. But as soon as he said, "I got my son, Hennessy, with me," he moved inside and there she was, looking sexy without even trying.

The sudden rush of heat to his loins, made Hennessy lightheaded. His eyes couldn't take her in fast enough. Mischievous smile, mysterious eyes, hair piled loosely on top of her head, full breasts, sexy hips wrapped in denim jeans—he couldn't decide which feature he liked most. He was suddenly a fat kid with the sweetness of Deja dangling in front of his eyes like candy.

"Hi, Hennessy," she greeted him.

Her voice was like music and did nothing to calm Hennessy's swirling rush of mad lust. *I'm staring*, he realized before finally remembering how to speak. "Hi."

"You coming in or what?" she asked, smiling devilishly.

"Yeah. Sure." His foot missed the last step and he had to grab the rails to keep from falling back to the ground. He cursed.

"Ya all right, boy?" Boozie turned.

"I'm fine." He played a few more of his favorite curses in his head as he walked past Deja. What was up with the clumsiness? This wasn't his first time seeing the woman.

"What brings you gentlemen to my doorstep this fine day," Deja asked, closing the door. "It's certainly unexpected." She sent a meaningful glance in Hennessy's direction.

Hennessy decided to leave the talking to his daddy while he tended his wounded ego.

"We brought something of Rayne's like you asked," Boozie said. "Give it to her, son."

Obediently, Hennessy offered the piece of clothing to Deja. "It's her jacket," he said, quite unnecessarily. He winced. Whatever was evaporating his brain needed to stop—immediately.

Deja took the jacket and studied it. "This should work," she said. She was struggling to keep her tone neutral. "But I really need to be able to focus to get a good reading." She looked back toward the closed bedroom door where her mamma slept. "I should try this at my shop."

"Don't you worry none about your mamma," Boozie said, following her train of thought. "I can hang out here."

"That'll be great."

"I'll take a nap and keep an ear out for Ivalou." He proceeded to kick off his shoes and stretched out on the couch. Hennessy got the feeling this wasn't the first time.

"Why don't you go with her, son?" Boozie gestured them both toward the door. "You don't have to if you'd rather stay," Deja said softly, biting her bottom lip.

Hennessy's eyes met Deja's. They sparked with invitation in total contradiction to her words.

"Oh no. I wanna come," he assured her. He couldn't get out of his chair fast enough. "I definitely wanna come."

Deja's Mini Cooper seemed smaller than usual as Hennessy pushed back the seat to accommodate his long legs. The smell of her soft scent drifted across the car, it wasn't overpowering, just enough to make him want to nuzzle her neck—and rip her blouse open—and run his hands along her smooth thighs.

Stop it, Hennessy, he chided himself.

Deja's breathing seemed a bit more rapid than usual. Hennessy wondered if she was feeling the same thing as he was. "So, how was California?" she asked.

Her question startled Hennessy and ended his internal debate over whether to cop a feel of her breasts or run hand along the jean-clad thigh nearest him. "Huh?"

"California," she repeated. "You did well there?"

"Yeah. We, uh, got a contract and cut a CD."

Her eyes widened with sincere delight. "That's great. You must be thrilled."

"I am," he said. But not as thrilled as he would be when he had her in his arms. He anticipated the taste of her kiss, the feel of her soft skin under his hands. "But, I missed you, Deja." He wasn't sure if he'd meant to say the words out loud. He'd laid his feelings on the table. It was Deja's move.

"I missed you too, Hennessy," she said.

Hennessy closed his eyes, relieved to hear her say it. "Then for God's sake, woman, pull over."

"What?" Deja's pulsed skipped around in her veins as she sensed desperation in his voice. "Here?"

"I don't care where." The gold around his eyes flared like the sun. "I just need you to stop this damn car."

"All right," she said. Need swirled in her eyes and Hennessy was feeling even more desperate. He looked around for the best place to pull over. The side of the road would probably not be the best idea.

"There." Spying the remains of an old apartment complex, Deja ducked the car between two huge piles of debris. "This is as private as we get, brother," she said, putting the car in Park. "But...Oh!" she cried out as Hennessy's hand slipped inside her jeans. "We can't do this in the car."

"Oh yes we can," Hennessy disagreed then greedily took her mouth with his own.

Her protests died beneath his kiss and he melted into her heavenly, mind-bending, soft and warm kiss. Magically, the large sunroof opened. Then, she was reaching over her to send her car seat into a prone position. "I didn't know it could go that far," he said staring deep into her eyes. "Look up at the sky, baby," he instructed in his hoarse, sexy voice. "I'm going to send you there."

"Promises, prom—"

He kissed the words from her lips and pulled off her jeans and panties in one smooth move hell bent on making his boast a reality.

Chapter Twelve

Deja saw more than the sky that afternoon. Making love with Hennessy in a Mini Cooper was the closest she'd ever been to Heaven. With both front seats laid back, the car wasn't too cramped. Of course, they hadn't stayed inside long. She smiled. Who knew it could be so much fun being a hood ornament?

"Thank goodness, it's dark now," Deja said, pulling on her clothes as the last of her Hennessy-induced high mellowed. "I'm pretty sure what we just did is illegal."

"Good thing the New Orleans police force ain't what it used to be then, huh?" He smiled wickedly, feeling more relaxed than he had in weeks. "But all of this could've been avoided if you hadn't been lookin' so sexy." He pulled her close and gave her a long, deep kiss.

"Mmm. This is nice," Deja said, running her hands along his broad shoulders. His dreads tickled the tops of her hands. "But, I have work to do. I was serious about needing to be at the *Deja's View* to get a reading on your sister's jacket."

A look of surprise passed briefly over his face. "I thought you were just makin' that up so we could…" His hand moved back and forth between them.

Disappointment settled in Deja's chest. He still wasn't taking her psychic gifts seriously. "You think I would lie to your daddy just to have you?"

"Well…" Hennessy smiled his gorgeous smile and puffed out his chest.

Deja could almost see his inflated ego. Of course, she had only herself to blame. She'd made her pleasure obvious the minute he'd walked in her door. Lord knew that man could push all the right buttons. "Get in the car, big head," she feigned disgust.

Too Much Hennessy

He did as she instructed, but made an unintelligible complaint under his breath about being called "big head" which made Deja smile. She liked having someone to talk to and joke with. She'd been so consumed with taking care of her mamma lately, of trying to find a contractor to fix the house, and trying to find a job. She was tired of these serious pursuits and having to be responsible all of the time. She hadn't realized just how tired until this moment. The past half-hour with Hennessy had been incredibly decadent and outrageously irresponsible. She hadn't had such a good time since he'd left. Which brought her to the question that had to be asked. "How long you here for?" she asked, holding her breath.

"A while," Hennessy said noncommittally.

"A short while, a long while?" she asked but tried to keep the question light. The last thing she wanted was to make him feel as if she wanted more from him than he was able to give, but he'd come back hadn't he?

"As long as it takes," he offered hesitantly. "I'm helping Daddy with the Blues and Booze. Thought I'd book my Trio here once we get the place up and running."

"Oh. Sounds like a good plan," Deja said sincerely. "The Marsalis family and other Jazz and Blues musicians are starting to book gigs here at the local places that are open. It's their part in bringing the city back."

"I heard." Hennessy nodded and looked absently out the window as they headed toward the Quarter. "I'm still not sure it's worth the effort."

"You don't mean that," Deja started.

"Yeah, I do." Hennessy offered no apology. "It's like I've been telling my daddy, the government isn't doing a damned thing to get the levees in shape to take on another category four hurricane, so whatever gets rebuilt today, gets destroyed again late summer or fall. I think it's ridiculous to rebuild a below-sea-level city that's surrounded by water."

"But New Orleans is America's history, from the architecture to the blend of races that make up the population. It's the birthplace of Jazz and Cajun cooking. It's contributed so much to the culture of this nation that it'd be a waste to let it all crumble in the wake of Hurricane Katrina. Can't you see that?"

Hennessy stared at her long and hard. "No. I don't."

"What about all those displaced people who want to come home?" she pressed.

"They'll make a new start where they are. People do it all the time."

"Hennessy," she sought his eyes. "Nothing feels the same as home. Nothing is as comfortable. Nothing is as good. That's why my mamma insisted on coming back. Don't you get it?"

"I understand what you're saying, Deja. But, honestly, I don't feel that way about the city." He stared at the windows as they passed by area after area that had been destroyed by the hurricane. "It just makes me sad to be here."

"Then why bother to come back and help your daddy?" she shot the question like a bullet. "Why come back at all?"

"Because it's important to my daddy and...I wanted to see you," he admitted.

It was meant to be a compliment. Deja knew that. She supposed she should be grateful he'd wanted to come back to see her, to make mad love to her, but she wanted so much more from him. She wanted him to stay with her forever, for a lifetime. And then, maybe, she could finally get enough of him. Deja had never wanted anything from any man before and she found her sudden neediness a little frightening.

Hennessy had made it clear there'd be no long-term commitments to her or to New Orleans, so Deja had a decision to make: enjoy the time they had together without demanding more or, keep as far away from him as possible. *Some choice.* Either way, she would end up brokenhearted, wouldn't she?

"Deja?" Hennessy's voice was low as he leaned over to kiss her neck. "I didn't mean to make you mad."

"I'm not mad," she lied, putting a death grip on the steering wheel. His lips were soft and warm against her neck and she could feel herself getting aroused again. The power he had over her libido was maddening and did nothing to soften her mood.

"What can I do to make it up to you?" he teased as his hand cupped a breast.

Too Much Hennessy

Deja pulled away from him without a word. She couldn't let him think that sex would solve everything. "We're here." She pulled into the parking spot and made short work of grabbing Rayne's jacket from the back seat and getting out of the car.

She's pissed, Hennessy thought as he followed her inside the building. When would he learn not to be so honest? *Never*, he decided. It had been the right thing to tell her he wasn't planning on staying in New Orleans. The last thing he wanted was to lead her on and have her thinking he'd be around forever when he most decidedly would not.

When the time came for him to go, he wanted it to be quick and easy, like the last time.

Yeah, right. Easy didn't really describe it. The last time, he'd needed all his strength just to get out of the bed and sneak out of her trailer in the middle of the night. Just thinking about it made his chest ache.

Which was probably why she was so ticked off right now, he decided. She thought he'd leave without saying good-bye again. Hennessy made a vow, then and there, not to do that. This time, he'd face the deed head-on.

He rubbed at the ache that had increased in his chest and decided to be as unobtrusive as possible as she went about preparing the room for her reading. Hennessy propped himself in the doorway and watched Deja. She walked around the room lighting vanilla candles calmly enough, but when she whacked the floor pillows mercilessly into shape, it confirmed to him his Lay Low strategy had been the right one.

Finally she sat, making herself comfortable on her cushions. She laid the jacket on the low table and closed her eyes as she held her hands over the object.

Hennessy studied the woman as if seeing her for the first time. She sat erect, breathing in and out slowly for several long minutes. Her breasts rose and fell in time to some inner rhythm she seemed to have found. The strained look on her face when she'd first began disappeared. Now she looked peaceful, tranquil. He envied her. His mind always seemed "on" and even when he slept, he found no real peace, only discordant dreams. But not Deja. When she slept she looked this way—calm and controlled.

188

When he'd left her that night, she'd looked just this way. When he left this time, he was sure her demeanor would be different. The newness will wear off in say two…three months. And by then, she'd grow tired of his staying out till all hours with the band and sleeping all day. She'd complain about him not paying enough attention to her and in that respect, she'd be like all the other women he'd ever dated. When being with him stopped being fun, their time together would end. That's the way he'd always played it. The ache in his chest worsened.

Deja's peaceful demeanor changed as if she'd just read into his last thoughts. She frowned intensely with her head cocked slightly as if she were trying to hear something. Intrigued, Hennessy moved quietly from his post at the doorway between the two rooms to sit at the opposite side of the table. He watched Deja closely, to see if she would acknowledge his presence.

She mouthed something—a question—into the air.

"What?" Hennessy asked.

A moment later, she did it again. This time Hennessy was able to read her lips. "Where are you?" she asked the air.

The question wasn't meant for him, but for Rayne. Hennessy wished for just a second he could be inside Deja's head, listening for the answer from his sister if there was one.

On impulse, Hennessy placed his hand next to Deja's over his sister's jacket. If something could be felt, maybe he'd feel it too. He cleared his mind, closed his eyes and thought of nothing else but Rayne. If Deja didn't get an answer, maybe he could. He was her brother, after all. *Rayne*, he thought. *Rayne? Where are you?* He mouthed the words the way Deja had. He felt himself sliding into a light, peaceful place. He felt quietness press in all around him. He felt cocooned in tranquility. Everything was so quiet he knew if an answer was coming his way, this was the right place to hear it. "Rayne?" he asked again. "Where are you?"

A wicked slap across his cheek brought Hennessy out of his quiet place in one second flat. He stared into Deja's glazed eyes. "What's wrong?"

"How dare you make fun of me?" she said between clenched teeth.

"I wasn't." He grabbed both her hands before she could slap him again.

"You think this is some game I'm playing?" she yelled and struggled to break free of his grip.

"No. Deja—"

"I'm doing this to help your family and all you can do is act like an ass." She was on her feet, on the table, about to kick him.

Hennessy rose with her, turned her back to him and locked her in his arms. "Would you listen to me damn it?" It was his turn to be angry. "I wasn't making fun of you. I was trying to see if I could feel something…something from Rayne."

"No you weren't," she argued.

"Yes, I was," he insisted, holding her tighter as she squirmed.

"Then what did you feel?" she demanded, her back stiff against his torso.

"Nothing," he admitted. "Not from Rayne anyway."

"But you felt something?" she asked, sounding interested.

"I felt calm, quiet, you know? Like if I was going to get an answer, I had to be really still to hear it."

"Then what?" She relaxed.

"That was it." Feeling the ease of tension, Hennessy released her arms. "Next thing I knew you were slapping the hell out of me."

Deja turned to look at him. She put a hand to his offended cheek. "Sorry about that," she apologized. "But you deserved to have something slapped out of you for not fully believing in my gifts. Especially since I've proven them to you again and again."

"How's that?" Hennessy really didn't want to pick a fight, but this needed clarification. "What have you proven?"

"I told you your father wasn't dead, didn't I?"

"Yes, but it could've just been a lucky guess since the body had been so badly deteriorated and no dental records or DNA identification had been done. We just saw the wisdom in doing that."

"Yeah, but I didn't know how badly the body had been bloated. And, remember, I told you your daddy was the one who killed the man in the casket? I found out from your daddy just the other week, he killed the man after he'd broken into the B&B the night of the hurricane." Hennessy remembered his daddy telling him the same thing. He'd said the man was a member of DeTron's gang and there was sure to be retaliation.

"You think that was a lucky guess, too?" Deja challenged. She continued before he could answer. "Then there's your sister's dream about the field of flowers. Coincidence again?"

Hennessy really didn't have a good explanation for her being right about so many things. Reluctantly, he knew the only thing he could do was throw in the towel. "I guess you'd have to be more than lucky to get all that right." He smiled. "Though you have no idea how it pains me to admit it."

"I'll accept your lame little apology since I know how much ego it had to get through to make it out your mouth," she said smugly. "Though you have no idea how it pains me to have my gifts trivialized."

Hennessy rubbed his still stinging cheek. "I think I have some idea."

"Good," she said without further apology. "And just for the record, you heard about Mayor Ray Nagin's comment about New Orleans becoming a Chocolate City?"

"Couldn't help but hear about it. It was all over the news the other day."

"I predicted that." Deja's puffed with pride.

"Really?" His eyebrow lifted with surprise.

She nodded. "Got a job with the *Times-Picayune* as a columnist because of it. Now, help me put out these candles," she said, blowing out the ones nearest the table. "We need to get back to the trailer. I know where your sister is and its not going to make Boozie happy."

"DeTron's still in town?" Boozie frowned at the news Deja had just imparted. "And, my baby's back with him?"

"Fraid so," Deja said, moving to sit beside her mamma on the couch.

"Prob'ly got that chile back on that junk." Boozie paced the trailer floor like a caged lion. "Jest when we 'bout had her clean."

Hennessy had seen his daddy in a mood like this before. He'd been about thirteen when he'd packed up his guns and left the house that night, his face full of anger and purpose. He remembered his mamma crying and begging him to stay home and not go to the club that night, but he said he couldn't back down—that they'd think he was a punk.

The front page of the newspaper touted him as a hero the next day. Said a local business owner had stood up against local hoodlums to reclaim the street. But, from what his daddy had told him, DeTron didn't sound like he was simply a local hoodlum. He was a gang member, Hennessy couldn't remember if his daddy had mentioned which gang, but that hardly mattered. Tangling with one was like hitting a hornet's nest with a stick. All the rest would be on you in a matter of seconds. "What're you thinking, Daddy?" he asked cautiously.

Boozie looked up from his pacing to send his son a steely gaze. "I'ma go get her, that's what I'm thinkin'."

Hennessy had been afraid of that. "You can't do that, Daddy. You'll be killed."

"He's right, Boozie," Deja offered. "These gang members would just as soon shoot you as look at you."

"What'm I s'pose' to do?" Boozie threw his hands up. "Jest let 'em take my chile?"

"Daddy," Hennessy stood up to face his father. "Rayne went willingly. They didn't take her." He remembered thinking how she'd clearly packed to leave when he'd looked around her room.

"You don't know that." He spat out viciously. "Soon's they heard I was back in town, that dirty dog DeTron prob'ly got ahold to Rayne and tole her she had to go back with him or I'd be hurt."

"If that's the case, we should call the police and tell them she's been kidnapped." Hennessy suggested.

"Police can't do nuttin 'bout this," Boozie argued. "They in cahoots with the gangs anyways, you know that."

Hennessy didn't know, but a part of him believed it. Many New Orleans police officers had run alongside civilians looting the stores after the hurricane flooded the streets. He didn't know how he would've reacted in the same situation. Would he have stayed as long as his daddy had? Would he have faced the men who broke into the bar on his own?

A part of Hennessy was shamed he hadn't been there to stand with his daddy. He'd known all along the man wouldn't evacuate for the hurricane. And yet Hennessy had chosen not to come back. Of course he had no idea what kind of trouble his father was in at that time. Now he was getting a better idea, and was determined not to let his father stand alone in this fight. Hennessy was ready to do whatever was necessary to get his sister back, if for no one else, but little Ray Ray. The child needed his mamma.

Still, they needed a better plan. Busting into DeTron's place with guns blazing would get them all killed and he said as much to his daddy.

"Yer right, son," Boozie sighed and ran a hand over his thick salt and pepper hair. "But, I'm fresh outta bright ideas. If you got any, let's hear 'em."

"I'd really like to know how much time we have," Hennessy said. "Deja, did you get a sense of how Rayne is doing? I mean is she on drugs? Is she being beaten or anything?"

Deja thought a moment before answering. "I can't tell you any of that, Hennessy, but I got the sense that she was scared...but not for herself," she said.

"Was she scared for Daddy?" Hennessy asked.

"No. I got the feeling she was afraid for her son."

A stab of fear pierced Hennessy's heart. "They're threatening to hurt Ray Ray?"

Deja shrugged. "I don't know that for sure."

"If they touch one hair on my grandson's head—" Boozie railed between clenched teeth, his pacing renewed.

"Calm yourself, Boozie," It was Ivalou who spoke. "Let your son think through this."

This was the first time Hennessy had heard Deja's mamma speak. He was surprised to hear such a strong voice coming out of such a thin woman. Hennessy thought she must've been pretty once, but time, and maybe her illness, had draped ugly bags beneath her eyes and sucked in her cheeks. What he could now tell about the woman was that she had steel for a spine. His daddy's glare didn't faze her in the least. Instead, with one look, she managed to stop his angry rant. Hennessy had never seen anyone stop the moving train that was his daddy before.

"Go ahead, Hennessy," Ivalou urged. "What were you sayin'?"

Hennessy remembered what Deja had told him about her mamma's illness; how it made it appear as if she were drunk when her blood toxins were high. She appeared quite lucid at the moment and very cordial. "Thank you, ma'am," he acknowledged, "but I'm not sure I have any great ideas. I think it's obvious we need to keep a close eye on Ray Ray, though." His daddy nodded his agreement. "I also think we need to get movin' on the B&B restoration. Maybe all DeTron really wants is to get back on the gravy train. We won't know until he contacts you, Daddy or we open the place up."

"Or, I get a better connection with Rayne," Deja offered.

"Right." Hennessy nodded at her.

"But what about Rayne?" Boozie asked. "What if he plans to kill her?"

"If DeTron was going to kill her to get back at you, he would've done it already," Hennessy was thinking out loud. "So, I think we can rule that out. In the meantime, let's trust that Rayne knows how to take care of herself."

"What if he starts beatin' on her again?" Boozie persisted.

"As I recall, my sister gave back as good as she got," Hennessy smiled. "She split the man's head open with his own baseball bat to get out of there the last time, right?"

The thought finally broke through the intense frown on Boozie's face. "Yeah, she did."

"Maybe DeTron accepted your offer of getting a take on the B&B just to get rid of her."

"You think?"

Hennessy chuckled. "I don't know, but it might've helped open his mind up to the negotiation."

"Oh, now you got jokes, huh?" Boozie couldn't hide the smile that started and stopped and started again. "Let's get outta here and check on the boy. We gotta tell Lila what's goin' on, too." He walked over and gave Ivalou a peck on the cheek. "I'll see ya later, gal. Try'n be good."

"I will." Ivalou beamed under the attention.

Hennessy hesitated as he looked at Deja. He wasn't sure if he should give her the good-bye kiss waiting on his lips. What the hell? He thought. His daddy was bound to find out sometime. He kissed her thoroughly before following his daddy out to his truck.

Hennessy knew something would be said, but they were well on their way back to his mamma's house before Boozie spoke. "Deja's a good girl," he said plainly.

"I know," Hennessy said, feeling a little hurt that his daddy thought he needed to be told such a thing. "I've got a lot of respect for her."

Boozie looked over at him. "Respect ain't all you feel for her is it?' The question felt like an accusation.

"No," he admitted. "I like her a lot."

"I can see that. I see she likes you back, too."

Hennessy wished the man would get to whatever point he was trying to make. "Do you have a problem with us being together, Daddy?" Hennessy asked, probing the old man's eyes for the answer.

"Can't answer that, son," Boozie sighed. "Really don't know how I feel."

"I'm not going to hurt her," Hennessy offered, knowing that's what he feared.

"Now don't do that, son," Boozie wagged his head from side-to-side. "Don't go sayin' stuff you can't back up."

"I'm serious, Daddy. I already told her when I was done here, I'd be leaving again. She understands."

"And that makes it all right?" Boozie slammed his hand on the steering wheel. The truck swerved slightly on the road.

Surprised by his daddy' reaction, Hennessy could feel his own anger rising. "Yeah, it makes it all right. It always has before."

"Some women's meant for playin' and some's meant for stayin', Hennessy," Boozie was almost shouting now. "Deja's the kind that needs a man to stay with her. You willin' to do that?"

"I'm not willing to do that for anybody," Hennessy countered. "I'm not built for staying in one place too long. I need the road. I need my music."

"Then ya need to be a man and let that girl go right now!"

His daddy had never given him an ultimatum before and Hennessy didn't like it one bit. "Why should I listen to you?" he demanded. "You trying to say you did the right thing by letting Mamma go? You hurt her, Daddy, and she still isn't over it."

"I ain't talkin' 'bout me and yo mamma—"

"Why not? You know I'm right, don't you?" Hennessy knew he was crossing the line, but he couldn't stop. All the things he'd ever thought, but had never said to his daddy were coming out in a rush. "My heart breaks to see the way she looks at you whenever you're around—like some starving pup waitin' for you to throw her a damned bone. She pretends to be mad at you so you can't see how bad she hurts. You left her, Daddy. You left after you'd promised to be with her 'till death do us part.' You think that was right?"

Boozie stared stiffly out the windshield. "Yo mamma's doin' all right. She got married again."

"You know what Antoine is, same as I do," Hennessy let his anger cool down to a simmer. "He's the band-aid hiding her wounds. That's all he is and I'm pretty sure he knows it."

"If that's how you see things, that's all the more reason you should listen to me," Boozie said, his gaze still beyond the windshield.

"Why's that?"

"So's you don't make the same mistake, son."

Hennessy sighed and sank low in his seat. He and Deja were different people in different circumstances. Unlike his daddy, he wasn't making any promises he couldn't keep. Not a single one. "I don't intend to, Daddy," he said. "I don't intend to."

Deja traveled that night. Not because she felt Hennessy calling her or because she had the need to connect with him. In fact, the opposite was true. She wanted to distance herself from him emotionally, needed to. That afternoon, she'd gone from reeling over Hennessy the sex god to "slapping the hell out of him," as he'd said. The whole thing was really messing with her mind. She usually didn't get so agitated and it certainly wasn't like her to hit someone. What in the world was wrong with her?

She flew over the city, bypassing the places she normally visited and headed toward the other plane. She stopped herself just before exiting and decided to stay closer to home. Perching herself on the flatter part of St. Louis Cathedral's rooftop facing Jackson Square, she stared at the open area, listening to the sounds of the night.

Deja wanted to sit there and think about nothing, but she'd asked the question now and the answer to what had caused her behavior knocked on her brain, demanding to be acknowledged. She hadn't slapped Hennessy because he didn't believe in her gift, or because she'd thought he'd been mocking her when he'd closed his eyes. No. The real problem was that Hennessy had told her he wasn't planning on sticking around. He'd told her this in the car. He told her this after he'd played her body like one of his instruments and after he'd sent her soaring to the heavens. Her need for him was insatiable and knowing the feeling wasn't reciprocated was a problem. If she let this little romance play out for the next month or two—or however long he was planning to stay—the harder it would be to let him go.

"Deja?"

She started and swirled in a little circle above the rooftop. "Hennessy?"

"Where are you?" his voice shot across the distance and reverberated around her.

He was traveling—on purpose—and he was looking for her. "I'm here," Deja barely thought the thought and Hennessy appeared beside her.

Hennessy looked around and seemed amazed to find himself hovering above the cathedral's roof with her. He gave a curse. "This is unbelievable. I just thought about you and then…followed your voice here."

Her heart soared. Her aura shimmered. "Yeah. Easy, huh?"

"So what now?" he asked her. His eyes danced with excitement at his newfound ability. "What do we do next?"

Deja laughed. "What do you want to do?" *Wrap me up and send me soaring again?*

Hennessy's expression sobered. "I wanna find Rayne. Can you help me?"

For the briefest moment, she'd thought maybe he'd come for her. Deja shook off the thought. "I…I can try," she struggled to cover her disappointment, "but if she's not a traveler…I dunno…I've never tried to find someone who wasn't already out here."

"Well, would you try?" he asked.

Looking into his eyes in this plane was like seeing into his soul. Caring and love was there…for his sister. Deja couldn't refuse him though a part of her was so jealous she could hardly think. "Okay," she said. "We can try."

"Now, where did you see her?" He scanned the empty streets before them.

"I couldn't tell exactly where she was," Deja explained. "I just got a sense of it, you know? I could feel where she was more than see it."

"Oh," Hennessy looked confused. "Well, could you feel her now? I mean if you concentrated?"

"I dunno, Hennessy. I mean our bodies are already asleep." She settled into a cross-legged position and closed her eyes. "Sit."

He did as she instructed…sort of. Was a person really sitting when they were hanging out on nothing but air? He couldn't manage the cross-legged thing, so just perched on the blue roof with his elbows on his knees. Not that his arms and legs felt real here. The whole thing was a little freaky.

They sat for long moments before Deja spoke again. "This isn't working," she said rising from the rooftop. She couldn't focus on anything with Hennessy being so close. "I can't find her."

"Do we have to sit?" he asked joining her in the night sky. "Can't we just…you know…fly around or something?"

"Sure, but…" Explaining how things worked here was difficult. "It's not like we're seeing the city in real time, you know?"

Hennessy shook his head. "No."

"It's like we see the world in a mirror, but it's only populated with a few of us."

"The ones who travel at night?"

"Exactly," Deja said. "We think things and they happen in the blink of an eye. The only things you find in this plane is other people who are looking."

"Why do we travel?" he asked. "I mean, what are we looking for?"

Deja stared at him for a long time, wondering why she'd never thought to ask that question. "I dunno, Hennessy. I think we're all looking for something different."

"What are you looking for?" The gold around his eyes intensified as he looked into her soul.

Surely he could see the answer. It had to be written all over her. All this time she'd been traveling she'd been looking for him. She knew it now, felt it in every part of her being. Even tonight, she'd convinced herself she needed to disconnect from him. Had she known somehow he'd come looking for her?

"Well?" he asked.

"I'm looking for something I don't think I'll ever have," she answered honestly feeling sadness creep coldly into her being. "I just can't seem to stop wanting it."

"What?" he pressed.

She was so tempted to tell him, just to lay it out on the line. But she couldn't bring herself to tell him all she wanted was his undying love and devotion. How do you tell someone that without losing your self-respect? Especially after the person has made it clear it ain't gonna happen? "It doesn't matter," she finally answered.

"What's that?" Hennessy spun in a tight circle.

"I didn't hear anything," Deja said.

Hennessy took off flying and Deja followed.

"What did you hear?" she asked.

"I thought I heard Rayne. I thought I heard her crying." He stopped abruptly and hovered over a street in St. Bernard Parish. "There it is again." He cocked his head to listen.

Deja couldn't hear a thing. "Wha—?"

Hennessy raised a hand to stop her. He strained to listen. "Did she say, Tron or Twon?"

The question wasn't meant for her and for the first time, Deja felt helpless. Usually she was the one who heard things no one else could. Was it possible that Hennessy was a bit psychic?

He took off flying again. This time he was low to the ground, checking out houses along the streets.

"What're you looking for?" Deja asked. "I told you we can't find someone who's not traveling."

"But I heard her, Deja," Hennessy shot over his shoulder as he searched wildly around the houses. "She was talking to somebody…she was crying."

"I don't think it's possible you heard her," she said to him.

He pulled up short and glared at her. "I don't believe this," he spat. "Why isn't it possible? Because you didn't hear it?"

That was exactly why, but Deja realized how egotistical it sounded. "Sorry. I didn't mean—"

"It doesn't matter," Hennessy sighed. "I lost her again."

His eyes continued to scan the neighborhood. "Wait a minute." He frowned. "What's going on here?"

Deja looked around. "What do you mean?"

"All of these houses are intact. It's like the hurricane never blew through here, but I know it did. I know most of these houses are destroyed."

"I know, but time and reality don't exist here, Hennessy. That's why you can't trust everything you see and hear."

"All right, well…" His shoulders sagged. "I guess there's nothing to do but get back then."

Deja could think of something to do and she dared him to look her in the eyes to see it.

But he didn't look. "How do I get back?" he asked.

"I'll show you," she said. She hoped she'd still be able to fly given how heavy her heart was feeling. "Follow me."

Chapter Thirteen

Something had changed and Hennessy didn't like it. Deja was going out of her way to avoid him—but for the life of him he couldn't figure out why. At first Deja gave him polite excuses not to spend time with him—she had to take care of her mamma or run errands. But last night she'd all but slammed the trailer door in his face. Maybe he'd been a little presumptuous to tell her he'd booked a hotel for them to use that night, but damn—he'd never seen a sistah get so mad.

Hennessy had taken to traveling on his own at night, had actually gotten quite good at getting around, but he missed Deja. And, he hadn't heard Rayne's voice again so his trips had been for nothing.

"Better watch what ya doin', son," his daddy warned.

Hennessy caught the blob of plaster before it hit the floor. He plopped the white paste back onto the trowel, wiped his hand on his jeans. He went back to sealing the drywall while cursing under his breath.

"Ya all right there, Hen?" Teardrop stood up and stretched his back. He'd built a new bar for the Blues 'N Booze, a beautiful mahogany one that he was now painstakingly engraving with a bold African theme. Hennessy couldn't remember the man being happier. "Ya got Californy on yer mind?"

"A bit," Hennessy answered honestly. He'd gotten several calls from Jack and Johnnie. Apparently, Terry Pryce had gone back on the junk and they were having a hard time keeping him sober enough to play. They wanted to know when the Trio would be playing gigs in New Orleans.

He looked around the bar. They'd made amazing progress in the three weeks he'd been here. New walls were up, the wood floor had been replaced and the doors and windows were repaired. Once the bar was done, the walls painted and the liquor re-stocked they should be ready to open. "Whaddya think, Daddy?" he asked. "We gonna make the grand opening the first week in March?"

"Heck yeah," Boozie acknowledged proudly. There was a smile on his face, but the heavy bags beneath his eyes betrayed how tired he was. Hennessy knew his daddy spent more time worrying about Rayne than he did anything else, including sleeping.

"You got that song I asked you for?" Boozie asked quietly.

"'Lovin' Hard'?"

"Mm hm."

"I got it," Hennessy said. "I brought you the CD."

"Naw. That won't do." Boozie shook his head. "Need a live band to play it. Need it fer openin' night."

"Perfect," Hennessy jumped on the opportunity. "I told Deja the Trio is available in March. We'll play it opening night and stay a couple of weeks if you like."

Boozie smiled and patted his son on the shoulder. "I'd be honored, son. Thank you. I'll check with my new manager to see who else she's got booked. I think she said she was calling on the Marsalis boys, too. They don't play the Blues, but nowadays any music we can push out the door is good."

"That'd be great, Daddy." Hennessy had met Wynton and Branford a year or so ago when the Trio had to stay over to open for them one night. They'd had a few beers after. It'd been good times. And to have anyone named Marsalis playing in his daddy's bar would add immediate notoriety to the fact the Blues 'N Booze was reopening and impress the hell out of Jack and Johnnie. He started to tell this to his daddy but the way the old man's eyes narrowed as he stared toward the front door stopped Hennessy.

Earl had walked in—barely. His feet were exactly one step inside the threshold and his hand gripped the door handle as if he was preparing for a quick getaway. He squeaked something, cleared his throat then tried again. "Boozie? Can I speak with you?"

"Yer not welcome in the B&B, Earl. I thought we was straight on that," Boozie barked.

"I know. I won't come in any further." Earl looked so unsteady it seemed a stiff wind would blow him over. "It's important."

The way he said it sent shivers of dread up Hennessy's spine. His daddy must've sensed the same thing, because he didn't pull out his gun and send him running.

"Come on back to the office," Boozie turned and headed that way.

Earl followed quickly, carefully avoiding Hennessy's gaze as he passed by.

Hennessy looked over at Teardrop. "What you make of that?" he asked.

"Whatever he's here for," Teardrop said, "It ain't good. Yo daddy tell ya he was stealin' from him?"

Hennessy shook his head. "Is that why he made Deja the new manager?"

"Yep." Teardrop went back to his carving. He was three quarters of the way around the huge bar. The piece would be a beauty once he had it all finished and stained. "I 'spect it ain't his old job he's after though. He got on with a friend of yo step-father's and been making good money. Good enough to get out that gov'ment trailer he used to have parked out back."

Hennessy remembered Earl leaving the week after he'd gotten back. It hadn't hurt his feelings in the least to have him gone. Every time he remembered how he'd left his sister naked and cold on his bathroom floor, he wanted to beat the hell out of him. He lathed more plaster on his trowel and was about to apply it when he heard loud thumps against the wall of his daddy's office.

Dropping the tool, he ran over to the door. "Daddy?" he shouted. He pushed open the heavy new door in time to see his father on top of the younger man, pounding his fist into Earl's pale brown face.

Hennessy winced, feeling a little sorry for Earl when the blood spurted from his mouth. "What happened?" he asked his dad.

Boozie cursed and lifted himself off the other man. "He tole me if I wanted to see my daughter agin…I'd best be sellin' the bar."

"Sell? To who? To him?"

"Man name of Cardoroy Humphrey—owns a property development company." Boozie's fist shook. Obviously he was trying to hold back another punishing blow.

"What's Humphrey got to do with Rayne?" Hennessy demanded of Earl who cowered on the floor, his arms prepared to block another punch.

"He…he's tryin' to buy up all kind of property 'round here 'cause the owners can't rebuild. He wants this block, startin' with the B&B."

"The B&B ain't for sale," Boozie shouted and landed a punch in Earl's side.

Hennessy had read about developers who were trying to get property under Eminent Domain—meaning the owners had abandoned the land. But that wasn't the case here. "You go tell this Humphrey that the B&B is being rebuilt—and so's the rest of the block. We'll call the police if he doesn't let my sister go," Hennessy threatened.

"I told him you wouldn't go for it, Boozie. I swear I did," Earl said.

"Let him up, Daddy," Hennessy helped his father off of Earl. They needed a lot more information and they wouldn't get it if the man was unconscious. "What's your role in all this?"

Earl pulled himself to a sitting position and pressed the back of his hand to his bleeding lip. "I'm just the messenger, Hennessy, man. That's all."

"What's this Humphrey guy got to do with Rayne?"

"The way I heard it" Earl pushed himself unsteadily to a standing position, "she went lookin' for a good time one night and ran into the man."

Hennessy planted a right hook across his jaw. "That's for disrespectin' my sister." He resented how he'd made it sound like she was nothing more than a hooker. "Now, tell me the rest and be careful how you talk about Rayne. Have you seen her?"

"Yeah, man," Earl said irritably, obviously growing tired of being beaten.

"Is she all right?"

"Yeah. DeTron only hits her if she tries to get on her cell or if she tries to leave." Earl leaned back over the desk a little, anticipating how upset Hennessy and Boozie would be at that news.

"DeTron, he's with her?" Hennessy asked.

"He's beatin' her?" Boozie asked at the same time.

Earl's Adam's apple bobbed up and down in his throat as he nodded. "Once or twice." He held up his hands. "But mostly they threaten to hurt little Ray Ray if she tries to call anybody."

"So why're you mixed up in all this" Hennessy asked.

Earl shrugged his thin shoulders. "Yo step-daddy, Mr. Ellis, tole me 'bout this job with Humphrey. I was telling him how I needed a job— but not just any job, you know? He said he knew 'bout a job that paid very well—you know so a brothah can live to the standard to which he's become accustomed and all that."

"This Humphrey fella got a till for you to steal from, too?" Boozie shot out sarcastically.

Earl frowned. "He told me I would be the front man for some of their real estate deals. Tole me I'd get commissions for makin' things happen. Sounded pretty good to me—like it was right up my alley. I did a couple deals for 'em last week and then this week…they asked me to come talk to you, Boozie. But, I had no idea till just yesterday they had Rayne."

"Where're they keeping her?" Hennessy demanded, growing angrier by the second at what a weak excuse for a man Earl was. "What's the address?"

"I…I can't tell you that," Earl said quietly. "I don't know."

"You just said you saw her!" Boozie shouted, grabbing the man by his shirt. "Tell the truth fore I beat it outta ya."

Earl swallowed hard. "They brought her out to a restaurant, that's where I saw here. They never tole me where they was keeping her."

Cursing a blue streak of profanity, Boozie released Earl and shoved him against the desk. "This don't make any kinda sense," he said, turning in a tight, frustrated circle. "How does this man know anything about me, about my bar, or about my daughter and Ray Ray? It's like the whole damn thing is a setup."

"I dunno, Daddy." Hennessy shook his head. Things weren't adding up. "Looks like DeTron had something to do with this." Which meant Deja had been right.

"He's just watchin' over Rayne," Earl clarified. "Her and Mr. Humphrey," he added, "Like he's their bodyguard or somethin'."

This whole thing was surreal. Hennessy couldn't believe his ears. "So, what now?" he asked his daddy. "You wanna find out where this Cordoray Humphrey is living? I'm sure the police can find him."

"If you call the police, Mr. Humphrey says…he'll kill Rayne," Earl said quietly.

"You think he'll do it?" Hennessy asked Earl.

The man nodded. "DeTron and his fellas got some serious fire power, man."

Boozie stared at the walls, his breathing coming quicker, his eyes welled with tears. "Earl, you tell Humphrey…" he began and stopped. "You tell him…he can have the damn bar."

"What?" Hennessy felt a crack in the universe. "No, Daddy. You need to think about this before—"

Boozie held up a hand. "This damn place ain't brought me nothing but grief since I bought it." His voice was thick with emotion. "It's high time I'm rid of it." With that, he rushed out of the office and then out of the bar.

Earl's hazel eyes went wide as saucers as he watched a tortured Boozie Walker leave the Blues 'N Booze. "I'll be John Brown," he said awestruck. "I uh…I gotta tell Mr. Humphrey he said yes," he said making his way out the office and through the bar. "Tell Boozie I'll call with the offer, hear?" He was racing toward his black Lexus a moment later.

Teardrop asked dropping his tools and stepping over to where Hennessey stood dumbfounded in the middle of the bar. "What's goin' on, Hen? What's that no good Earl up to?"

Hennessy couldn't speak. It was as like a bad Hollywood movie where he'd just been told the world was coming to an end and nothing that anyone could do would stop it. His daddy without the Blues 'N Booze? Rayne being held hostage? It was a damn nightmare.

He pushed his fingers through the thick roots of his hair and looked around at the walls, at the floors, at the windows. It was still here—magic. He'd felt it again when he'd first stepped inside as a child and felt the music that lived inside the walls. This place had been a constant in his life, the place he'd been most comfortable. The place he'd felt the most joy. The B&B had been his school, the artists who'd played here had been his teachers, and jamming onstage with them had been his playground.

Now, everything was going to change. And for what? Because some no-account man was trying to hustle his daddy. Someone who'd obviously thought pretty long and hard about the best way to make it happen.

Not Earl. He was exactly what he'd said—a front man. The man didn't have enough brains to think of this plan. It could be this Humphrey guy, but Hennessy didn't think it made any sense for a complete stranger to resort to kidnapping a woman to leverage a business deal. No. This was a personal attack.

Who hated his daddy this much?

DeTron? Again, it didn't seem to be the man's style, plus he appeared to be taking orders the same as Earl. That left one last name that Earl had mentioned—Antoine Ellis.

The thought made Hennessy's eyebrows lift. Was his father-in-law the brains behind all this? Did he really hate Daddy that much?

"Hennessy?" Teardrop stood directly in front of him now, his hands folded across his chest, an irritated look on his weathered face. "Son, you gonna tell me what's goin' on or do I have to put my foot up your behind? Don't think that I can't do it just 'cause you're bigger'n me."

"Sorry, Teardrop. I'll tell you the whole story, but first, what do you know about Antoine Ellis?"

"A bit. Why? He got something to do with what's goin' on?"

Nodding, Hennessy took to staring out the door again. "I think so. Tell me what you know about him…and start from the beginning."

Something didn't feel right, but Deja couldn't figure out what. She looked up from the schedule she was making on her computer and stared out the big window in their small living room for the fifth time that hour.

"What's wrong, baby?" Ivalou looked up from her crocheting. "You been starin' out that window all day."

"How would you know?" Deja smiled at her mamma. "Every few minutes, you nod out and start snoring. It'll be a miracle if you ever finish that thing you're making."

"This new medicine the doctor gave me makes me tired," Ivalou said simply, not stopping her handiwork. Jazmeen had taken to napping in her lap every chance she got. The two of them seemed to be hitting it off nicely. "And I'm making a nice runner for the table we'll have when we move back in our house."

"You sure are optimistic," Deja said, looking out the window once again. She halfway expected to see someone arrive—but she didn't know who. "It could be months before Boozie and his crew finish our house and we move in."

Ivalou peered over her reading glasses. "And you don't think I'll be around that long?" she asked quietly.

Realizing her error, Deja quickly apologized. "I didn't mean that, Mamma. I just meant the way you're going it'll take you a year to finish."

Sighing, Ivalou put down the needle and the thin yarn. "We should talk about this, Deja. I'm dying, baby and that isn't a secret to either one of us."

"Right," Deja acknowledged sadly. "So what's to talk about?"

"Not a lot," she said. "Just a couple of important things I think you ought to know."

"Like what?"

Ivalou pulled the glasses from her nose and looked her daughter straight in the eyes. "Like how proud I am of you."

The words went straight to Deja's heart where they overwhelmed her. Mamma had never been sentimental at all, so she didn't know quite how to respond.

"You're a remarkable woman and you've taken better care of me than I have of you," her mamma continued. "I regret that, but can't do much about it. I have a very good life insurance policy that should help you get back on your feet when I pass."

Deja was horrified. "I don't want money, Mamma. I'd much rather have you."

"And I'd rather stay here, believe me. But, not like this." She waved her hands wearily over her slight frame. "I've made a mess of myself, Dejanette. I'm just eternally grateful God saw fit to keep me from makin' a mess of you."

"Oh, Mamma." Deja let the tears spill freely from her eyes as she went over to hug the older woman. A startled Jazmeen leapt to the floor. "I love you," Deja whispered. She couldn't remember ever telling her mother that before and it felt good to finally get her feelings out in the open. "I'm gonna miss you so much when you leave."

"Me too, baby," Ivalou also wept.

They held each other for a long while. When it started to get uncomfortable, Deja pulled away. "I guess I'd better get back to work," she announced.

"Maybe you should take a break from work," Ivalou suggested. "You've been cooped up in here for days. Why don't you go over and see that handsome Hennessy. He seems to brighten your day."

Deja would like nothing better than to see Hennessy, but she'd made a decision—she was giving him up. She'd decided the night they'd last met traveling and had been keeping away from him like a bad drug ever since. "I have to make sure I've got bands booked for the next three months, Mamma. I don't want Boozie to think he's made the wrong decision making me the manager of the B&B. The little bit of money I'm getting from the paper for my columns won't help ends meet when the government money dries up."

"Boozie'd never think that," she said, dismissing the thought. "So how's it going? You finding some good bands still in town?"

"Some," Deja acknowledged. "But, most of them aren't big names."

"Are they any good?" Ivalou wrinkled her nose. "You don't wanna open up with bad bands."

"Actually, I've made a couple of really good finds." Deja warmed to the subject and stuck a CD in her laptop. "Listen to this."

"Heyyyy," Ivalou smiled and swayed in time to the slow, soulful Blues song. "This here's all right." She closed her eyes and snapped her fingers. "Reminds me of the old days."

"If you think they're good, listen to this one." Deja exchanged CDs and a livelier Blues beat resounded in the trailer.

"I like the vocalist on this one," Ivalou offered. "She's got a rich voice."

"I agree," Deja sat back in her chair satisfied. "I've booked each band for a month and I have some smaller groups opening for them."

"What about your Grand Opening, though, baby?" her mamma asked. "That's the most important."

"I agreed to let Hennessy's Whiskey Sins Trio play." Deja looked out the window again.

"Are they any good?"

"Pretty good."

"Well, let's hear 'em," the older woman insisted. "You know Boozie asked me to be his date opening night. I want to know what I'll be dancing to."

She didn't want to be reminded of Hennessy, his beautiful voice or his beautiful song, but she knew if she didn't play it, her mamma would know something was up. The last thing she needed was to have her prying into her personal business. Reluctantly, Deja slid in the CD Hennessy had given her the day she'd visited with Booze at the B&B.

And there it was, "Lovin' Hard," the best song on the disc. Deja recalled the way she'd felt when she'd first heard it. She'd known Hennessy had written it just for her and she'd been wrapped up in his love, life and music that night they'd traveled. She closed her eyes and indulged in the feeling once more of soaring in the heavens with him. She knew back then that she'd never get enough of him.

When they'd made love here, when he'd moved inside her, she'd felt whole and connected to him like no other person on earth. The thought made her ache for him and she was grateful he was nowhere around for her to act on her feelings.

"I like this song," Ivalou said from across the room. "And Hennessy…well his voice is sexy as hell for a little boy, isn't it?"

Deja could feel her eyes piercing her, prying for the truth. "Yeah, Mamma. He's got a very sexy voice, but he's hardly a little boy."

"I suppose you'd know about that." Ivalou gave her a devilish smile. "So, why're you avoiding him? You slammed the door in his face so hard yesterday I thought you were mad at him."

"I didn't slam the door, Mamma. The wind caught it," Deja lied. The truth was, she'd had a sudden desire to throw herself into his arms and slamming the door was the only other option she could think of at the time. "I just told him I had things to do."

"Which was a damn lie," Ivalou called her out. "What're you afraid of, baby?"

Deja sighed in frustration. "You're not going to be happy unless you're all up in my business, huh?"

"I have nothing else to keep me happy," she acknowledged. "So, out with it."

"Fine. If you must know, I'm not avoiding him. I'm just trying to keep my distance, that's all."

Ivalou looked at her like she was crazy. "What's the difference?"

"The difference is that I can't avoid him. We have to see each other. The closer to Grand Opening time, the more we'll have to work together. I'm just making sure he knows we can't be—physical anymore."

"What's the fun in that?"

"Mamma!" Deja was hardly a prude, but her mother always seemed to cross the lines she thought weren't supposed to be crossed between a mother and daughter.

Ivalou persisted. "Why don't you want to have sex with him anymore? Is he bad in bed?"

Deja felt herself warm with embarrassment. "No. He's leaving."

"Ahh." A look of realization dawned on Ivalou's face. "I see."

"What do you see?" Deja demanded, irritated that she'd been forced to confess her secret.

"That you don't wanna get hurt," Ivalou said with a shrug.

"Is something wrong with that?"

"No," Ivalou said unconvincingly.

"I know what you're thinking," Deja rose from her chair. "You think I need to loosen up and live in the moment, right? Just enjoy him while he's here."

Ivalou let a slow, wicked smile curve her thin lips. "That's the way I always played it—fast and loose."

"I know," Deja blew out a breath wishing she felt more comfortable living in the moment instead of planning out everything. "I should be more spontaneous."

"But then again," Ivalou added, "Fast and loose has left me sick and tired. I ain't hardly recommendin' it," she teased.

Deja stared at her, trying to figure out what she meant. "So, I shouldn't take advantage of him while he's here?"

Her mamma laughed. "I'm the last person you should take advice from, baby. I'm afraid you're gonna have to make up your own heart on this one."

"Great," Deja said, letting her hands fall to her side as she stared out the window once again. Her heart was just as confused as her head where Hennessy was concerned.

"Tell you what," Ivalou rose from the couch. "Let's get outta here for a while."

"Where do you wanna go?"

"Take me to the B&B. I wanna see how it's coming along."

"But Hennessy's there," Deja argued.

"Your problem, baby. Not mine." Her mamma slid out of her house shoes and put on her low heels. "You coming?" she asked opening the door.

"Looks like I have no choice," Deja answered following her. "But you can't stay long."

"I know, I know." Ivalou waved an impatient hand. "We'll be back before my medicine wears off."

"Would you look at that?" Ivalou said as they drove up to the Blues 'N Booze. There was a beehive of activity when Deja and Ivalou reached it around dusk. The neighbors had gotten off of their day jobs and had now assembled to put the finishing touches on the resurrected bar.

Several people were clearing trash from around the yard and throwing it in huge dumpsters. Others were re-grouting some loose bricks while others rinsed paintbrushes and rollers. Sister Alveta Flowers had cooked dinner for the entire crew once again. She figured the food at the makeshift grocery store they'd created at the church was put to good use in this endeavor.

Three huge pots of Gumbo and the remainder of two pans of corn-bread was laid out on long tables in the middle of the street. Young men and women whose T-shirts proclaimed them students of Tulane, were putting away healthy bowlfuls of the stew and smiling as Sister Alveta and her niece, Pam, pulled two cakes out of the backseat of a car.

"Looks like we're in time for Sister's famous 7-UP cake," Ivalou said walking over to greet the woman. "How you doin' today, Sister?" she called out to the woman.

Deja's eyes stopped on a lone figure standing just to the side of the table, staring at the activity as if he hadn't seen it every day for the past few weeks. He made a striking figure with his wide stance and broad shoulders silhouetted by the red-orange sky on the horizon. Despite his paint-splattered shirt and jeans, Hennessy was easily the best looking man in all of New Orlean's parishes. At least, that was Deja's opinion.

Still, he looked stiff, almost rigid. Once again she got the sense of something being out of sorts. Despite her decision to keep him at arm's length, she walked up beside him and touched him gently on the shoulder. "The B&B is looking good," she said. "Why're you lookin' so down?"

He turned his amazing gold-rimmed brown eyes in her direction. She saw pain there and disappointment.

"What's wrong?" she asked.

"What isn't?" he said sourly. "Look at this." He spread his arms wide to take in the entire scent. "My daddy did this. He brought all these people together and sold them a dream. A dream of rebuilding a better New Orleans for themselves and look at what they've done?"

"I think it's great, don't you?" Deja countered not understanding his bad mood.

"I do. It's great." His voice held wonder. "But I can't find the words to tell them the dream is over. That it's dead."

"What are you talking about, Hennessy?"

He proceeded to tell her what Earl had told him and his daddy only hours before. That Rayne and maybe Ray Ray's lives depended upon the sale of the B&B to some man named Humphrey.

"Did you call the police?" Deja asked. "That's kidnapping. That's extortion. We can't let this happen."

"We call the police and Rayne gets killed," Hennessy offered soberly. "Whatever we do, we won't get a second chance at it."

"Where's Boozie?" Deja looked toward the bar. "What's he think?"

"He's letting the man have the bar. Said it's caused him nothing but trouble since he bought it."

"He can't mean that." Deja saw too many things unraveling if Boozie gave in to the demands of this man. She wouldn't have a job, but more than that, the hope of the community would die and they'd all lose their houses. "We've got to think of something."

"I've been trying." Hennessy frowned when he looked at her again. "It surprises me you want to help at all since you've been giving me the cold shoulder lately. I got the feeling you don't want anything to do with me anymore. Am I wrong?"

It was more challenge than question. If she was going to make do without him, now was the time to tell him. But looking into his eyes, seeing the hurt and knowing she was only going to cause more pain was so hard. *Broken heart now—broken heart later,* she chanted to herself.

Broken heart now, she decided. She had to get it over with and stop agonizing over him. "I'm sorry, Hennessy…" she struggled to find the words.

His frown deepened.

"I…I think we should end things now…before they get too serious. But that doesn't mean we can't work together. And I'll do whatever I can to help you find Rayne," she offered, hoping to salvage some part of their relationship.

"That's the biggest load of bull—" The last of his words died in the wind. "I don't believe this, Deja. You of all people, I didn't expect to play this game. You're gonna deny me sex hoping I'll give in and make a long-term commitment."

"I don't want anybody who doesn't want me. Who do you—" His palm nearly hit her nose as he pushed it in her face.

"I don't have time for this," he said, storming off toward the bar.

Deja crossed her arms and fumed. "Egotistical jackass," she hissed.

"You told him, didn't you?" her mamma was moving to her side.

Deja nodded, "Okay, so maybe I could've picked a day when he wasn't already kissing the concrete, but I didn't think he'd take it so hard."

"Any man with an ego takes rejection pretty hard, baby. Now that it's done, all you can do is wait."

"Wait for what?"

"For him to come after you."

"I wouldn't take him back after that." Deja knew it was a lie, but it felt good saying it out loud.

"'Course not, baby. Why would you?" her mamma's tone was patronizing.

"Great," Deja folded her arms in disappointment. "Take his side."

"Do me a favor, Deja," Ivalou patted her daughter's arm. "Don't beat him away with a stick like I did Boozie. Learn something from your mamma's mistakes, all right?"

"What're you talking about, Mamma? Boozie didn't stay away. He'd still have you if you let him," Deja said, wondering if the thought had ever occurred to her.

Ivalou smiled. It was a smile that reached her eyes and filled the hollows of her cheeks. "I don't deserve that man's love," she said. "Never did. But, I'm keeping him away for his own good now. Not mine."

"But you're like best friends. You can talk about anything," Deja argued. "Besides, right now, I think he may need you more than you need him."

Ivalou frowned. "I seriously doubt that."

"No, really. I think he does," Deja argued. "Get in the car. I'll tell you on the way to his house." Deja told, or Deja filled her she'd heard from Hennessy. In less than ten minutes they reached Boozie's house, which was being repaired in tandem with the B&B. But not this evening. Only one lone truck was parked in the drive beside the house.

Deja and Ivalou knocked and rang the bell, but there was no answer. Closing her eyes, Deja put a hand to the door of the house, trying to get a feel for if he'd done harm to himself.

"You feel something, baby?" Ivalou paced the front porch anxiously.

"He's not dead," she offered.

"That's something," Ivalou said. "But why won't he answer?"

They continued banging on the door and calling his name. Finally, he opened the door. Boozie swayed a bit on his feet in the opening. He wore only a white T-shirt and a pair of shorts and a skewed smile. He was clearly drunk. "Heyyyy. Day-zha. How you doin I.V. Lou?" He motioned for them to enter. "I'm havin' a drink. You wanna drink?" he asked as he stumbled toward the living room table. He captured the half-empty bottle of Jack

Daniels in one shaky hand and tried to pour the liquid into the glass held in the other.

"Let me have that, Boozie." Ivalou walked over and took the bottle and glass from his hand. She sniffed the bottle and closed her eyes appreciatively. "Hello, Jack," she said reverently. "I sure have missed you."

"You gonna drink it or you gonna shpeak to it?" Boozie asked, seconds before falling backwards onto the couch.

Deja also worried about what her mamma's intentions were toward that liquor bottle. "Mamma—"

Ivalou gave her a look. "I can't drink this stuff, Boozie. You know that."

"Well, here." He held out his arms unsteadily to take the objects from her hands.

"You've had enough," she told him and walked the bottle into the kitchen.

Deja couldn't see it, but she suspected her mamma was pouring the liquor down the sink.

"I.V.Lou you bring dat back here now," he hollered, making no attempt to rise from the couch. "I'm havin'a bad day."

"Tell you what, sweetheart," she said sweetly from the kitchen. "Why don't I make you a cup of coffee and you put on your jamas and tell me all about it?"

Deja wondered how many times she'd heard Boozie tell her mamma that exact thing over the years. Clearly he was in no condition to talk to her about what could be done to save Rayne and his club. The most sober man she'd ever known was completely tanked and it saddened her. He'd made his choice. He'd chosen to save Rayne, but it was clear the thought of losing the Blues 'N Booze was eating him alive.

Ivalou came out of the kitchen and took Boozie's hand. "Come on, big guy. Let's get you in bed." He struggled to his feet and threw an arm over her thin shoulders.

Deja was sure the woman would buckle under the weight, but somehow she managed to steer him toward his bedroom.

"Dejanette," she looked back at her daughter. "Bring me my medicine. Looks like I'll be stayin' over tonight."

Chapter Fourteen

Hennessy sat in Rayne's car staring at the house his mamma lived in with Antoine Ellis. Teardrop said Antoine had come to town when he was about twenty. He was from Los Angeles originally and used to tell stories about his life in a gang. Teardrop couldn't remember which one, but knew it was one of the worst ones in the city at the time.

Antoine used to tell everyone how he rose to the top after several members had died and he'd managed to survive three years without getting thrown in Juvenile Detention. He'd taught the other kids how to run numbers, sell drugs and kill other gang members without getting caught by the police. Apparently, he'd been forced out of the city one night when a rival gang came into their turf and did multiple drive-bys. He got out with the clothes on his back and several thousand dollars he'd managed to keep stashed.

He went legit in New Orleans, starting his own car wash business with the money he had on him. It had been widely rumored at the time that he'd used means, both legitimate and illegitimate, to build his small fortune. It was a matter of public record that Antoine Ellis sold the car washes and Laundromats just ten days before Katrina hit. He'd told his wife he was retiring.

Hennessy was convinced his mamma had no idea what kind of snake she was married to otherwise she'd have been long gone. His own dilemma was how did he go back in to this house knowing what he knew now? Should he confront Antoine directly and ask what he'd done with Rayne? Should he ask him up front why he was stealing his daddy's bar out from under him?

The curtain of the front window lifted and Ray Ray peeked out. His little face lit up when he saw his uncle and he waved and bounced up and down. He could tell the boy was shouting, making no secret to the people inside the house that he was there.

Hennessy exited the car. He'd just play it by ear where Antoine was concerned. The front door opened when he was halfway down the sidewalk. His mamma bustled out in a colorful orange and yellow outfit.

"Hi, baby," she kissed and hugged him. "I'm off to play cards with the ladies. I made some dinner. I think Antoine and Ray Ray left you some. I'll see you in a few hours." She waved and headed down the street as Ray Ray jumped on his uncle's leg.

Clutching denim, the little boy chanted. "Hen-see, Hen-see, Hen-see."

Hennessy lifted his nephew and gave him a kiss on the cheek. "How you doin', man? You get your grub on?"

"Yep." The three-year-old gave an exaggerated nod.

"Didya save me some?" he asked as they entered the house.

"Yep." Ray Ray slid out of his arms and tugged on his hand. "C'mon. I'll show you, Uncle Hen-see."

Hennessy eyed Antoine who was slumped comfortably on the couch watching *CSI.* "How you doin, 'Twon?"

"Good, good," the old man said, scratching his thin belly. "Jus watchin' the show here."

"All right," Hennessy nodded and let his nephew lead him down the hallway to the kitchen, although he wasn't really hungry. He thought about racing back into the living room and punching the man's face in and asking him where the hell he got off kidnapping his sister and threatening his daddy's livelihood, but the truth was, the man looked harmless. He never said much, never did anything to call attention to himself and Hennessy wondered if he'd just been frontin' the whole time he'd been married.

Hennessy ate dinner, talked with Ray Ray and cleared his dishes before heading back to the living room. Antoine was still on the couch watching TV, which was highly unusual. By now, the man was usually fast asleep, either on the couch or in his bed. "It's about time for you to be in bed, isn't it old man?" he fished, hoping the question sounded casual.

"Yeah. Guess it's that time all right." The old man checked his watch and sat up as if he was going to bed. "Say, how's yo daddy's club comin' along?" he asked.

Hennessy felt the hairs on the back of his neck go up. Not once had Antoine Ellis ever asked about the progress of the B&B or anything else he'd been doing. He decided to tell him the truth about what happened today to see how he responded. "It's goin' all right, but something bad happened today."

"'S'that right?" Antoine moved closer to the edge of the couch, seeming very interested. "What happened?"

"The man who kidnapped Rayne sent Earl in to talk with us. You remember Earl don't you?"

Antoine pretended to be racking his memory. "He's the fella used to run the place for your daddy, ain't he?"

Hennessy nodded. "He came in and said he's working for some guy named Humphrey. He said Rayne's being held hostage and won't be let go unless Daddy agrees to sell the bar to him."

"That don't seem right," Antoine offered without emotion. "Did ya call the police?"

"Naw. The bas—, the man said he'd kill Rayne if the police were brought in."

"So what's Boozie gonna do?" he asked a little too anxiously.

This is what he wanted to know, Hennessy decided. He was trying to see if his dad was truly going along with the plan. "He's gonna sell the bar to the man. I can't believe it, but he's gonna do it."

Antoine gave a nod and rose to his feet. "Sounds like the best thing to do. You don't wanna tangle with them big-time developers. Seems like they got the city government in they back pockets."

"You think he's a developer?" Hennessy asked, knowing he'd left that detail out of the story.

Antoine stopped short. "Isn't he? I jus figured he was."

221

"If he is, it doesn't make sense," Hennessy pressed. "Why would he stoop to kidnapping Rayne to get what he wants? If he's got the city on his side, he could do something political instead of something so personal."

Antoine shrugged. "Don't know, boy. Either way, I wouldn't tangle with him."

"I told Daddy not to do it," Hennessy said, testing the waters.

Antoine stopped once again. "Why you tell him a fool thing like that?"

"I think the man's bluffing," Hennessy challenged, staring straight into his stepfather's eyes.

His eyes were bright, sharp and black as the night. His brown face paled and his lips drew up into a tight thin line. "What if he ain't?"

"No legitimate businessman would risk his reputation to commit murder," he said quietly.

Antoine's eyes narrowed and his voice was barely above a whisper. "You want your sister to die, Hennessy?" It wasn't a question. It was a threat.

Hennessy shot across the room and grabbed Antoine's shirt in tight fists. "Where is she?" he demanded.

The older man didn't flinch, just stared straight into Hennessy's eyes. "That ain't something I need to know," he said, through clenched, crooked teeth. "Now, what you want to ask yourself, boy, is do you really wanna wake up Ray Ray by having me shoot you?" He gave a nod to the child who'd fallen asleep in the chair.

He felt something hard pressing into his gut. "You wouldn't dare," Hennessy attempted bravely.

"You don't think so?" Antoine's voice was cold, steady. "Man has a right to protect himself in his own home. The police usually go for that excuse…'specially when they don't have time to investigate shit."

Hennessy wanted nothing more but to beat the man down with his bare hands right then. But, that didn't help him find his sister or protect his family.

"Fine," he acquiesced, releasing the man. "But Rayne had better be with you when my daddy signs the deed over."

"You don't give me orders, boy. She'll be there if I say so," Antoine spat, letting his weapon drop slowly to his side. "I'm goin' to bed. See that you put that child in bed, too so's your mamma don't give me hell about it." He retreated to his bedroom.

Whatever had been keeping him steady during his close encounter with the true Antoine Ellis suddenly wore off. Hennessy's legs gave out and he sank onto the couch like a stone. He laid an arm protectively over Ray Ray. How could he ever leave the child alone again in this house? Or his mamma?

As if on cue, Lila came bursting through the door. "Hey, babee," she said cheerily.

"Hey, good lookin'." He forced a smile, not wanting her to know the trouble they were in.

"You still awake, dahlin?" She came over and kissed his cheek. "Why don't you put that baby in the bed?" she scolded. "He'll wake up cranky tomorrow and then what'll I do with him?"

"'S'that you, Lila?" Antoine called from the bedroom.

"You awake too, Antoine?" She put down her purse and headed down the hallway. "What's the matter? You got heartburn again?"

He didn't want her finding out what he was up to was more likely, Hennessy thought to himself. He suspected she was better off not knowing for the moment anyway. She was probably safer that way.

Resigned to the fact he could do little that night, he carried Ray Ray to his bed and covered him. He kicked off his shoes and lay on the bed beside him. He was a light sleeper and if Antoine, or anyone else came in, he'd kill them with his bare hands before he'd let them hurt his nephew.

Hennessy had never been more afraid for his family. He rolled to his side and stared at the sleeping child. He ran a finger along one smooth brown cheek and fluffed the soft curls on his head. If anything happened to this baby or to his sister, he didn't know what he'd do. For the first time in his life, he wished he'd taken his daddy's advice and gotten a gun. Unlike Rayne, he'd never thought he'd have a need for one.

Deja lay awake, staring at the ceiling in her trailer. She had to do something. She couldn't imagine Boozie losing his bar. For purely selfish reasons, she'd been looking forward to managing the nightly operations, but she knew how much the business meant to the man who'd helped her all her life. She knew how much it meant to everyone in the neighborhood. Rebuilding the Blues 'N Booze had become symbolic of how the community could overcome adversity through self-empowerment. They weren't asking the city or federal government for a handout, but for a hand up. Mayor Nagin had embraced it and had moved heaven and earth to find funding for Boozie and his neighborhood crew. There was a rebirth of pride in the community and without Boozie Walker playing a key role, she was afraid the movement would die.

Deja thought back to the day she'd tried to find Rayne by focusing on the energy coming from her jacket. She'd gotten many images, but had focused mainly on DeTron's presence. If she thought about it now, maybe she could remember other details she'd overlooked at the time. If she could figure out where Rayne was, and somehow free her from her captors, then there'd be no reason for Boozie to make a deal with this devil named Humphrey.

She'd Googled Cordoray Humphrey on the Internet and had found his name alongside other managing partners under a company called A. E. Development. There was a corporate address in town for his development company, but little else. Chances were, he was just another opportunist trying to take New Orleans citizens for a ride like the contractors who'd taken her money and left town.

A thought occurred to her. Even if this man wanted to buy the B&B, he'd need someone to manage it. Heaven knew she still needed a job — so it would be a natural thing for her to show up at the man's office and request a meeting. She'd lobby to keep her management position and see if she could get a read on where he might be holding Rayne Walker Williams. It wasn't a great idea, but at least it was something.

Satisfied she had a plan of action, Deja closed her eyes and tried to force herself to sleep, but so much could go wrong, clearing her mind was difficult. She wasn't at all sure if she would be making things better or worse with her plan. All she knew was that she had to try.

Two things surprised Hennessy when he arrived at his daddy's house the next morning with Ray Ray in tow. He was surprised to find his daddy nursing a hangover and equally surprised to find Ivalou Devine to be the one mixing his cure. "Tryin' something new, old man?" he teased.

Boozie squinted at him through red-rimmed eyes. "Now I 'member why I gave up drinkin' years go."

"Well, you up to talking?" Hennessy grabbed a chair, letting Ray Ray run into the living room to race his toy car on the new wood floor. "I have a plan."

Boozie winced. "Naw, son. There's no need for a plan. I'm signin' the place over and that's that."

Hennessy said angrily. "In case you've forgotten, I own half that bar. You put my name on the deed."

By the old man's expression he'd forgotten that detail. "Don't matter. You're signin' if I'm signin'," he said. "We ain't putting your sister's life in danger over a club."

"Just listen, Daddy. My plan is that you sign off on whatever the agreement is so they think you're going along with the deal. Nobody knows I'm on the deed 'cept us. They'll think the deal is done so we get Rayne back. Once she's safe, I take legal action to get them put in jail."

"And they'll shoot you before we ever see the inside of a courtroom," Boozie challenged. "I'm not havin' it."

"Just think about it, Daddy. The Blues 'N Booze is more than just a club. It's become a symbol of this neighborhood, of this city, rising from the ashes. It's too important to this community for us to let it go without a fight."

"The club'll still open. Earl never said they intended to shut it down or anythin'. The community will still have hope."

"It's not the same, Daddy. The B&B without you won't be the same. Besides, you're the one pullin' everyone together to rebuild homes and businesses. They need you to continue removing the red tape around the city government's processes. Heck, you've got the mayor himself listening to you and giving you permits and resources just because of your reputation. This thing doesn't work without you and the B&B."

Boozie stared into the bloody red mixture in his glass for long moments. Finally, he spoke, "That's a real nice speech, son. But, ain't no way I'm putting my little girl's life on the line. What if it don't work?"

"Then, I sign the damn contract and we're done with it. I don't want anything to happen to Rayne either. But, if there's any way for us to keep the bar and save Rayne, I think we should do it."

His daddy gave him a tortured look. "What if we sign it over and they still hurt Rayne? I couldn't bear it, Hennessy. I couldn't—" his voice broke.

"They'll give us Rayne," Hennessy assured him. "This is personal. Antoine Ellis is behind this whole thing. He doesn't want Rayne. He wants to hurt you."

"What makes you say that?" Ivalou had taken a seat at the table and held Boozie's hand. "How do you know he had anything to do with this?'

"A legitimate developer would've gone through legal channels to cut this deal. They'd have no reason to leverage a woman's life over a piece of property. And last night—last night he put a gun in my gut and threatened to kill me."

"He what?" Boozie's face grew stormy. "He tried to kill you? He confessed to taking Rayne? Why didn't you call me?"

"Because I didn't want you comin' over with guns blazin' and maybe makin' things worse. We don't need a war, Daddy. We need a plan. We need to do this my way."

"You sure all he wants is the bar, son?"

Hennessy nodded.

"Did you tell yo mamma?" Boozie asked.

"No. I figured she was safer not knowing. I can't have her acting funny around her husband. 'Sides, Antoine made sure I didn't have a chance to talk with her alone."

"How're we gonna keep everybody safe?" Boozie asked, running a hand over his thick hair.

"We tell Earl we want to see Rayne when we sign the papers. We make sure Mamma's somewhere safe and that we have Ray Ray in our possession." Hennessy reiterated. "Before they figure out the deal isn't legitimate without my signature, we get everyone out of the city. In fact, we should buy airline tickets today."

"You're gonna go with 'em," Boozie said.

"You're coming too," Hennessy countered.

A look passed between Booze and Ivalou. "I got reason to stay, son," he said gently. "Don't you worry 'bout me."

Hennessy thought about Deja. He wished he had a reason to stay, but she'd been clear, she wanted nothing more to do with him. "I want to end this before it gets too serious," she'd said. He'd been so mad he'd literally saw red. He'd expected more from her, not this childish game she was playing to try and trap him. That's the reason why he was still bothered by what she'd said, he decided. Otherwise, he'd have forgotten about it and let her go like he'd let go of all the others.

His daddy's voice brought him back to the moment. "If we gonna do this son, set a time with Humphrey. Let's get this over with and get the family outta here."

Too Much Hennessy

Lila Walker Ellis stared out the window at the business people walking the streets of the Central Business District. Her head pounded and her stomach was queasy. She didn't know if she could go through with the plan, though it seemed to be a pretty good idea when Antoine had cooked it up weeks ago.

"I can't believe you're doin' this, Mamma," Rayne seared her with a look of disgust and hatred. A look she'd yet to abandon even after so many weeks of confinement inside the office building.

Shamed, Lila turned her back on her daughter. "Antoine hasn't done you no harm, child." She said it to ease the guilt not to argue the point.

"Antoine didn't, but DeTron's used me as punchin' bag, in case you forgot. But I guess the bruises on my arms and back didn't cause me no harm, huh?"

"This ain't about you," Lila wheeled around angrily. "How many times I gotta tell you that? This is about your no-good daddy who thinks he can just crap all over folks and walk away."

"What's he done to you?" Rayne countered. "Divorce you? Lots of people get divorced."

"He disrespected me," Lila said crossly. Her long brown curls bobbed angrily about her shoulders. "He's been carryin' on with Ivalou Devine since the day he married me. I've had to suffer rumors in the church and around the town for over thirty years now."

"Mamma, you're re-married—have been for five years. There're no rumors," Rayne argued. "It's all in your head."

"I ain't crazy," the older woman shouted. "Though Lord knows Boozie Walker nearly made me lose my mind."

"I don't believe this." Rayne rose from the chair and paced the blue-green carpet of the nearly empty office. "But what I really don't believe is how you let Antoine talk you into this. What's in it for him? Isn't he rolling in the dough 'cause of all those laundromats and carwashes he sold?"

"He's doin' it because he loves me," Lila said simply. "He wants to prove to me he's a better man than Boozie, that's all."

Rayne made a noise and rolled her eyes. "No doubt."

"What's that 'sposed to mean?" Lila demanded.

"You know why he needs to prove his worth, Mamma?" Rayne challenged. "'Cause you've been measuring him against my daddy since the day you married him. I may not know much about men, but I know that's not something their egos take lightly."

Lila remained silent, though her mouth moved from side to side as if chewing on the thought. If she'd planned to say something, the opportunity disappeared when DeTron Williams entered the room.

"What ya'll B's talking bout?" he asked, eyeing Rayne suspiciously. "Don't get no ideas 'bout tryin' to escape."

"Watch how you speak to me, DeTron," Lila scolded.

"I'll talk how I like, ho," his face contorted into a menacing scowl. "Only reason I put up wid your mouth all this time is on account of your old man paying me big cheddar."

"I told you he ain't good for the money," Rayne sassed. "But you don't listen to me."

DeTron rushed up to her and stood inches away from her face. "If you didn't have to be presentable for your daddy, I'd slap the hell outta you right now," he threatened. His breath smelled sour and the gaudiness of the gold grill on his teeth looked ridiculous to Rayne, but she didn't say anything. One thing she knew was DeTron wasn't shy about using his fists and she didn't want to be on the receiving end of his vicious backhand. It hurt even worse when her mamma just stood by not doing anything about it.

"Stop givin' me all your damn lip and sit down," DeTron pointed at one of only two chairs in the room.

"Fine." Rayne sat back down. "How long's this gonna take?"

"How the hell would I know," he said irritably. "Some chick just came in talking 'bout she needs a job. Ho is throwin' off the schedule." He pulled a cigarette from the pocket of his oversized plaid shirt and lit it.

In times past, Rayne would've killed for a pull of a cigarette to ease the pain of her drug withdrawal, but no more. She'd been more sober in the past few weeks than she could remember being in years. DeTron thought he was torturing her when he and his thugs did drugs in front of her. But, the funny thing was, the more she saw them high, the less she wanted to be high. Her daddy would say there was some kind of irony there.

Her daddy. She'd thought a lot about Boozie Walker while she'd been held captive. One of the things she'd come to realize was that the man may have lied about being her blood relative, but he'd never lied about anything else. From the time she'd taken her first steps, till the time she'd taken her first fall, he'd been there to brush her off and encourage her to try again.

This past year, she'd fallen again—big time. Drugs had kicked her behind and she'd sunk to the lowest low, and he'd been there. He'd sent her to detox, talked to her about self-love and self-worth. He'd started making payments to DeTron to save her from her mistake of a marriage and her husband's almost daily beatings.

And he would be here today, she thought. This time he was making the ultimate sacrifice: he was giving up the Blues 'N Booze. He was giving up the place that had been his life-long love in order to save her. If she'd had any doubt about the depth of his love for her, it had been totally erased. He'd always been on her side, while her mamma…well Lila was all about Lila.

Rayne put a hand to her chest, missing the little pistol she'd tucked firmly into her bra strap between her breasts. DeTron had found it there when he'd patted her down the first day. But Rayne knew he had it on him. She'd seen him tuck it into the left leg pocket on his jeans. It sagged noticeably.

She had to get her pistol back.

Deja stepped out of her Mini and stared at the office building. It was an old building, but looked to be in good repair. Instantly when she walked inside the cool interior, she knew Rayne was inside somewhere.

She sensed that someone close to her wished her harm—or maybe someone wished her harm who was close in proximity to her. The vibrations she was getting were mixed.

She took the elevator to the second floor and found the office listed on the Internet. The temporary sign taped to the door saying A. E. Development was the first sign this probably was a fly-by-night operation. She pushed inside the office and found a man sitting at a desk, flanked by a man she thought to be Lila Ellis' husband. He'd been with Hennessy's mamma the day she'd caught Deja hugging Boozie in a restaurant. "Oh, hi. Is that you, Mr. Ellis?" she asked, stepping up to the desk.

He frowned. "Yes...you're...you're..."

"Deja Devine." She offered her hand.

His palm was warm and sweaty and Deja had to resist the urge to wipe her hand on her skirt when she pulled her hand away.

"Is there something we can help you with?" Ellis asked, not bothering to introduce the other man who sat watching her carefully. He looked a little like a large water bug with his round eyeglasses, wide brown eyes and a sweaty bald, brown head.

"Well, I heard from my friend Hennessy Walker that his daddy is selling the Blues 'N Booze to your company."

Ellis' eyes narrowed. "Yeah?"

"I was hired to be the manager by Boozie and I'd like to keep the job. I want to know how I sign up with you," she said, keeping her tone light.

The water bug man shifted a bit in his chair. He seemed extremely uncomfortable.

"We've already got somebody to run the place," Ellis said. "He ran the place before the hurricane—I figure I'll go with experience."

"You talking about Earl?" she asked wrinkling her nose. "You know he never booked any of the groups, right? Boozie did that."

Ellis looked irritated. "But he managed the joint other than that."

"You don't have anything to manage if you can't secure the talent, right? I've already booked bands through Memorial Day, but that all goes away if I'm not the manager. The contracts'll be no good…you don't open on time…you lose money."

"We…we don't have time for this," water bug said to Ellis. His voice was very proper and barely above a whisper. He was afraid of something…or someone. "They'll be here any moment."

"I know," Ellis snapped back. "Miss, uh—"

"Devine," Deja reminded him. She noticed the closed door on the left side of the room and knew Rayne was behind it.

"We have another appointment, so how 'bout I think on your offer and get back with you."

"Okay. That's fine." Deja opened her huge bag and dug around for her business card holder. "Here it is," she announced, pulling it out of the depths. She handed a card to Ellis. "That's my cell. It's always on."

"Good. We'll call ya," he said, turning his attention back to the papers on the desk in front of water bug.

Deja knew she couldn't leave yet. Rayne wanted to be out of that room. No. It wasn't that she wanted out; she needed to out. Otherwise, something bad was going to happen. Closing her purse, she walked toward the side door deliberately. When her hand touched the handle, Antoine Ellis yelled.

"That's not the way out, Ms. Devine."

She opened the door a crack. "Oh. I thought it might be a restroom." She turned to face him, trying to look innocent. She saw it clearly then…something wicked in the depths of his dark eyes slid past his irises and chilled her.

A man in an oversized plaid shirt and jeans pulled the door open further, throwing Deja off balance. The man, she was sure was DeTron Williams, caught her. He then took the opportunity to check her out thoroughly. "What's up, E? Who's this chick?"

"That's my ex-husband's cheap mistress," Lila Ellis stepped up, hands on her hips. "I shoulda known you'd show up, ya gold diggah. You tryin' to steal my new husband?"

Deja stood blinking at her.

"Mamma, stop trippin'. She ain't Daddy's mistress." Rayne strode across the small, nearly empty space to join the other three huddled in the doorway. "If anybody's groovin' on her, it's Hennessy."

Deja wanted to say that Hennessy wasn't grooving on her anymore…not after she'd made him angry the other day. Of course, he'd accused her of trying to trap him, which still bothered her.

But there was no time for talking, Antoine Ellis had rounded the desk and was shouting out orders. "DeTron, dammit! Get all of these women back in that room and keep your eye on 'em."

"Don't be bustin' my ass, old man." DeTron countered, grabbing the very low crotch of his jeans. "I'm doin' all this as a favor to you. A favor that's gonna cost you big time, hear?"

Antoine's face was like stone. "Just do it," he said in a dangerously low tone.

"Ready, old men?" Hennessy looked to his daddy on the left and Teardrop on the right as they stood in front of the office building. "Put your game face on."

"Son, this ain't no game. This is about people's lives—remember that."

The thought sobered Hennessy significantly. "I know, Daddy."

"C'mon, then. Let's do this." Boozie took the lead, pushing open the doors and heading into the building. "'Drop, you got your blade?"

"Don't leave without it," the old man let the switchblade fall into his palm just a bit, before pushing it back up his sleeve.

"Hennessy, you know what to do with that gun?"

"Yeah. DeTron or one of his boys'll frisk me and take it away…what's to know?"

Boozie stopped and turned on his son. "You need to know what to do after that. What'd I tell you to do after that?" he pressed.

"If the transaction turns sour, I jump on him and beat him to the ground since there're no bullets in the gun."

"That's right. Element of surprise. Me and Drop'll take down the rest."

"You sure this'll work?" Hennessy was beginning to doubt. He'd never been in a situation like this before.

The old men passed a look between them that told him they weren't strangers to this kind of situation. "It's always worked befo'," Drop assured him with a nod.

They found the office with the sign taped to the door and walked in.

Hennessy registered the fact that his sister and mamma were present, but what drew his complete attention was DeTron cursing and shoving Deja into another room while Rayne pulled at his pants legs trying to get him off the other woman.

He started to go after the man, but his daddy's firm grip on his arm stopped him from going more than a step.

"So, this *was* your doin', Ellis," Boozie said loudly, startling everyone on the other side of the room.

Antoine spun around and pulled a gun from his jacket.

DeTron pulled a long barreled gun from beneath his baggy clothes.

Rayne turned away from DeTron to slip something down her bra, a small smile of satisfaction graced her lips. Hennessy was sure he was the only one who noticed.

Boozie held up his palms and took a cautious step forward. "Now, there ain't no need for guns, gentlemen," he said calmly. "I came here to do business, that's all."

Antoine's harsh frown softened slightly. "Glad to hear that, Walker. If you're willin' to be civilized, I see no reason not to do the same." He tucked his gun back inside his jacket. "Have a seat."

Boozie eased into one of the chairs at the desk.

Antoine pushed aside the bald, black man with bug eyes and took the chair behind the desk. "My man Humphrey here," he lifted his chin at the man, "he drew up the papers. They're all nice and legal." He turned the document to face his wife's ex-husband.

"You…uh…don't mind if I have my daughter look these over with me, do you?" Boozie asked. "She's gotta little pre-law under her belt. She been handling my contracts for years."

Antoine's eyes narrowed suspiciously. ""S'that true?" he asked his wife.

"Yes," Lila confirmed, moving to stand behind her husband's chair. "She and him was always lookin' over contracts for the bar."

Hennessy couldn't believe his eyes. Something hardened in his chest as he realized his mamma knew about—and apparently condoned—what was going on here. Had she helped him plot this dirty deal, he wondered?

Rayne didn't wait for an invitation, she quickly moved to sit in the empty chair beside her daddy.

Boozie took her hand immediately, pressing it to his lips. "You look good, dahlin," he said closing his hand over hers. "You doin all right?"

"Never better, Daddy." She leaned over and gave him a kiss. Hennessy could see she whispered something in his ear.

"We ain't got time for family reunions," Antoine said irritably. "You gonna look those over or not?" he asked Rayne, stabbing at the papers.

She sighed and pulled the document in front of her and started reading the first page. "This is it?" She looked up at Antoine. Hennessy couldn't see her face, but knew her tapered eyebrows were raised in a look of disbelief. "A quarter of a million for the B&B? Are you kiddin' me?"

Smiling, Antoine sat back in his chair. "You looked at the price of real estate in New Orleans lately?" His voice was dredged in smugness. "That's more than fair."

"It's highway robbery for a piece of property that's fully renovated," she argued, shoving the contract across the wood to him.

Antoine motioned Humphrey over to his side. They whispered conspiratorially for a while. Lila interjected something and they broke apart.

"We thought you'd reject our first offer," Antoine said, apparently ready to make a counter offer. "So, we're willing to drop the price to two hundred thousand instead."

"You crooked sonofa—"

"Hennessy!" Boozie stopped him with a look. "I see how this is gonna go," he said turning back to the man across the desk. "I'm willin' to sign your contract as written," he said, pulling the document back. "My child's life ain't worth the argument."

Hennessy was angry, but he'd expected this. His daddy said he wouldn't put Rayne's life in jeopardy. Even though they now had her in their sights, they were far from safe.

Boozie dropped the pen and pushed out his chair. "It's done." He took Rayne's hand and motioned to Hennessy. "Let's get out of here."

Deja had made her way around DeTron and over to Hennessy's side, though he wasn't sure when. They all turned to leave the room.

Hennessy was relieved. Plan "A" had gone exactly as planned.

Chapter Fifteen

W "ait a minute," It was Lila who spoke, stopping all of them just as they reached the door. "What about you, Hennessy?"

Hennessy's heart skipped. Whatever his mamma was about to say, he had a feeling it wasn't going to be good. "What about me?"

"You gotta sign, too."

Boozie cursed softly. Teardrop blew a long breath.

"I remember you signin' the place over to Hennessy a few years back," Lila said nastily to her ex-husband. "That's the first thing you took away to make sure I was left with nothin', Boozie Walker." Her eyes narrowed to slits and her mouth tightened into a thin pale line. "Then you cheated on me and had people talking 'bout me behind my back. You left me alone every night while you ran off to that damn bar and your little hos. I had no choice but to divorce you."

"Lila, I didn't mean—" Boozie was cut short as his ex-wife's tirade continued.

"And all I wanted for Rayne was for her to do right. I knew the child was born of sin and didn't know right from wrong, but when I tried to punish her you'd go behind me to let her off the hook. Now, look at her." Her face twisted with distaste as she looked Rayne up and down. "She turned out to be a slut and a drug addict. And…she loves you more'n she loves me."

"Listen, Lila," Boozie pleaded.

"No!" She came around the desk to confront him. "You took every-thin' precious away from me, Boozie Walker. It's time I got what's owed me. Takin' away your bar ain't even enough to start makin' it up to me."

"Mamma?" Hennessy had to speak. "You were my heart—I always loved you," he said, placing his hand to his chest. "But, this…you betrayed us, Mamma—all of us. Daddy never took nothin' away from you. You pushed him and Rayne away…just like you're pushing me away now. How can I ever look at you again with anything but disgust?"

"Oh, baby." Lila's eyes welled and spilled over when she turned her eyes to the floor.

Hennessy hoped her tears were due to shame. He was completely destroyed to find out his mamma let jealousy turn her into someone so ugly. Just then, he felt Deja's warm and comforting hand slide inside his. He clutched it gratefully.

Antoine cleared his throat and took his wife by her shoulders. "Come on, Lila," he said soothingly. The man was truly evil, but there was one thing that was plain as day…he still loved his wife. He sat her in a chair and took the pen and thrust it toward Hennessy. "Son, let's be done with this mess."

"I ain't your son." Hennessy stepped up, grabbed the pen and flipped through the typewritten sheets angrily. He got to the signature page and stopped. "I'll sign once my family is gone."

"Hennessy…" Boozie's warned.

Hennessy refused to look back at him. "I'm serious, Daddy. Leave. Now." He could hear shuffling and whispering, and finally, the door closed behind him.

"You want me to follow 'em?" DeTron asked.

"What the hell for?" Antoine shot out irritably, which sent DeTron cursing into the next room. He slammed the door shut.

Antoine turned to Hennessy. "They're gone. Sign."

Hennessy stared hard at the paper. All it would take was his signature and their whole neighborhood would be lost. Antoine Ellis wasn't interested in anybody's success but his own. The pressure of the gun at his back reminded Hennessy that there was always plan B. He stood and took a step back. "I ain't feelin' this."

"Where do you think you're going?" Antoine barked.

Pulling the weapon from his slacks, Hennessy pointed it first at Antoine then at the man named Humphrey who just stood there looking wide-eyed like a bug.

"Hennessy. No, baby," his Mamma turned in her chair and pleaded. "This ain't you. Don't try and be like your daddy."

"I'd be honored to be like my daddy," he said to her, backing up slowly toward the door.

"DeTron!" Antoine shouted.

Hennessy's eyes shot to the door that had opened. Several things happened all at once…and all in slow motion. The tip of DeTron's gun came into sight. Hennessy turned and ran toward the door. The sound of a gun's safety being switched off sounded loud in his ears. He reached out for the door handle, but the door opened away from him. He stumbled then fell at his sister's high-heeled feet. Rayne shouted, "DeTron look at this!" And then, the sound of a bullet being fired resounded in the room like a cannon. His mamma screamed. And then there was another.

"Get out, Hennessy!" Rayne screamed.

He scrambled out of the door on his hands and knees before rising to his feet. "Rayne," he shouted. "Come on."

She ran out of the room, her blouse flying open as she sprinted down the hallway. Hennessy struggled to keep up with her as they flew down the stairs and out the front door where their daddy, Teardrop and Deja stood anxiously waiting.

They wasted no time sorting themselves into cars. Hennessy hopped into the Mini Cooper beside Deja without a second thought. Rayne piled into the truck between her daddy and his best friend. They all tore out of the parking lot. Hennessy was impressed by how much get-up-and-go the little car had and how well Deja maneuvered it in and out of traffic.

"Where we going?" Hennessy asked.

"Airport," she said. "Your daddy said you've got to get out of town for your own good."

"That's right." He snapped his fingers, not knowing how he'd forgotten that detail. He'd booked flights for everyone, except his daddy, who'd absolutely refused to go. Hennessy checked his watch. It was two o'clock and their flight left at three-thirty. Pam Flowers, who'd been watching Ray Ray, would be waiting with the child in the terminal by now. He flipped open his cell phone and confirmed they were there and she'd checked him in.

"Headin' to California?" Deja asked, trying to sound nonchalant. She knew this was going to happen—was inevitable—but she couldn't help but feel sad about him leaving again.

"Yeah," he acknowledged, but didn't expand upon it. "At least for now."

Wanting—no needing to change the subject, Deja said, "That was a either a really brave thing you did back there, or really stupid."

Hennessy gave a half chuckle. "It was really stupid. The gun I had didn't have any bullets. But, I couldn't see letting the B&B go to Antoine Ellis…and my mamma," he said the last bitterly. "I still can't believe she was in on this."

"Well, I hate to tell you this, but you didn't have to worry about them taking over the B&B even if you had signed the contract." Deja bit her bottom lip.

"What're you talking about?"

"Your daddy signed the bar over to my mamma yesterday after you left his house."

"I went through all of that for nothing?"

"Yeah. But he figured you'd sign the papers like you'd planned." She lifted a chastising eyebrow in his direction. "Your sister ran back to save you. She said she just knew you'd do something…"

Hennessy gave her a sideways look. "You can say it."

"Egomaniacal," she finished, trying to suppress a smile.

"Yeah, well, that was the only big word she learned when she was in college for two years. I guess she had to use it some time. What I was tryin' to figure out was why you were there," it was his turn to raise an eyebrow. "I don't remember us pulling you into the plan."

"I had to do something," she said. "After everything your daddy's done for me and Mamma, I couldn't let him lose the Blues 'N Booze and all those people he's helping…anyway. I just couldn't bear it."

"I know how you feel." Hennessy nodded. "But I tell you what. When DeTron shoved you to the floor into that room, I was fixin' to run over and beat the hell outta him till my daddy stopped me."

"You were?" Deja couldn't help but be flattered.

He looked over her and the heat in his brown eyes nearly melted her soul.

"That's a fact," he said, his expression soft, but serious. "He didn't hurt you did he?" He ran the back of his hand along her cheek.

Deja felt her insides soften and her head begin to spin. Not good while she was driving. "No. I…I'm fine."

"I'm sorry about what I said to you when…"

"That's good. I'm glad you're sorry," she said swallowing hard. "Because I wasn't trying to trap you. I don't play games like that, Hennessy."

Hennessy looked ashamed. "I knew that even when I said it. I was just so mad."

"Why?" She really wanted to know.

"Because," he shrugged, "you're the first woman who's ever broke off with me before I…broke off with her."

"Shoe doesn't fit so good on the other foot, huh?" She didn't feel sorry for him. Her heart was breaking a little more every mile closer they got to the airport. "I just thought it'd be easier."

A heavy silence fell between them as an unspoken question lingered in the air: Easier for whom?

They didn't say another word until they reached the airport.

Hennessy sighed and placed his hand on the door handle. "Thanks, Deja. For everything," he said. "Hopefully, I'll see you for the grand opening."

"I've got you booked," she said. "Don't ruin my debut as a manager by not showing up, all right?" She willed him to get out before she let the tears stinging the backs of her eyes spill out.

"I'll do my best. " He leaned over and kissed her gently on the cheek. "Take care of my daddy, would you? I'm worried about him. I don't trust Antoine and DeTron as far as I can throw 'em."

"I'll try."

"And, Deja…" he took hold of her hand and paused as if struggling to find words to say. "Take care of yourself, too."

She could only manage to nod because her voice was stuck behind a lump in her throat. He climbed out of the car and disappeared into the building.

Deja pulled away from the curb and headed out of the airport. The temperature was about 68 degrees outside and a bit warmer inside her car. She refused to roll down the windows or open the moon roof, however. She wanted the smell of Hennessy's cologne to last as long as possible… at least as long as it took to cry him out of her system.

"There it is. Bigger than life." Hennessy slapped the front page of the *New Orleans Times-Picayune* and dropped it on the table for Jack, Johnnie and Rayne to see. "The legendary Blues 'N Booze opens again March 1."

"'S'bout damn time." Jack snatched up the paper. "Our last gig was a week ago and my funds are getting low. Jack Harris Daniels can't roll that way." He winked at Rayne and gave her a smile filled with gold grille.

Rayne gave her brother a You-Better-See-Bout-Ya-Boy look and went back to eating her bacon and eggs. Seeing her appetite return in the few weeks they'd been in California was nice. And the little bit of weight she'd put on made her look healthy and less pitiful.

Hennessy was also glad to see how much more Rayne interacted with her son these days. She took him to the hotel swimming pool every day and read books to him every night. Ray Ray loved the water and was flourishing under his mamma's attention.

Rayne picked up the paper now abandoned by Jack whose attention had shifted to a pretty Mexican woman at the table next to them. She was dressed in a low-cut blouse and tight pants. From what she'd seen in the past few weeks that was just his type.

242

Rayne flipped through the paper as her brother ordered himself breakfast and played with Ray Ray. The obituaries weren't usually her thing, but a name caught her eye and she had to read further.

Hennessy was digging into a fresh plate of pancakes, now and she didn't want to ruin his appetite, but he needed to know about this.

"Hen," she said, nudging his arm. "Did you see this?"

He leaned her way, his jaws working. The moment he saw the name, his entire body froze. "Damn," he cursed softly. "Damn."

"I know." Rayne stroked his arm.

"What?" Johnnie perked up. "What happened?"

Hennessy looked at his band mates. "I have to go back to New Orleans."

"Heck, yeah, man. We all goin', right?" Johnnie asked.

"I have to go today."

"Naw. Not again, man." Johnnie shook his large head back and forth. "Why you gotta go now? Ain't we playin' this weekend in San Jose?"

His complaining brought Jack's attention back to the table. "You leaving us high and dry again, Hennessy?"

"A friend of mine's mother died. I have to go to the funeral."

"Another funeral," Jack asked. "Who else you know is fixin' to die?"

"You will if you don't close your ghetto-grilled mouth," Rayne shot back.

"Stop complaining," Hennessy said. "I'll be seein' you fellas in a coupla weeks when we open at the B&B. Rayne'll help you get settled once you get in town."

"You gonna leave us with her?" Jack whined. "She's hostile like a mug."

Hennessy looked over at Rayne and smiled, thinking about how she saved his life the day they left New Orleans. "You don't know the half of it." Fortunately, or unfortunately, she'd only wounded both Antoine and DeTron with her little pink pearl-handled pistol. They'd gone to the police and filed a complaint on her, but that had backfired on them. Antoine had been doing shady deals all over the city and DeTron, well, his past finally caught up with him. No one had heard from Earl Grant. Maybe he'd gone back to San Antonio to live off his brother.

"I'ma gonna make plane reservations and try to make it back for the funeral," Hennessy rose, leaving half his pancakes uneaten.

"You goin', bye-bye, Uncah Hensee?" Ray Ray asked from his booster seat where he'd been busy putting away his own pancake.

"Yeah, little man." Hennessy went over and kissed the boys soft curls. He looked over at his sister who was smiling adoringly at her son. "Hey, Sis?"

"What?"

"I meant to ask you. When you told DeTron to "look at this" what were you talking about?"

"My tits, of course."

Jack spewed the coffee all over table in front of him.

Well, that explained why her blouse had been open when they ran out of the building. "Was that really necessary?" Hennessy asked.

"It worked." Rayne shrugged. "It's been my experience that no matter what a man is doin', bare breasts—or in my case, nearly bare breasts—stops him cold. Besides, I had to get to my gun. It was under my bra strap."

Jack and Johnnie were simply staring at her in disbelief.

"What?" she challenged them. "Bare breasts trump everything, right fellas?"

They only took a second or two to think about it.

"Works for me," Jack acknowledged.

"Absolutely," Johnnie added.

Hennessy thought about Deja's breasts. Yep. They'd stop him in his tracks no matter what he was doing. He was sure of it. "When you're right, you're right, Sis."

"This friend of yours," Jack licked the front of his ridiculously gold gilded teeth, "She's a real Playa Slaya, huh?"

"I didn't tell you she was a 'she'," Hennessy defended.

"Didn't have to," Johnnie interjected, smiling his big smile. "We know you, brah. Know you got it bad for somebody. Has to be this friend you're goin' to see."

Embarrassment heated Hennessy. Was it that obvious how much he'd been missing Deja? He looked over at Rayne.

To her credit, she said nothing. But the tilt of her head and her sideways glance told him she'd noticed too how much time he'd been off alone. He'd been composing. Something he did when he had things messing with his head he needed to work out.

"Whatever, ya'll," he tried to play it all off. He made a quick excuse and headed off to his room to make the plane reservation. *Playa Slayer, huh?* The thought started a two-beat in the back of his mind. *Playa Slayer, I'm knockin at your door…*the lyrics spilled into his brain…*Listen baby, don't wanna play these games no more…*

If Hennessy had been depressed about his last trip to New Orleans, this one was far worse. Ivalou Devine had passed away three days ago. Her funeral was this afternoon. Hennessy had a delay with his connecting flight and was afraid of being late. He checked his watch. Almost four. He was already speeding in the rental car. He didn't want to risk a ticket, but he had to get there on time. Deja was probably devastated. He had to be there for her.

Be there for her. He thought about the words and all they implied. Would it be so bad for him to be there for her forever? For a lifetime?

At four-fifteen he finally pulled into the parking lot of the funeral home. He raced inside and walked soberly down the aisle as some woman sang a lovely, but sad gospel song. Hennessy was about to duck into an open seat near the back, but changed his mind. If he was going to be here.…He walked along the side until he reached the front row. Only two people sat on the right side: his father and Deja. Hennessy took a seat next to Deja and covered her hand. He could feel the cold damp tissue wadded in her fist.

She turned to look at him. Her eyes were sad, sober. "Hennessy…"

"I'm here," he said firmly. "I'm right here."

Too Much Hennessy

The service didn't last too long, and the procession proceeded to the burial site. An elderly couple, Deja introduced as her grandparents, rode in the family limousine with Deja, Boozie and Hennessy. Hennessy noted that Ivalou's parents seemed sad, but cold the entire ride. After the pastor said a few words, they filed past the open casket. Hennessy followed behind his daddy. He thought Ivalou looked plastic, like some macabre doll lying in a satin box. He noticed on her left ring finger she wore a ring. He recognized it. It was the diamond ring he'd seen in his daddy's safe deposit box. So...the ring had been for her all along. He placed a hand on his daddy's shoulder as the old man lingered over the body.

Ivalou Devine had been his one and only love, of that, Hennessy was certain.

Hours later, Hennessy led an exhausted Deja out of her grandparent's grand, newly renovated, southern plantation-style house and into his rental car. "Ready to go home?" he asked.

She turned teary eyes to him, "I don't have a home anymore, Hennessy."

His heart shattered with sadness for her. He leaned over and kissed her gently on the cheek. "Don't say that, baby."

"What am I gonna do now?" she asked hopelessly. "I've spent my whole life worrying about Mamma, taking care of her every need. Now she's gone...what am I supposed to do?" She was completely distraught.

Hennessy was in uncharted territory. He wasn't sure what was the right thing to say or do, so he punted. "I'll tell you what," he put the car in Drive, "you don't worry about what you're gonna do today. Worry about it tomorrow or the next day. In the meantime, let me take care of you, all right?"

Deja blinked tear-soaked eyes a few times before answering. "Okay."

If she was dreaming, Deja never wanted to wake up. Hennessy had checked them into a hotel suite, she wasn't sure where, but it didn't matter. She remembered soaking in a hot tub with flower-scented water and falling blissfully asleep. Hennessy woke her, dried her in huge fluffy towels and carried her to a bed of clean, soft linens. She fell asleep again, only to awaken now to find herself nestled in his arms. She snuggled closer, enjoying his warmth and the feel of his bare skin against hers.

She didn't think, only acted, as she kissed his chest and rubbed her hand along the hairs just below his navel. His erection was nearly immediate as it pulsed enthusiastically against the back of her hand. She wrapped her hand around him and he moaned his approval.

Unlike their previous encounters, on this plane or the other, their lovemaking wasn't full of passion and fire. This time, they were slow and patient as if they were getting to know one another, their likes, their dislikes and taking note of them for future reference. Yet, as always a craving, an insatiable need to have more, to take more, to give more rose between them. Soon their needs grew more intense and their bodies moved faster, their passionate moans grew louder, and they both raced for the ecstasy they only found when they were together.

And then it happened. Hennessy went rigid and sent his life, his love, his all into Deja. She closed herself around him, and accepted it all as her Chakras exploded with light and energy.

Hennessy fell limp on top of her and panted heavily in her ear. "We're lucky one of us doesn't have a heart attack when that happens."

Deja put her arms around his shoulders. "I love you, Hennessy James Walker," she said softy. "You know, don't you?"

Hennessy raised himself to his elbows and looked deep into her dark eyes. "I know. But, then again, there's no way you couldn't."

"I was being serious." Deja frowned slightly.

"I am, too," Hennessy assured her. "I dreamed you into my life, Deja Devine. That means I loved you first. You had no choice but to love me back."

She smiled with him this time. "I don't want you to leave me again," she said. "I'm not tryin' to trap you…it's just how I feel. Is that bad?"

Too Much Hennessy

Hennessy shook his head, causing his dreads to sway. "Naw. If it is, it's the right kind of bad." He kissed her forehead then the tip of her nose. "Did I tell ya what Jack and Johnnie called you?"

She shook her head.

"Playa Slaya. They knew I was hooked on you before I ever did."

"Player Slayer?" she chuckled. "I kinda like it."

"Then say it right," he insisted. "Don't say it all proper like you did, it's Playa Slaya."

"Playa Slaya," Deja exaggerated the pronunciation.

"Ooh." Hennessy closed his eyes and bit his lip. "Say it one mo' time for me, baby."

"Playa Slaya," she said sexily.

"Lord have mercy," he teased. "I think we gonna have to go another round."

When he made love to her the second time, Deja wrapped herself tight around him, hoping to never have to let him go.

Epilogue

It was like old times at the Blues 'N Booze. Every seat in the house was filled and folks were cutting a rug on the dance floor. The sound of Jazz and Blues vibrated the walls and spilled out into the street to draw passersby inside.

Boozie Walker was working the room and shootin' the breeze with everybody like they were all his best friends. And, many of them were these days, Hennessy decided. Four square blocks around the bar had been renovated a house at a time through the efforts of the St. Bernard Parish Krewe as the mayor now called them. And many more neighborhoods were following suit.

Hennessy leaned back against the walls and sipped his rum and coke. The legendary Marsalis brothers were on stage now, rocking the house as they ended their last set. He still didn't know what magic strings Deja had pulled to get them for a week, but he'd always known she had some sort of magic over everything she touched.

He looked over at the office, where she stood in the doorway, enjoying the fruits of her labor. She was more beautiful than she'd ever been if such were possible.

The Marsalis brothers were met with thundering applause and a standing ovation. The time had come for the Whiskey Sins Trio to go in and play...they were now the house band, playing nightly. "Come on, fellas," he shouted over the din at Jack and Johnnie who seemed reluctant to leave their females guests...but there wasn't anything unusual in that.

Rayne walked in and gave him a nod. She'd re-enrolled in pre-law classes at Tulane, newly determined to get her degree and go to law school. The best news was that she was sober. Chances are she'd nurse a couple of Diet Cokes tonight like she'd done every night she's stopped by.

Once they were all set, Hennessy took the microphone. "Good evenin' New Orleans, how ya'll doin?" As expected, the crowd erupted into applause. They were here to have a good time.

"I'd like to give a shout out to anybody in the St. Bernard Parish Krewe." More shouts when up. "And to all ya'll who're visitin' our fair city, welcome to the Blues 'N Booze!"

The walls rocked with the intensity of the shouting and applause this time.

"I'ma play a song, my daddy wrote," he said strumming his guitar as Jack started the rhythm on his drums. "It's called 'Lovin' Hard'. It's about the woman he loved all his life...but who died recently." His eyes met his daddy's who was sitting with a table full of people in the middle of the room. "Sorry I never got to play it for her in person, Daddy. But here it goes."

He sang the song like he'd never sung it before. The audience swayed and popped their fingers in time with his rhythm. Several women had their eyes closed, to let the groove take hold of their souls and that's when Hennessy knew he had them. And, he had Deja. She'd come into the bar area while he was singing and was now leading the applause with tears glistening in her eyes.

"Thank you." Hennessy bowed. After a while, everyone sat down except one lone figure in the middle of the room. Boozie clapped until he must've worn his hands raw. He put a hand to his heart and then pointed at his son.

"I love you, too, Daddy," Hennessy said. His heart was full. He was finally home and settled. It felt good. "I have another song to sing if you all will indulge me."

His audience let him know they were more than willing.

"This song is about a woman. No...not just any woman. A Playa Slaya." He smiled at Deja. "I wrote it for the woman who stole my heart while I was dreaming and captured my soul when I was awake. I gave up all other women for her, but not until she kicked me to the curb."

Jack and Johnnie hooted "oh noo's" from behind him and punctuated their words with their instruments. "It's all right, fellas," he said good-naturedly to them. "I'm hanging up my Playa card. Now, I'm in a whole new game."

Jack opened with a bit on his drums and Hennessy started singing to the woman he loved. *"Playa Slayer I'm knockin at your door,"* he sang to Deja, *"Listen baby, don't wanna play these games no more. Playa Slaya you gotta let me in. 'Cause if I lose your love, dahlin' it'll be mooore than a sin…Oww!"* He walked from the stage as the audience hollered. He walked until he stood directly in front of Deja. The warmth in her smile and the lights dancing in her eyes told him all he needed to know.

"Playa Slaaa-ya, I know you're feelin' me," He pulled her close with his free arm. *"I don't know how you strip me, baaaa-by, of all my dignity. Hah, but let me tell you Playa Slaya, you bet-ter let me in. 'Cause I'm fallin' to my knees un-til you say your givin' in!"*

Hennessy dropped to his knees and the women in the crowd started screaming. Deja laughed and to his surprise, pulled the microphone from his hand.

Shouts of "uh, oh, playa. Uh oh" came out of the crowd.

"Now, listen Playa," Deja spoke it to the beat rather than sang it, but she did it with feeling. *"You have yet to prove a thing."*

"Tell it, sistah." And "Go 'head," rang out from the audience.

"You say you love me. But I don't see no wed-ding ring!" She held up her left hand to show everyone it was bare.

The audience went wild.

Hennessy's jaw dropped as he stared into her all-knowing eyes. It should've spoiled the surprise she'd seen this coming, but somehow, it only made it sweeter.

Taking back the mike, he decided to play along.

"All right, Playa Slaya, since you've al-ready got my heart," he improvised, pulling the little box from his pants pocket. *"How 'bout you take this ring un-til death do we paaart?"*

He opened the box.

Deja nearly passed out at the size of the square-cut diamond flanked by a half dozen baguettes.

"Take it, girl! Take it," someone hollered out. Followed by another woman who yelled, "I'll take it if you won't."

Deja had never been happier. The only thing that would've made this night better was to share it with her mamma. Of course, she knew she'd be seeing her soon...maybe even tonight. She extended her hand to the man who was on his knees before her. Nothing would make her happier than to be his wife.

Hennessy set down the microphone and slid the ring onto her finger. Rising, he pulled her into his arms and gave her the kiss that would begin a lifetime of kisses.

And the Whiskey Sins Trio played on. Giving the patrons of the B&B Blues, Booze and a little bit of love to take home with them that night.

Group Discussion Questions:

1. Which of the characters in the book was most in love with New Orleans?

2. What role did the Blues 'N Booze club play in the story?

3. What lesson(s) did Hennessy Walker have to learn in order to grow as a person?

4. What drove Lila Ellis to take the actions she took?

5. Why did Deja Devine think Hennessy was "too much?"

6. At what point did Hennessy fall in love with Deja?

7. What did it take for Rayne to finally overcome her addiction?

8. What role did Boozie Walker play in the story?

Note from the Author

This book is more than a romance between two characters; it's also about the romance felt for New Orleans, one of our most beloved United States cities. As this book is written, there are efforts going on to rebuild New Orleans post Hurricane Katrina, but there is still much to be done.

No one was prepared for this disaster. Not the government, and not the people.

My hope is that by the time of this book's publication, the city will be well on its way to rebuilding its magic…and reinforcing its levees. Only then will the Crescent City be able to once again "Let the good times roll."

About the Author

T. T. Henderson was born and raised in Denver, Colorado. She currently resides in San Antonio, Texas. She became a fan of romance after attending a writer's conference in Colorado Springs in the early 90s. Her second year attending the conference she won the Contemporary Romance category and was awarded the prize by the amazing best selling author, Nora Roberts. Ms. Henderson has written multiple romances (all with great reviews from readers and *Romantic Times Magazine*) while raising two children and a husband and maintaining a full time job as a vice president at a *Fortune* 500 company.

Parker Publishing, LLC

Celebrating Black
Love Life Literature

Mail or fax orders to:

12523 Limonite Avenue
Suite #220-438
Mira Loma, CA 91752
(866) 205-7902
(951) 685-8036 fax

or order from our Web site:

www.parker-publishing.com
orders@parker-publishing.com

Ship to:

Name: _____

Address: _____

_____

_____

City: _____

State: _____ Zip: _____

Phone: _____

Qty	Title	Price	Total

Shipping and handling is $3.50, Priority Mail shipping is $6.00
FREE standard shipping for orders over $30 — Add S&H

Alaska, Hawaii, and international orders – call for rates — CA residents add 7.75% sales tax

See Website for special discounts and promotions — Total

Payment methods: We accept Visa, MasterCard, Discovery, or money orders. NO PERSONAL CHECKS.

Payment Method: (circle one):   VISA   MC   DISC   Money Order

Name on Card: _____

Card Number: _____ Exp Date: _____

Billing Address: _____

_____

City: _____

State: _____ Zip: _____